WARNED OFF

'Dick Francis better look out . . . *Warned Off* is a novel that evokes the tense excitement of the racing game'

The Sunderland Echo

'This galloping novel set in the world of horse-racing flies over the hurdles, keeping readers gripped to the finish'

Oracle

'A very professional racing thriller . . . lots of rough stuff, plenty of racing background and action mixed up with a love interest all combine to provide a good fast-moving story'

Publishing News

'A winner for all racing fans, *Warned Off* marks the debut of a formidable writing partnership'

Kent Today

About the authors

Richard Pitman has done everything with race-horses except eat them, and thinks he may even have done that unwittingly. He rode the winners of over 470 races over jumps including the Champion Hurdle, Hennessey Gold Cup, Mackeson Gold Cup and the King George VI Chase twice. He has owned and bred three winning horses and hopes to see more come from his small stud in Oxfordshire. The author of three previous books, he has been a broadcaster for the past seventeen years with the BBC, writes on racing for the *Sunday Express* and is currently writing his second novel with Joe McNally.

Joe McNally's life-long love affair with steeple-chasing started when he played truant as a 13-year-old to work in Jim Barrett's racing stable in his home village of New Stevenston, Lanarkshire. He's always been employed in the racing/betting game and now works for Satellite Information Services as a Regional Manager. He's published some short fiction and numerous articles on racing. With long suffering wife Mary and sons Ryan and Kevin, Joe, 38, has been exiled in Kidderminster, Worcester, since 1989.

WARNED OFF

RICHARD
PITMAN
JOE
McNALLY

CORONET BOOKS
Hodder and Stoughton

Copyright © Richard Pitman and
Joe McNally 1992

First published in Great Britain in 1992
by Hodder and Stoughton Ltd

Coronet edition 1992

Printed and bound in Great Britain
for Hodder and Stoughton Children's
Books, a division of Hodder and
Stoughton Ltd, Mill Road, Dunton
Green, Sevenoaks, Kent TN13 2YA
(Editorial Office: 47 Bedford Square,
London WC1B 3DP) by Clays Ltd
St Ives plc. Typeset by Hewer Text
Composition Services, Edinburgh.

British Library C.I.P.
Pitman, Richard
   Warned off.
   I. Title   II. McNally, Joe
   823[F]

ISBN 0-340-569174

CHAPTER ONE

Back in December, two days before Christmas, I'd been stumbling across a wintry Newmarket Heath trying to find the way home after spending most of the night in the bar of a cheap hotel. Cold, tired, penniless, lonely and hungover, the last thing I needed to find was a corpse.

The grey-white grass and sky had frozen out the horizon and I followed a wide stream hoping to find a crossing place that would save me trying to skate to the other bank. I was watching my toes, half mesmerised by the sound of my boots crunching through the crystalled grass.

The body was lying face down, white with frost. His head was under the ice which locked him in like a big solid necklace. I bent down ... Three inches of flesh showed between the bottom of his trouser leg and the top of his brown sock and a single thin water reed was frozen onto the bare skin.

I touched the leg. It was bone hard. You could have knocked on it and heard the sound fifty yards away. I turned round and headed wearily back towards town and the police station.

The sergeant who broke the ice with a hammer and pulled the corpse's head out recognised him by the gold stud in his ear: Danny Gordon, twenty-seven years old, late of the Horseracing Forensic Laboratory, Newmarket.

1

His face was the colour and texture of tripe and his throat was cut so deep his head had almost come off.

The whisky that had tasted so good only hours before changed to bile and I turned away trying to swallow it back down.

The police took me back to Newmarket for questioning. What were you doing on the Heath so early? Going home. Where had you been? Visiting my sister. Where does she live? I don't know, she used to live here but they tell me she moved away a couple of years ago. You didn't know? No. How come? It's a long story, officer, return of the prodigal and all that. You were going home – the address you gave is at least fifty miles away; how were you planning to get there? Hitch a lift. Why? Because I have no money.

His sympathy was unaroused. They kept me most of the afternoon. I'd hoped they'd fix me a lift back to the caravan at Bartlett's place, but they didn't. I answered the questions and signed the statement and they said they'd be in touch and to notify them of any change of address.

It was early evening when they let me go. My feet were cold and wet, I had a day's growth of beard and the hangover was still there.

The shops in the High Street were brightly lit and busy. As their doors swung open and closed bursts of Christmas songs clashed in the dusk. It started snowing lightly, big flakes, and the shoppers smiled and mouthed at each other, 'White Christmas!'

An image of Danny Gordon's almost severed head came into my mind . . . thoughts of his wife as she told the kids that Daddy wouldn't be home for Christmas. Tidings of comfort and joy.

About nine weeks later McCarthy came to see me. I didn't recognise him when I first opened the caravan door; the only light came from a weak gas lamp hanging behind me, and though he looked up when he spoke his face was still in shadow.

I stepped to one side. The lamp swung and flickered in the wind but enough light fell on his face to identify him in my memory as Peter McCarthy, Racecourse Security Services investigator.

'Hallo, Eddie.'

The surprise at seeing him kept me silent.

'You remember me, don't you?'

I nodded. 'What do you want?'

'Just to talk.'

'The last time we talked it cost me my licence and eighteen months in jail.'

We stared at each other. The rain blew into his back and pattered in bursts on his wide-brimmed hat. 'Give me fifteen minutes,' he said. 'If you're not interested in what I've got to say after that you can throw me out.' I moved aside. He pulled the door open wide and came in.

As he took off his hat, rainwater ran from the brim onto his wrist and up his sleeve. He shook his arm quickly and pressed his jacket sleeve against it. 'Hell of a night, eh?' I didn't reply. Taking off his long heavy coat, he looked around him.

'There's a hook behind the door,' I said. Pulling a plastic chair from under the fixed table I left it for him, and went to sit on my bed in the corner. McCarthy hung his coat up then fished in his jacket pocket and pulled out a handkerchief.

He held it up to the light. There were dark smears and blotches on it and he was trying to fold it over to a clean bit. He saw me watching. 'Nosebleeds,' he said, 'been getting them since I was a kid.'

You'd have thought he'd carry more than one hankie but as I remembered he'd never been a man of particularly clean habits. Not that I'd had that much to

3

do with him, but he used to be a standing joke among the lads.

They said he was RSS's most effective man and that people would rather stick to the rules than face an interview with him. When he got excited, which was often, he was a fast, animated speaker who found it difficult to keep all his saliva and any unswallowed food remnants to himself.

He burped indiscriminately, though he did follow up with an automatic 'Pa'n me.'

About six feet two and three stone overweight (most of it on his belly, straining at the buttons of his shirt), his face and untidy curly hair had a greasy sheen even after he'd wiped away the rain (and some sweat) with his hankie. Before putting it back in his pocket he stuck his little finger up his nose, pulled something out, looked at it then wiped it on the hankie.

Finally he sat down, rested his arms on the table, clasped his hands and looked straight at me like I was a camera and he was about to start reading the news.

'Doesn't today's date give you a clue as to why I'm here?' he said.

The morning paper lay on the floor by my bed. I picked it up and read the date, '27th February'.

McCarthy smiled. 'That's right.'

'You've brought a late Valentine card.'

His smile widened. 'Nice to see you've kept your sense of humour.'

'It was more sarcasm,' I said, straightfaced, which made him uncertain. He dropped the smile and got serious. 'Your ban expired yesterday.'

'I know.'

He waited for me to say more. I didn't.

'I wondered what your plans were.'

'Why?'

He shrugged. 'Maybe I can help you out.'

4

'What makes you think I need help?'

He looked around the caravan. It was old. God knows how many of Bartlett's stablehands and labourers had used it before me. It was damp and dingy and full of holes which I'd plugged to get me through the winter, though the winds coming off the fields still found their way in.

'Not what champion jockeys are used to,' McCarthy said.

'Ex-champion . . . I get by.'

He sat straighter and unclasped his fingers. 'Come on, Eddie, how much longer do you want to be stuck in this box in the wilds of Northamptonshire?'

'I'll move on when I'm ready, without any help from you.'

He sat back and stared at me. 'You're bearing old grudges,' he said.

'Damn right I am.'

'You're being silly. What's the point? It won't do you any good.'

'It gives me personal satisfaction.'

'That doesn't pay the rent, does it?'

'The accommodation's free.'

'Nothing's free, Eddie.'

I looked at him. 'Does that include the "help" you're so keen to give me?'

He half smiled, half shrugged. 'We should both get something out of it.'

'Surprise, surprise.'

I got up to get a drink. All I had was a third of a bottle of whisky in a cupboard under the sink. Unscrewing the top I half-filled a small glass, feeling no more hospitable towards McCarthy than when I'd opened the door, but I did offer him a drink.

'Coffee, if you've got some. Milk and two sugars.'

As I filled the small tin kettle through the spout and

5

lit the one gas ring that worked I tried to figure what McCarthy's angle was.

The last time I'd seen him he'd been investigating my 'involvement' in a doping ring. I'd had nothing to do with it, but they didn't believe me. They took away my jockey's licence for life and warned me 'off the turf' for five years. Whatever he was here for it wasn't to say sorry.

The kettle bubbled and I sloshed some boiling water into a mug and left McCarthy to stir it.

Taking the whisky back to my bunk I sat down and drank. Swilling the liquid round my mouth I waited for him to start talking again. He looked across at me; I wasn't so sure he could see me in the dark corner but he raised his mug slowly. 'Cheers,' he said.

I nodded and waited to hear him slurp the hot coffee, but he sipped almost silently before taking up his newsreader's pose again. 'How close a touch have you kept with racing in the last five years?'

'None. I've no reason to.'

'You've been away most of the time, haven't you?'

'For a while.'

'Ireland, wasn't it?'

I nodded, unwilling to give him the satisfaction of me saying he was well informed.

'And you've been back in England, what, about eight months?'

'Last June. Almost nine.'

'Heard anything on the grapevine since then?'

'I'm a warned-off person, Mr McCarthy, people are not exactly rushing to my door with the latest gossip.'

'Were a warned-off person,' he corrected.

I sighed. 'You're using up a lot of your fifteen minutes splitting hairs.'

'Okay, okay. I was just trying to work out how much I had to tell you without covering old ground.'

6

He sipped some coffee, settling himself lower over the table.

'Towards the end of last flat season we heard from a good source that a new drug was being developed for use on racehorses. It's a powerful stimulant and is supposed to be undetectable. The plan as far as we know was to have it ready for the new flat season which is now, what, about three weeks away.

'We got on to it fairly sharp and we were making reasonable progress till just before Christmas when things came to a dead end with a guy called Danny Gordon.' He stopped and held my gaze.

'The same Danny Gordon I found with his throat cut?'

'The same. I think the man who had him killed is the man behind the new drug. Gordon worked in the lab at the Horseracing Forensic Laboratory.'

'I know.'

'He was last seen alive leaving a Newmarket pub with two men. That was three days before you found him. Now, it turns out the same two men, or at least we're pretty sure it's the same two, were responsible for a couple of serious assaults about a week before Gordon's death.

'A small-time crook called Elrick was visited at home by two blokes. We don't know what they wanted because Elrick won't talk, but before they left they systematically pounded his ankles, feet and toes with a builder's hammer. He had to have both feet amputated.'

McCarthy watched for my reaction. Involuntarily my toes wiggled. He wasn't finished. 'A week later the same two men, we think, went to see a guy called Ruudi Odin at his house on the Kent coast. Now, Odin's a much bigger fish than Elrick; he's been involved in syndicate fraud in England and bribing jockeys in Sweden.

'Again, he won't say what they wanted but they carefully slit his eyelids open with a scalpel. They taped cotton-wool pads over his eyes and soaked them in weedkiller . . . Blind for life.'

I drank. 'Is that it?'

'Then they killed Danny Gordon.'

'Who's going to be next?'

'There may not be a next, not if they got what they wanted from Gordon.'

'And how are you going to find that out?'

'By catching the man who's running the operation.'

'Good luck.' I raised my glass to him and drank. He watched me.

'You haven't asked where you come in.'

'Where do I come in?'

'We want you to find the killers.'

CHAPTER TWO

It stopped me in mid-swallow and almost made me choke. I put down the glass and picked up the battered alarm clock from the floor. 'Your fifteen minutes are up, McCarthy, good night.'

'Hear me out, Eddie.'

'No thanks, I've heard enough.' I got up, finished my drink at the walk and rinsed the glass out under the tap.

'Eddie, listen . . .'

'Look, Mac, you've won the bet or the contest or whatever it was you came here for. The let's take the piss out of Eddie Malloy trophy is yours, that makes you a dual winner. Now finish your drink and go away and amuse yourself somewhere else.'

'Eddie, slow down, slow down, for God's sake, I'm trying to help you.'

'Sure you are, just like you helped me five years ago?'

'Oh, come on, Eddie, be fair!'

'Me be fair! What do you know about fairness? How much did I get from you and your people?'

'Listen, I never agreed with your conviction or your punishment, it was way over the top. But I had to do the job I was paid for. What would you have done in my place?'

'I'd have spoken up, that's what I would have done, said my piece before your bosses decided to take away my livelihood for the rest of my days!'

9

'I did speak up! So did Charles Gilbrandson who sat on the Disciplinary Committee. Your riding ban was for life. They wanted to give you the same length of warning-off but Charles and I kept that down to five years.'

'Bully for you. It wouldn't have mattered if it was only a ten-minute warning-off; what would I want to do on a racecourse except ride? I'm banned from riding for life . . . that was all that mattered. Banned! . . . For what? For being "associated" with dopers. Associated, in my case, was socialising, having a few drinks with them, for God's sake!

'How the hell was I supposed to know what they were doing? But for your people guilt by association was enough. What was the phrase? "On the balance of probability." That was it, I was convicted "on the balance of probability". And you sit there trying to defend that!'

He was halfway to his feet but, sinking back into the chair, he looked down into his coffee mug, slowly swirling what liquid was left. The silence made me realise we'd been shouting. I turned and lifted my glass again and poured another drink, regretting I'd lost my temper. I'd never wanted them to see what they really did to me when they took my licence away.

Turning his head, McCarthy looked up at me. He spoke quietly. 'Do you want to sit down? I'll explain the whole thing.'

I stared at him.

'Ask me anything you want. I'll be straight with you.'

I walked slowly back to the corner and sat down. McCarthy looked across and with a half-shrug and open hands he said, 'Where do you want to start?'

Breathing out slowly I tried to relax, tried to gather my thoughts. 'Everything you've told me so far, it's all for real?'

He nodded. 'Every word.'

'Why did you come here?'

'To ask you to help find whoever is behind Danny Gordon's murder and the attacks on Odin and Elrick.'

'Why would you think I could help?'

'I only started thinking about it when your name came up in connection with the Gordon case. Up till then, to be honest, I'd forgotten you'd even existed.'

'Go on.'

'Well, we have a budget which allows for some "outside help" from time to time if we feel it's needed and when I saw your name linked with Gordon I started thinking . . . Remember Mr Kruger?'

I nodded slowly. 'What's he got to do with it?'

'It was more what he had to do with your case. You were convinced it was Kruger who set you up, weren't you?'

'He was the man behind the doping ring, I know that. I wouldn't have said he set me up. It was nothing personal, he just didn't care who was involved, who went down, as long as it wasn't him.'

'But you got him for it?'

'Oh, I got him all right. It cost me eighteen months in jail but it was worth it. If you guys had got him before you took my licence away then we wouldn't be having this conversation.'

'We tried.'

'Not very hard, though, did you? I managed to find him.'

McCarthy slugged down the last of the coffee though it must have been stone cold. Burping, he patted his stomach, 'Pa'n me.' He got up, carrying the mug. 'Mind if I make another?'

'Help yourself.'

He talked as he tried to light the gas. 'It wouldn't have mattered if we'd found Kruger, there was no real

11

evidence against him. The three others banned along with you denied your claims that Kruger had anything to do with it.'

'They were scared of him.'

'And that's why they wouldn't incriminate Kruger?'

'They told me that themselves. They said they wouldn't repeat it to you people, but they told me Kruger was the man and I told you and if you'd dug deep enough you could have found something to tie him in.'

'We didn't have enough grounds, Eddie, you know that, and we didn't have the time.'

'Well, you should have found the time, Mr McCarthy . . . you should have found the time! If it had been someone "important" instead of just an upstart jockey you'd have found it, wouldn't you?'

He was ready to come back at me with a direct answer but he stopped himself. 'Eddie, we're just getting into another shouting match. It's pointless. We'll be here all night if we keep raking through the justices or injustices of it. I know you're bitter . . .'

'Damn right I am.'

'. . . but what's the point, it's not going to get your licence back, is it?'

'Maybe not, but . . .'

'Eddie, please, let's get this business over with. Hear me out and decide what you want to do, then, if you want to blow your top completely over your own case, I'll listen . . . If it'll make you feel better, I'll listen.'

I threw back the rest of my drink and nodded slowly.

'Okay?' he asked.

'Okay.'

The kettle started its thin whistle and McCarthy fixed himself another coffee. Stirring the sugar in he turned towards me, 'Tell me how you tracked Kruger down.'

12

'By asking questions, travelling around, making a nuisance of myself; threatening, cajoling, bribing, following things up . . . By never being willing just to let it drop, by wanting it badly enough.'

'And you finally found him at home?'

The memory brought a smile to my face like it always did. 'Yep, at home in his nice big mansion in Kent, all alone.'

'I thought there were witnesses.'

'That was Kruger's story in court when I came to trial. He conjured up two girlfriends who he claimed were with him and saw me assault him.'

'But he was on his own?'

I nodded. 'And I beat the shit out of him.'

'And tried to drown him?'

'I was just cleaning him up a bit. There was a lot of blood on his face so I shoved his head down the toilet and flushed it a couple of times.'

McCarthy slurped some more coffee. 'They said in court he could have died, didn't they?'

'Yep, and I couldn't have given a toss if he did.'

'Any regrets?' McCarthy asked.

'About Kruger?'

He nodded.

'Absolutely none.'

'You showed a lot of good qualities.'

I didn't reply.

'Persistence, cunning, imagination, ruthlessness . . .'

'Mmm . . .' My mind was still back there. 'Maybe.'

'Think you could do it again?'

'What do you mean, if it happened all over again?'

'I mean now.'

I stared at him.

'This case we're working on now, the new drug. We got our hands on some of it in an incomplete form, sort of halfway through processing, if you like. We got it just before Danny Gordon was killed. It took about two weeks to analyse properly and when the report came through it . . . well, it seems like a lot of the techniques used in the processing of these drugs can be very individual, peculiar to one man or one team and sometimes this shows up in analysis.

'Well, what it comes down to is, if you were right five years ago and Kruger was behind the dope ring then, it looks like he's at it again. This stuff bears all the hallmarks.'

My mind was beginning to race. 'So what you're saying is, if Kruger is behind this and he gets caught there's every chance you can pin the old one on him?'

'Probably.'

'Would that exonerate me?'

'You know it wouldn't. You went down because you were a bit-part player. Correction, because you were thought to be a bit-part player. Your only chance of exoneration as far as I can see would be if Kruger admitted you had nothing to do with it.'

'And if he did?'

He shrugged. 'Who knows?'

I sat forward on the bed. 'Would I get my licence back?'

'We have to find him first.'

'Mac! Would they give me back my licence?'

He cradled the coffee mug and smiled. 'There'd be a hell of a stink if they didn't.'

CHAPTER THREE

I was finding it hard to control myself. If emotions travel through your body like blood then none had flowed through me for five years, the well had dried up. If they had started just trickling back I'd have been able to handle it better but they were gushing. I was almost shaking, I felt panicky. I got to my feet and started pacing, almost marching, up and down. Glancing wildly in all directions I couldn't keep my eyes still. I covered them with my hands, rubbing them hard, massaging my face, still striding up and down.

McCarthy mistook it all for impatience. 'Eddie, slow down, you can't start tonight.' I didn't answer. 'You're going to have to be fully briefed.'

I shoved my hands into my pockets and kept pacing. 'Tell me more about Kruger.' My voice sounded high-pitched, almost strangled.

'Later.'

'Now!'

'Eddie, you're building your hopes too high. Be realistic. If you do catch him he's going to hate you enough to want to kill you . . . probably already does. The last thing he'll want to do is clear your name.'

'I'll take my chances. Tell me everything you've got on him.'

'Slow down, man! Kruger is the main suspect but the evidence on the whole case is too scant to pin anything on anybody just now.'

'Just tell me, Mac!'

He got up. 'Look, if you're taking this on let's do it right. We'll arrange a meeting and you can have the full file on the case.'

'Tomorrow, then.'

'For God's sake, Eddie, slow down!'

I stopped pacing and faced him. 'Tomorrow, Mac. I've taken it easy and slowed down for five years . . . I want this bastard Kruger and I want my licence back. Meet me tomorrow.' I felt as if my eyes were bulging. My face was hot, it must have been deep red. McCarthy stared at me.

'Where?'

'What about the Red Ox?' I said.

'Fine. That's not far from my house. Okay, around 12.30?'

I nodded.

'Have you got transport?'

'I can probably talk Bartlett into lending me his car for the day but I'm going to need one long-term.'

McCarthy hauled his coat on and pulled the brim of his hat low. 'We'll talk about it tomorrow.'

'Okay.'

As he turned towards the door his hat hit the lamp and started it swaying to send a pool of yellow light up and down his body. He held out his hand and I grasped it. 'See you tomorrow, then?'

I nodded.

He smiled as the light flooded his face and I could see a small clot of dried blood just inside his left nostril. 'One thing, to stop you building your hopes too high, Kruger hasn't been seen for two years.'

He waited for a reaction. I didn't give one. As he opened the door the wind grabbed it, slamming it against the wall of the caravan. Outside, McCarthy held his hat on with one hand and as the lock banged

16

into its catch a last gust of wind killed the flickering lampflame and it went dark.

I lay awake for hours. Thinking of the future . . . Thinking of the past . . . Listening . . . to the wind . . . the rain. For the first time in years I closed my eyes with some hope for the morning.

Rising at dawn next day, I shivered as I dressed. I boiled some water and the coffee mug warmed my hands as I stood at the window.

Bartlett had only four horses in and it didn't take long to feed them and muck out. I'd known him have up to ten in at the one time. Horses out of training, ex-point-to-pointers, young unbroken ones, old rogues – they all had one thing in common, problems. Bartlett tried to sort out the physical ones and he expected me to deal with the mental ones.

I didn't plan to tell him I was leaving. I needed to borrow his car for the day and it was grudgingly lent, as things stood. It was a ten-year-old Saab and it started first time. Pulling out into the rutted farm road I checked the petrol gauge, half full. A thin drizzle started and I tried out the lights and indicators before I found the wipers.

By the time I reached Lambourn the rain was pelting down. I drove through the valley. On the downland gallops trainers would be working their second or third lots of the morning.

Up the slope to my right a string of fifteen or more walked steadily along the ridge, their riders in all colours of plastic capes hunched against the driving rain. They looked like Apaches coming home from an all-night party.

As I approached the village I passed half a dozen in single file, hooves splashing through the puddles, their scowling riders soaked, big wet patches on the light green rugs embroidered with the trainer's initials. I used to ride for him . . . long time ago . . . My warning-off had meant I wasn't even allowed to pick up droppings in his yard.

The Red Ox is a white-walled pub by the river Lambourn, its pebbled car park no bigger than a large front garden. Pulling in beside the only other car there, a brown Volvo, I killed the lights and switched off the wipers.

The bar was small, warm and thickly carpeted. On the walls were racing prints and a dartboard with a large tumour around the treble twenty.

McCarthy was the only customer. He sat in a corner by the window. His big coat hung near him on a stand. He nodded as I approached and sat down facing him, and I could see his fingers were politely trying not to drum on the heavy oak table.

'Am I late or are you early?'

'I'm early,' he said. 'I've got to be in London for two o'clock, something's come up.' He looked across at the barmaid. 'I've ordered sandwiches, will that do?'

I nodded. 'Sure.'

His briefcase was on the floor beside his seat. He bent and flicked it open and came up with a cardboard file thinner than a folded newspaper. Laying the file on the table he looked at me.

'What's that?' I asked.

'That's what we've got on the case so far.'

I picked it up. It weighed under a pound. I dropped it and it slapped back onto the table. The barmaid looked across from her sandwich making and seemed to spread faster. 'Won't be long, gentlemen.'

McCarthy gave her an apologetic smile, 'It's okay, no hurry.'

I pulled the cardboard folder towards me. 'Bulging with reports, eh?'

'I told you, our information dried up months ago. That's the result of only a few weeks' investigations.'

The barmaid brought the sandwiches and two glasses of beer. She was small and dark haired and she smelled nice.

I took a sandwich. McCarthy took two. I bit into the pink ham and swallowed some beer. McCarthy's was gone in a couple of bites. I tried not to watch his Adam's apple. He sipped some beer and the froth stayed on his lips.

'There's not really much else I can tell you. It's all in there,' he said.

I nodded slowly, watching him.

'Since I'm stuck for time, would you mind if we didn't discuss it now? Could you take it away and read it, then phone me with any questions?'

'Sure,' I said and he managed a small smile and seemed to relax. I smiled back. He picked up two more sandwiches and started chewing.

'Can I ask you one question just now?' I said.

He raised his eyebrows, chewed and nodded.

'How much are you paying?'

Six more chews, a swallow, a mouthful of beer and he replied, 'For what?'

'For me.'

'As in?'

'As in wages, salary . . .'

'How does six hundred a month plus expenses sound?'

'Mean.'

'It's a hard item to place on the budget, Eddie.'

'That's your problem, Mac. I've got to live.'

'How much is Bartlett paying you?'

'Bartlett asks me to break horses, you're asking me to catch murderers . . . and Bartlett throws in board and lodgings.'

19

He picked at his teeth with a fingernail. 'I'm arranging that for you, and a car.'

'Where will I be staying?'

'A friend of mine has a holiday cottage in the Cotswolds. I should have confirmation this afternoon that you can use it.'

'And the car?'

'A hire car will be delivered to you, just tell me where you want it and when.'

'Bartlett's place, 9 a.m. tomorrow.'

'Okay.'

McCarthy continued working on his teeth and looking at me, expecting more questions. I didn't ask any.

'We're agreed on six hundred a month then?' he said.

'And a five grand bonus on Kruger's conviction.'

He shook his head quickly. 'You're kidding, Eddie, there's no way I can authorise that.'

'Look, Mac, five grand is peanuts compared to what it'll cost if Kruger starts using this drug on the racecourse.'

'You've got Kruger hung out to dry and you haven't even opened that file.' He grabbed two more sandwiches and bit into them.

'It was you that said Kruger was the chief suspect,' I reminded him.

He drank and chewed, swallowed and burped. 'Pa'n me . . . only on the evidence we've got. Anyway, he's supposed to be your big motivation, not the money.'

'Mac, you said last night you had the budget for it.'

He wiped his mouth with the back of his hand and belched loudly again. 'Pa'n me . . . not that sort of money, for God's sake!'

I gripped his arm and he stared at me. 'Listen, Mac, at the end of this, if I'm not dead or crippled I'm going to have to live on something till either my licence is returned or I find another job. Trainers will hardly be queuing up to sign me – even with my licence it's going to be a long road back.'

He shook his head again, slowly this time. 'Can't do it, Eddie, not five grand.'

'Okay.' I pushed the file towards him. 'Let's forget it.'

'What do you mean?'

'I mean forget it, I'm not doing it, I don't want the job, it doesn't pay enough.' I took a drink.

'We can't forget it, where does that leave me?'

'Get your own guys to do it.'

'I can't.'

'Why not?'

He looked away without answering. Getting up, I walked round the table and leaned over him. 'Why not, Mr McCarthy?'

'They're too busy.'

'Bullshit.'

He forced himself to look up at me. 'Tell me why, Mac, tell me why your boys won't do it.'

He looked away again, silent.

'Then I'll tell you why – because they're scared. Isn't that right? Elrick's crippled, Odin's blind, Danny Gordon's dead and your guys are shit-scared!'

He was still avoiding my eyes. I went on. 'I was thinking about things as I drove here and the one thing that bothered me was the reason the RSS boys weren't dealing with this themselves.' I straightened up and walked slowly to the window. 'I can't believe I took in all that crap you gave me about how good a detective I was. What was it again? . . . Persistence, cunning, ruthlessness . . .'

McCarthy cut in, 'Those were the main reasons, Eddie, honestly.'

'Main reasons, my arse. The main reasons were that

21

you'd get me to take the chances your boys wouldn't because I was a worthless has-been and it didn't matter if I went the same way as the other three.'

I walked back to the table and stood in front of him. 'Am I right, Mac?'

'I am having a bit of trouble getting someone to take it on,' he mumbled. We were silent for a full minute then McCarthy spoke quietly, 'I'll pay the five grand if you still want the job.'

I moved back round the table and sat down. He pushed the file slowly towards me. I let him stew for another minute before picking it up.

'Good,' he said, smiling as he rose and reached for his coat. Putting it on he slung a business card across the table. 'Call me at that number around ten tonight and I'll give you details of the cottage.' I slid the card into my top pocket and drank some more beer.

'Must rush,' McCarthy said. 'I'll pay at the bar before I go.'

He walked towards the bar but stopped after about five paces, turned and came slowly back towards me. 'Eddie . . .' he said quietly. I looked up, smiling smugly, expecting an apology. '. . . Eh, you won't be wanting that last sandwich, will you?'

CHAPTER FOUR

It was mid-afternoon when I got back home and Bartlett was in the yard yelling at someone. His son stood scowling in front of him, a broken halter trailing from his hand. The boy was a thin pale sixteen-year-old with a moustache like a baby's eyebrow.

Bartlett was pushing him, thumping his chest with his open hand, shouting each word that synchronised with the blows. Knowing I could wind Bartlett up at the same time, I decided to rescue the boy before he got bumped into the next county.

'Mr Bartlett, sorry to interrupt the family get together but can I have a word?'

Bartlett spun and faced me. He was an ugly sod with an uncommonly large head sporting more hair than a man his age was entitled to. His thick lips were always wet and he opened them showing a mouthful of teeth that should have been given to one of his horses.

'What is it?'

He was still almost shouting but was concentrating on me rather than the boy, who took the opportunity and made a swift, silent exit.

'Holidays,' I said. His scowl had been pretty bleak but he dug hard and came up with another wrinkle on his forehead. 'What?'

'Holidays, Mr Bartlett.'

'What about them?'

'I'd like some.'

'Don't be daft.' He turned, looking for the boy. 'Benny!' he yelled. The only reply he got was a slight echo from an open box at the bottom of the yard. 'Benny! Don't you show your face back here without that filly!' He turned back to me. 'He spent an hour in the field catching her then, as soon as he gets through the gate, the silly little bastard lets 'er give 'im the slip ... I'm ashamed to admit he's my own flesh and blood.'

'Never mind, if he doesn't catch her, at least you won't see him again.'

He grunted and started walking towards the house. I fell into step with him. 'About the holidays, Mr Bartlett . . .'

He didn't stop. 'I don't pay you to take holidays, son.'

'I need a month off.'

'I can't afford to give it to you and you can't afford to take it.'

'What does that mean?'

Stopping at the front door he turned to look at me. 'It means, Malloy, that the first morning you don't show in this yard for work, you pack up your troubles in your old kitbag and get your arse out of my caravan.' He smiled and went into the house, slamming the door in my face.

Leaving in the morning was going to be a pleasure.

Reading the RSS file on the case didn't take up much of my evening. The evidence against Kruger was far from conclusive. It was based mostly on my allegations of his connection with my case five years ago, a reported sighting of one of his henchmen speaking to Danny Gordon a month before he died and a strong rumour that Kruger had been in Austria for the last two years (his son, who worked for a large drug company, controlled a research lab in Vienna).

A report confirmed that Kruger hadn't been seen in England for two years, that the henchman had disappeared since last seen talking to Danny Gordon and that neither the crippled Elrick nor the blinded Odin would answer 'relevant' questions.

On the two suspected murderers there was little information; brief physical descriptions which, in essence, said, both big, fit, white and English. The only recent clue to their whereabouts was an unconfirmed report that they'd been seen leaving Sandown racecourse three weeks ago with a jockey called Alan Harle.

I knew Harle, he'd been one of the bread-and-butter jockeys when I'd been riding. We'd had the odd drink together, the occasional sauna and I'd given him a lift to the races a few times. RSS had not yet interviewed him so he looked the most promising lead.

The rest of the file consisted of reports on the assaults on Elrick and Odin and on the murder of Danny Gordon. There was a photograph of his body.

It made me think of iced ponds and cut throats, and suddenly six hundred a month plus expenses seemed as crazy as Russian roulette with five bullets.

At ten o'clock I walked to the pub and phoned McCarthy.

'Eddie. Been through the file?'

'Uhuh.'

'Any questions?'

'Yes, am I mad?'

'No, just desperate.'

He was right. 'If I end up dead, scatter my ashes on Cleeve Hill.'

'Don't be morbid.'

'Tell it to Danny Gordon.'

He tried to change the subject. 'The car'll be there in the morning.'

'What about the cottage?'

'I'll tell you about it . . .'

McCarthy had said the place was isolated, he wasn't

kidding. It lay in the heart of a thick wood, the track leading to it barely wide enough for the silver Rover he'd hired for me.

The cottage had grey stone walls and a small garden, one bedroom, one kitchen, one living-room all furnished and decorated in greens, browns and greys. The inside walls were bare stone and six dark varnished beams split the ceiling into lanes. Faded cushions covered the stone seats of a deep inglenook fireplace.

A hand-written note was propped on the mantelpiece. 'Firelighters in kitchen cupboard. Logs in shed outside. Chimney may need to be swept.' It did.

The nearest village, eight miles away, was a village in name only, as I found on my first visit. It had fewer buildings than a two-quid Lego kit.

The next few days were spent organising. The phone wanted reconnecting, the chimney had to be swept, I needed logs for the fire, food, some new clothes and footwear. When everything was done I started looking for more to do, more mundane necessities, and I realised I was just putting off the moment when I'd actually have to start doing what I was being paid for – 'investigating', but I didn't know where or how.

I thought back to the last time I'd tracked down Kruger. I'd just been running around crazy then, asking everyone anything till I got what I needed. This time I couldn't work that way.

I sat down to think. It was dusk, windless but still cold. I built a fire and the clean chimney sucked at the firelighter flames and wrapped them round the ash logs. I washed the greasy paraffin film from my fingers, poured a large whisky, with ice, and sat down by the fire.

Holding the cut-glass tumbler I looked through the golden liquid and silver ice cubes at the flames. The room was dark except for the firelight which cast flickering shadows on the back wall.

I drank and tried to plan. The only definite links at the moment, apart from Harle, were Elrick and Odin. They hadn't volunteered anything to McCarthy's people and there was no reason for them to treat me differently, but I had to try. Elrick lived up near Nottingham. I would visit him tomorrow then go to Kent the day after to see Odin.

Even if I came up with nothing from those two at least I'd have made a start. I drank some more and thought some more and wondered about what was to come. The fire burned hot now and I eased off my shoes and closed my eyes.

CHAPTER FIVE

I found Elrick living with his sister in a run-down house near a village called Clipston. The gate was broken and swung both ways as I pushed through it. Elrick watched me from his wheelchair at the front door, a heavy coat and flat cap protecting him from the cold and an old blanket covering his legs. Allowing for his three or four days' beard growth he looked to be in his mid-forties.

As I walked up the path towards him the door opened and his sister came out carrying washing in a red plastic basket with a vertical split in one side which opened and closed like a fish's mouth as she came down the short ramp.

When she saw me she stepped in front of her brother's wheelchair, shielding him.

'What do you want?' she asked, holding the clothes basket in front of her now as if to protect herself. I stopped a few yards from her. 'Is it okay if I have a word with Mr Elrick?'

'No, he's not seeing anybody.' She was big and serious, maybe five years older than her brother.

'It won't take long – I've come all the way up from London,' I lied.

'Well just turn round and go all the way back,' she said. Elrick spoke. 'It's okay, Margaret, let him in.' I saw his hand on her hip, easing her aside. She scowled and stamped back into the house with her basket.

I walked up to him and offered my hand. 'Eddie Malloy.' He shook it.

'Thought I recognised the face.'

There was the trace of a foreign accent. 'David, isn't it?' I said.

'That's right.' His thoughts, suddenly, seemed miles away.

'How have you been?' I asked.

'I remember you, you were a fair jock.'

'Thanks . . . Look, I'm doing a favour for a friend and . . .'

'Used to ride Sandown well, as I recall.'

'Yes, thanks . . . Listen, David, I . . .'

'You got sent down, didn't you?' He was staring into the distance and hadn't looked at me once.

'That's right,' I said.

'Got you in the end, eh?'

His questions were rhetorical. I may as well not have been there.

'David, do you remember the man who did this to you?'

'I landed a real nice touch at Sandown once, Whitbread day it was.'

I sat down on the ramp beside his wheelchair. Our eyes were on the same level. 'Look, David, I'm trying to help catch these guys, I need . . .'

'Wasn't the big race, right enough. Last race of the day as I remember.'

I spent another five minutes on the same lines with no result. Either he was putting on a helluva good act or they'd screwed the guy's mind up completely. The latter was favourite. He was still rambling when I left. '. . . They'd given her a gallop too many, too, by mistake, and she still won easing up – funny old game, eh?'

Yes, Mr Elrick, a funny old game.

I decided to go to Kent that evening and find out if Ruudi Odin would be any more helpful. It was pointless putting it off till tomorrow; the time with Elrick had been wasted and I didn't want to waste any more.

Odin lived right on the shore. I got there just after 7 p.m. It was dark and the wind blew cold off the sea as I approached the unlit cottage. The curtains were drawn on the front windows and there was no sound from inside. The doorbell was a mechanical pull type; I pulled it. The chimes sounded, slow and hollow. I waited. No one came.

I rang again. Waited. Nothing. I walked round the back. The rear windows were heavily curtained and I tried looking for gaps, searching for some light inside. There was none. Not my day for meeting people.

I was surprised Odin wasn't at home. As far as I knew he lived alone except for his new guide dog and I'd been told he'd become a virtual recluse since being blinded.

He'd dropped what friends he'd had and if he went out at all it was only to walk on the beach.

Where was he then? Assuming he wasn't asleep in bed, I decided to find a pub and pass a couple of hours before coming back to check again.

The landlord of the Ancient Mariner had enough time on his hands to be throwing darts at the board in the corner. He had no opponent. Only two other men were in the bar. One was slumped in a chair by the gas-fire either asleep or dead and the other sat (perilously close to the dartboard considering the number of empty seats) eating crisps and reading *The Times*.

Mine host stopped throwing long enough to pour me a whisky, fold the fiver I gave him into a wad in his pocket and give me change. He came back my side of the bar and resumed his mechanical throwing.

'Fancy a game?' he asked.

'Don't play it,' I said.

He threw quickly; scored 60.

'Pity,' he said, recovering the darts.

'Mmm.'

He threw again: 57.

'We've got a good pub team here, y'know,' he said, dropping a dart as he pulled them out.

'Yeah?'

'Yep.'

No more chat, six more darts: 101 and 73.

'On holiday?' he asked, throwing again; scored 61.

'Visiting a friend,' I said.

'Local?' 90.

'A mile or so down the front, Ruudi Odin.'

'A close friend?' 81.

'Why do you ask?'

'He killed himself yesterday morning.' Bullseye.

The lady who'd been training Odin's guide dog had found the labrador whining below his dangling feet as he hung by its leather lead from the doorway.

She told the police Odin had become increasingly depressed since his 'accident' and the police said they were not seeking anyone else in connection with Odin's death. There was no suicide note.

Odin was dead. Elrick had a mental block. The only lead left was Alan Harle who'd been seen with the two men I was looking for. I hadn't wanted to approach Harle so early as there was every chance he was involved, but it seemed I'd little choice. I would just have to be careful.

I tried to contact him through a mutual jockey-friend but he was 'in France, looking after some horses for his guv'nor'. I was told he'd be back for the Champion Hurdle at Cheltenham, but that was eleven days away.

Eleven days with nothing to do but contemplate what it would be like to be back on a racecourse, the course I'd loved above all others, back among the people I'd known so well. I wondered how I'd handle it, how I'd cope . . . I was sure I'd get by.

Now here I was, high up in the new stand, feeling the wind, breathing deeply, watching everything below me, envying the jockeys, hating McCarthy, not coping, not coping at all.

CHAPTER SIX

I went to the Arkle bar and ordered whisky. The place was beginning to fill but I found a space by the window and unfolded *The Sporting Life*. The headline said: 'Spartan Sandal to Trample Rivals.' This was their tip for the Champion Hurdle, the biggest race of the year for two-mile hurdlers. There had been a time when I'd have known every runner's form by heart, but these past five years I'd deliberately deprived myself of racing information of any sort.

I had a lot of catching-up to do. I read on: 'Spartan Sandal looks to have a favourite's chance, in what appears to be a sub-standard Champion Hurdle, of landing the prize for the Essex stable of Jim Arlott.'

The writer went on to dissect the form but a piece near the end of the page took my attention. 'Castle Douglas, one of the outsiders, will be a first runner in the race for second season trainer, Basil Roscoe, who enjoys the exclusive patronage of the mysterious Louis Perlman, with whose horses he's done so well this year. A first ride in the race for Alan Harle, Castle Douglas would have to show mighty improvement to figure here.

'Still, if the miracle happened, surely Mr Perlman would at last come out of hiding to receive the trophy from the Queen Mother. Despite 23 winners this season Perlman has yet to be seen on a racecourse, or anywhere else for that matter.'

I'd never heard of Perlman or his trainer Roscoe and, when I was riding, Harle would never have had a chance of a ride in the Champion Hurdle. He hadn't been getting fifty rides a season five years ago.

I finished my drink and watched the bar fill up with bodies and noise and smoke. Little had changed. The women still wore furs and drank champagne and asked their men deliberately silly questions about horses, which they thought made them seem innocent and girlish.

The debutantes were still ever so wide-eyed, peach-skinned and plummy-tongued and when they heard a thick Irish accent they still giggled like they were at the zoo seeing some strange animal for the first time.

The Irishmen were still Irishmen. Talking fast, drinking faster, half their money already won or lost on the boat trip over and the rest ready to plunge between now and Thursday evening.

If you sat and listened you could hear other accents: Scots, Yorkshiremen, Brummies, Scouse, Welsh, Cockneys and a few who'd need interpreters when they went to have a bet.

I saw many people I didn't know and a few I did. I wondered how many of those who remembered me would take avoiding action when they saw me.

My glass was empty and I didn't want another drink. The bar was packed now, anyway, and I was drawing impatient looks from ladies waiting for somewhere to rest their drinks. I moved away and three old vultures swooped for my empty space. I didn't wait to see which one landed first.

Drifting around the course over the next couple of hours I saw a few familiar faces. Some stopped, some nodded, embarrassed, and some ignored me. To the ones who spoke I told them simply that since my ban was now up I planned to come racing occasionally for old time's sake.

An owner I used to ride for asked if I'd be getting my licence back, too. I told him I doubted that very much and he touched my arm and looked sympathetic. Sympathy riled me but I appreciated the gesture.

Watching what I could of the first two races from bad vantage points I saw an easy victory for the Irish in the first and a three whip finish of necks in the novice chase. I reckoned if I'd been on the runner-up he'd have won by a length. Dreams.

Twenty minutes before the off of the Champion Hurdle I was in the stand. This was one race I wanted to see from start to finish. Leaning on the barrier I passed the time hunting with my binoculars for familiar faces in the masses below.

By the time the big race runners came under orders the crush was really on around me. Tight against the railing I had drawn the short straw for immediate neighbours: three men, all big, all heavy, one behind me and one either side.

The race itself was uneventful, run at a fair pace with no casualties. The finish though was very interesting.

Spartan Sandal and Kiri jumped the last together and were having a hell of a tussle till halfway up the hill. That's when Alan Harle brought along the horse I'd been watching throughout, Castle Douglas, on the outside.

Castle Douglas, with Harle riding as though the devil were at his heels, flew past the battling pair halfway up the run-in and won going away by four lengths.

Twenty-to-one winners of the Champion Hurdle are seldom greeted with ecstasy by racegoers and Harle's was no exception. He galloped past the post to cries of 'What the hell's that?' and walked back in applauded by small polite sections of the crowd.

Raising my glasses I focused on Harle's face. He was wiping his nose on his sleeve and smiling. Leaning forward he slapped the horse three times on the neck and ruffled the delighted stable lad's fair hair.

Harle had certainly prospered since I'd left racing. He'd come into the game as a kid straight from the orphanage and had been riding for almost a decade when I first came on the scene, round the gaffs mostly, on bad jumpers nobody else would ride.

In consequence he'd suffered more than his share of bad falls but had always seemed to bounce back. From what I remembered of his personality he was an easy-going type who took opportunity where he found it. He liked drink and women, both in frequent doses.

As jockeys go he was not, or hadn't been, particularly ambitious or dedicated, nor did he ride for the thrill of danger. He never concentrated on one thing long enough to be scared of it or to realise that one day a horse might roll on him or kick his head and he'd never get up again.

To see him come back in on a Champion Hurdler, unless he had turned over a palm-size new leaf, stretched credibility to new lengths.

The stand cleared quickly as people hurried to see the winner being unsaddled. I didn't feel like joining the pack so I climbed to the top level which gave me a view of the paddock.

Harle dismounted to hearty congratulations from a camel-coated man and a brassy looking blonde in a tight black skirt. He was probably the trainer, Roscoe. The lady would be either his wife or girlfriend. I raised my binoculars.

He was fairly young, early thirties maybe, and, from his fair styled hair to his brown Gucci shoes, impeccably dressed. Arms out of the sleeves, he wore his coat like a cloak and maybe I was just imagining it but I swore I could smell his aftershave.

A handful of Pressmen surrounded him and the blonde who looked older, maybe forty. I tilted the glasses slowly: good legs, good figure, good dentist. Her mouth got a lot of exercise between smiling, pouting and talking and I decided she was Roscoe's girlfriend.

The MC for the presentation put me right when he picked up the microphone. 'Your Royal Highness, ladies and gentlemen, unfortunately the winning owner, Mr Louis Perlman, cannot be here today and so I now call on Mrs Basil Roscoe to receive the Champion Hurdle Challenge Cup on his behalf.'

The blonde minced forward, her stiletto heels murdering a few worms as she crossed the lawn. Her husband watched, smiling smugly, and I wondered what kind of owner Louis Perlman was and what pleasure he took from his horses if he never went to watch them run.

What was Roscoe's past history? He was a new one on me. The Press bar was only one floor below me so I put my glasses down and went looking for some information.

CHAPTER SEVEN

There was only one hack in the Press bar, Joe Judd of *The Sportsman*. Seated at a table he looked engrossed in a magazine held in his left hand. With his right hand Joe was breaking small pieces from the crust of a mince-pie and carrying them slowly towards his mouth.

Beside the pie was a pint of beer minus two mouthfuls. Occasionally Joe's hand would play tricks on the pie, heading for it, flexing its fingers, then at the last second passing over to clutch the handle of the beer glass. Not once did his eyes leave the magazine. The guy was a pro.

'You're supposed to write those not read them,' I said as I sat down across from him. He looked at me, cow-like, still chewing. With his black hair, brown eyes and sallow skin he looked of Latin stock. He wore a constantly perplexed frown as if he'd just been told he'd failed his driving test. He finally spoke. 'What do you know, Eddie . . . They told me you were back, what's the story?'

'No story, my ban was up a month ago, though the riding ban still holds . . . I'm just trying to get back into circulation.'

He nodded at the same pace he was chewing. 'Good, I'm pleased for you.'

His eyes went back to the magazine and his fingers to the mince-pie. Reaching for the plate I slid the pie slowly away from him. His fingers followed, though he didn't look up. I lifted the pie and bit into it, it was almost cold. Judd kept reading, though he spoke. 'That's my lunch, Eddie.'

'It's almost four o'clock,' I said through a mouthful of mince.

'Still . . .' he said.

'Shouldn't you be in the paddock doing interviews?'

He looked up. 'Nah, I don't worry about that. I'll get all the quotes from one of the lads.' He began reading again.

'How many races have you seen today?' I asked.

'None.'

'They still paying you three hundred a week plus expenses?'

'Four.'

'A fair day's work for a fair day's pay, eh?'

'That's my motto.' His right hand, still deprived of the pie, brought the beer to his lips.

'Want your lunch back, Joe?' I asked.

'Please.'

'Give me a minute of your attention then and the answers to a few questions.'

'Will you go away after that?'

'Yes.'

He put the magazine down and gave me the benefit of his frown.

'Basil Roscoe's horse just won the Champion Hurdle,' I said.

'Good for him.'

'What do you know about him?'

'He hasn't been training for five minutes, he's an upstart and if he didn't have a wife I'd say he was a poof.'

'What's his background?'

'Ex-public school, ex-city, ex-Wall Street, ex-directory.'

39

'You don't like him?'

'None of the lads do. He won't talk to us unless it's on the racecourse. See him in the street, he'll walk past. Phone him at home, he won't talk.'

'And he won't tell you about his big owner, right?'

'Perlman? . . . Yes, that's been a long-running battle. Every time someone asks about him Roscoe just taps the side of his nose with his cute little finger and says, "Mr Perlman values one thing above all others, privacy." Creep.'

'I hear he's got a dozen of Perlman's horses.'

'That's right, they're all winners too.'

'Perlman got horses with anyone else?'

'Nope, Roscoe's virtually his private trainer.'

I didn't want to press too much, Judd was beginning to look interested. There was just one more thing I wanted to find out. 'How long has Alan Harle been riding for Roscoe?'

Judd considered. 'About six months, I'd say.'

'What was he doing in the six months before that?'

'Scraping his usual living, I suppose. At the start of the season he was still bumming around the gaffs.'

I smiled. 'So everything comes to he who waits, after all, eh?'

'So they say, Eddie, so they say.' He looked at his lunch. I was still guarding it. Sliding the plate across the table I left it halfway there in no man's land. He looked again at it. 'Thanks,' he said, drily.

I got up. 'You're welcome.'

Leaning on his elbows, hands clasped, he looked up. 'You know, if I didn't want rid of you so quick I might be interested in why you're asking questions about Roscoe.'

Pushing the chair in I rested my hands on the back. 'I think he might be my long lost brother,' I said.

Judd didn't smile. 'Your sense of humour has not benefited from your prolonged rest.'

'My bank balance isn't too healthy either,' I said. You could almost see Judd's ears prick. 'You got something on Roscoe, money-wise?'

I laughed. 'You're adding two and two and getting five, Joe. Evil minds are bad at sums.'

He frowned on, unconvinced.

'Between you and me,' I said, 'it's actually Harle I'm worried about. He's an old buddy of mine and I'd hate to see him fall into bad company.'

'Sure you would.'

I nodded. 'Mmm.'

Judd's elbows began to spread and his chin sunk lower over his stone-cold lunch. But his eyes kept looking up at me.

'If he's such an old buddy of yours, why don't you go and ask him questions?'

I shrugged. 'Can't get near the guy since he went up in the world. He's a bighead.'

'Pinhead, more like.'

His chin came to rest an inch above the pie, his eyes still watching me. I straightened. 'Thanks for your time, Joe.'

He grunted and lowered his eyes. The frown didn't waver.

'*Bon appetit,*' I said.

He was still staring at the pie when I left.

There wouldn't be a chance of getting near Harle while he was celebrating his big win so I bought a card from one of the stalls, scribbled a congratulatory message and asked a passing jockey to give it to him.

I walked on through to the ring, the bookmakers' stronghold. The next race, an amateur's steeplechase, was fifteen minutes away and I had decided to go on to the course and watch it from ground level at the last

41

fence. A stroll among the betting boys would pass the time nicely.

There were about eight rows with twenty-five bookies in each. Every pitch had a betting board and two wooden stools, one beside the board on which stood the bookie and one behind it supporting his clerk.

The clerks stood, head bowed, over their big open books, solemnly jotting details like a weary St Peter on a busy day. The bookies chalked the odds up on their boards, frequently chopping and changing and barking their offers out of throats blistered by years of calling prices.

Up and down the rows punters moved slowly but almost constantly, milling like cattle. Occasionally a maverick would break loose and move fast, jostling his way through to the bookie showing the best price for the horse he wanted. Sometimes a few broke simultaneously in different directions causing a minor stampede as others tried to follow to see what they might be missing out on and try to have some of it before the bookie wiped it off.

When the men on the stools adjusted the prices according to the weight of money, the crowd would settle again into their uneasy milling, waiting for the next break.

I knew a few of the bookies and some nodded recognition as I wandered among them. None looked surprised to see me. I walked to the rails where the real big money boys bet. Rails bookies weren't allowed to display boards, nor did they need to; most of their customers were known to them by name and bank account number.

At the end of this line was an old and very familiar face which opened in a big smile when it saw me.

'Eddie, my old son, come 'ere!' The battered voice hadn't changed. I walked up smiling and shook hands with Wilbur Slacke. He clasped my hand in both of his which were cold and white with thick blue veins.

'Still skinning the punters then, Will?' I said.

'Just enough to keep the wolf from the door as usual, Eddie, though the bugger's getting a bit too close to the front gate recently!'

'Does that mean you'll have to sell one of the Mercs? My heart bleeds.'

He smiled even wider, showing his own teeth still, though they'd seen better days. His eyes watered in the cold wind as he stepped rheumatically off the stool to lean on the railings.

'How's business with you?' I asked.

'Not so bad, Eddie . . . Can't complain really.'

'The big winner must have been a good one for you.'

'Brilliant result. Best one I can remember in the Champion for a long time . . . We all won a few quid except that big bugger at the end.' He nodded down the line of bookies towards a sour looking character handing someone a wad of notes as thick as a sandwich.

'The big guy with the black hair?'

Will nodded, still smiling. 'A right mean bastard.'

'I don't remember him from when I was riding.'

Will coughed from somewhere deep then turned away to spit. 'Nah,' he said, 'Johnny-come-lately from up North – shouldn't even be here. He's never been on the waiting list for that pitch. Claims he's operating it on behalf of Sammy Wainwright but I'm sure he bought Sammy off. Still, he's took a few doings with results recently so maybe he'll get skint soon and crawl back into the hole he came out of.'

I'd never heard Will call anyone down so much. I looked at the guy again. He was taking money this time but didn't look any happier.

'What's his name?' I asked.

'Stoke. Howard Stoke.' He started coughing again and I slapped his back gently. When he stopped his face was crimson and his eyes full of water.

'A nice glass of malt would quieten that down,' I said.

'Likely.' He nodded.

'Half a dozen would kill it stone dead.'

His smile returned. 'And me with it.'

'There are worse ways to go, Will.'

'You might be right,' he said as another coughing fit bent him double.

Out on the course, away from the crowds, the grass was lush on good to soft ground which gave an inch under my heels. I stood by the open ditch way over on the far side of the track. The black birch was tightly packed between the white wings that led the horses in. The fence sloped away, inviting them to jump.

The field approached. Sixteen thoroughbreds. Eight tons of horseflesh moving at thirty miles an hour. Watching the leader, a big bay, his ears pricked as he came to jump, I found myself counting the stride in with his jockey . . . One, two, three, kick – up and over he goes.

The rest reach it now, closely grouped, the jockeys' colours mixing, meshing with speed. The thunderous hoofbeats shake the ground and the birch crackles like a long firework as their bellies brush through. Cameras click and whirr, jockeys shout and whips smack on flesh. They land, their front feet pushing into the turf. Hooves slide and a big brown head goes low. The rider cries out but his mount recovers. They are last by a length as the runners gallop away.

Silence now. Emptiness.

In the depths of depression I head home.

CHAPTER EIGHT

Back at the cottage I poured a drink stiff enough to splint a fracture and sat down. It was cold and gloomy. I lit a fire. After five minutes' spitting and crackling the logs caught properly and began to warm the room.

I drew the curtains, closing out the dusk, and filled my whisky glass. I left the lights off, the fire was bright enough.

I stood in front of it staring down at the burning logs. Then at myself in the mirror above the mantelpiece. The flames weaved and jumped, casting light then shadows on my face and shoulders ... I looked tired ... ghostly.

After another drink I began to feel warm inside as well as out. Pulling the chair nearer the fire I sat down and started thinking ... It had been a bloody melancholy day.

Tipping the glass towards me I looked through the liquid at the soft yellow gold of the flames. I stared. All that looked back was my self-pitying face. Finishing the drink in one gulp I shut out all the old pathetic thoughts and faced up to reality.

I was no longer a jockey. Maybe I'd never be a jockey again. There was a job to do and it had to be done on the racecourse as much as anywhere else.

I had hated that place today because I wasn't the big shot any more. I would always hate going to racecourses now like a deceived husband would hate

attending parties thrown by his ex and her lover –
after having to watch them fawn over each other all
evening nobody would even say goodbye when he left
because nobody would notice he'd gone.

Well, I would damn well just have to get used to it
because it was the only way back for me.

Pouring another drink I tried piecing together the
day's events. I hadn't been able to talk to Harle.
He'd been tied up with interviews, celebrations and
all the other demands which fall on Champion Hurdle
winners.

How direct could I be anyway, when I did meet
him? How long before people would start asking
questions about me asking questions? I'd gone over
the top a bit with Joe Judd. He was definitely suspicious and though he was lazy, he was shrewd
enough. If Joe smelt an exclusive for his paper he'd
start asking questions of his own. I'd have to be
careful.

I thought about Harle's connections: Roscoe and this
phantom, Perlman. Strange bedfellows. Harle himself,
his rapid rise to fame.

I had been out of racing a while, I know, but things
don't change that much. There are jockeys who are
bound for the top from the first time they sit on a
horse and there are some who make a decent living
after three or four years.

But I'd never known one to bum around as long as
Harle then find himself employed by a powerful new
owner as first jockey. I made a mental note to find
out who rode the ones Harle wasn't available for and
how many outside rides Harle's new-found fame had
won him.

What goes for jockeys goes double for trainers. They
don't come from nowhere to training for a top owner.
Roscoe was even more surprising than Harle, who'd at

least had the experience of bumming around the gaffs. But here he was up with the guys who'd been training Festival winners before he could keep his nappy dry for a whole night, training a Champion Hurdle winner. I wondered how long he'd known Harle.

As for the elusive Mr Perlman, I'd heard of one or two shy owners in my riding days but they'd never stuck the game long. They were the people who had inherited horses or rich folks pressed into it by poorer friends. Owning racehorses was not a pastime for shrinking violets.

It stretched credibility to breaking-point to believe that Perlman wouldn't make at least a token appearance to be presented by royalty with the Champion Hurdle winner's trophy.

If he were patronising one of the big stables I'd have been inclined to believe he was simply an extreme eccentric but the fact that Harle and Roscoe were involved made me very sceptical.

Perlman had to have something serious to hide. Maybe under another name he'd been warned off. If so, what offence had he committed?

Perlman would have needed Jockey Club clearance before being accepted as an owner and I wondered if he'd ever been interviewed. I'd mention it to McCarthy at the first opportunity and see if he could turn up anything in his files.

Harle would be staying at the Duke's Hotel in Cheltenham. That was where the top-notchers went. The racing snobs never stayed anywhere else. Roscoe was certain to be bedding down there with Mrs Roscoe and where he was, Harle wouldn't be more than a couple of lengths behind.

There would be a party tonight with the Champion Hurdle under their belts and everybody who thought they were anybody would be there. The tales passing among the loose tongues would be worth hearing. I decided to invite myself.

It was 7.30. My glass was almost empty. I swallowed the last of the whisky and decided to sleep for a couple of hours before tidying myself up to gatecrashing standard.

A steady drive into town, a meal somewhere and the party would be in full swing by the time I got there. I put down my glass and relaxed in the chair. The logs burned brightly and the shadows jumped faster on the back wall. It was very warm. I drifted into sleep.

The Rover's twin beams lit up the narrow twisting hilly roads which didn't straighten till near the outskirts of Cheltenham. The town was busy. The population must treble during Festival week.

I parked and found a restaurant with Regency decor and a fair to middling chef. After eating an acceptable if unspectacular meal I remembered to ask for McCarthy's receipt.

The white front of the Duke's Hotel was illuminated by a row of floodlights in the gardens facing it. This was my first time through its doors for six years. Inside, nothing had changed: twenty guineas a roll wallpaper and thirty quid a yard carpet. Teak, leather, brass and silk in dignified doses.

At reception a dark-eyed, cream-bloused twenty-year-old told me Mr Roscoe had taken the Directors' Suite for the evening, that it was on the third floor and if I was Mr Glenn I was to go right up.

I didn't tell her I was Mr Glenn and I didn't tell her I wasn't. I just went to wait for the lift.

The Directors' Suite was big enough to hold maybe fifty or sixty people. The walls were oak-panelled, shiny, the carpet thick and luxurious below groups of small chandeliers. The room was longer than it was broad and I guessed that a large conference table had been hurriedly removed to accommodate Roscoe's ravers.

There were at least fifty people too many for comfort. A smoke haze hung low under the lights like a bank of smog, staying a foot above the tallest heads, though you somehow thought if the constant chatter stopped below, it might drift down and smother everyone.

They had all, according to taste, dressed for a party, some of the women with much care, but that had been hours ago. By now there were distinct signs of staleness; a carelessly rubbed eye leaving a mascara smear, a few straggling tendrils escaping from a blonde bun, a vee-shaped frock front which had taken an uneven dive showing a tanned, wrinkled cleavage. If all the jewellery were real there was a million pounds' worth.

I recognised a number of jockeys, conspicuous anyway by their short stature. The other men were all shapes and sizes and in varying stages of undress, some missing ties or jackets or both. Some leaned against walls and flirted with women. Some leaned against walls and thought about flirting with women. Everyone held a drink.

The men smoked cigars, the women cigarettes – not a place for bronchitis sufferers. It was warm and stuffy from too many bodies. A sweaty affair.

I sidled through the throng to where I'd guessed the bar was. It was makeshift: two long tables pushed together and covered with embroidered linen. Two bar-maids in black uniforms were pouring champagne at a hot pace. Working my way through I lifted a glass.

Someone spoke in my right ear. 'Take two.' Something in the voice zoomed straight into my memory bank and locked on immediately. I knew who it was before I started turning round, someone I hadn't seen since I was fifteen years old, someone I'd had such a crush on at school I hadn't even been able to speak to her.

I faced her. Charmain. The auburn hair was pinned up showing small ears and the fine jawline, as I remembered it, along with the green eyes and the wide lips, just thick enough to give the impression of a permanent pout. She was lightly made-up, a natural flush colouring her cheeks.

I had never really forgotten her over the years. She'd been my first love and it hadn't mattered all that much that it was unrequited. I had often lain awake especially in prison, thinking about her, dreaming of meeting her again and fantasising about the outcome.

The scene had been well rehearsed in my mind; we'd look at each other for a long moment just like we were doing now then she'd say, in a voice mixed with curiosity and desire, 'Aren't you Eddie Malloy . . .?'

All my old feelings for her came flooding back as I waited for her to speak. Her look turned to one of slightly puzzled recognition. 'Don't I know you?'

I nodded, trying to look cool. 'I'm Eddie Malloy. We were at school together.'

Her eyes widened. 'Oh, I remember . . . of course.'

But I could see she didn't remember so I pretended, childishly, that I couldn't recall her name properly. 'And you're, eh, is it Carol . . . ?'

'Charmain,' she said, unoffended. 'Carroll used to be my surname but I'm married now.' She held out her left hand. The fat solitaire over a wide golden wedding band put the seal on my past like a trap-door closing.

I stared at the rings. 'When did that happen?' I asked, unintentionally making it sound like some kind of tragedy.

'Six months ago,' she said, smiling radiantly.

I caught myself about to ask if she really loved him.

I was getting sillier by the minute. She made me feel even worse with her next question. 'What are you now?' she asked. I frowned. 'I mean, are you a trainer or a jockey or something?'

Obviously just a something, I thought . . . In her eyes, anyway. 'I used to be a jockey,' I said.

'Were you good?'

'Yes.'

'Is that all?'

'What more do you want?'

'You don't just say yes to a question like that.'

'I do.'

She looked perplexed.

'You're funny,' she said.

I stared at her. 'Thanks.'

'Why did you stop if you were good?'

'The Jockey Club took my licence away.'

'Why?'

'They said I was involved with a dope ring.'

'Were you?'

'What do you think?' I said, my childishness showing again.

She shrugged, looking slightly hurt at my attitude. 'I don't think you'd have done it,' she said.

I suddenly felt a great tenderness for her which was quickly snuffed out by a hefty bump from behind which made me spill my drink. Some splashed down into an empty glass but most stained the white linen tablecloth. The offender pushed past without apologising.

I recovered and looked round. A large man had his large hand on Charmain's bare arm. Four thick fingers gripped her upper arm so tightly that the flesh between them showed white and bloodless.

She looked surprised and embarrassed. He looked very angry.

51

About six feet two and fiftyish, his bluish-black hair colour was as natural to an Englishman as chappatis for breakfast. It looked greasy and hung over his collar. His sideburns were dyed the same colour and stretched over his pale skin to two inches below his ear lobe. His eyes were a thick cloudy grey.

He wore a fawn jacket over a stomach that was held in only by a large ego. His feet, in crocodile shoes, splayed badly, the heels almost touching but the toes wide apart.

He looked as mean as he had when I'd seen him earlier that day at the races paying out a lot of money.

'Howard!' Charmain said, half pleading. His grip was hurting but she didn't try to pull free.

'Where have you been?' His voice was level but threatening. I guessed he'd had a lot of practice containing a nasty temper in public. I was having some trouble containing mine.

'I just came to get another drink, darling!' She looked up at him and turned on a full wattage smile, though he was still hurting her. I watched his fingers, they began to relax.

'Good,' he said and released her arm. Her hand went up to cover the thick white fingermarks, though she kept smiling. His ugly mouth smiled, showing teeth yellow near the gums and white at the biting end but his eyes stayed mean.

Charmain introduced us. 'Oh, Howard, this is Eddie, he used to be . . . a jockey.' He looked down and the smile left his mouth. He didn't offer his hand and he didn't say pleased to meet you. Charmain tried it from my side. 'Eddie, this is my husband, Howard Stoke.'

I smiled my most pleasant smile. It upset him.

'Who invited you?' The growl was still level.

'I'm a friend of Alan Harle's.' I was still being pleasant.

'I could have guessed that,' he said. I waited for the punchline.

'You jockeys all have the same dumb look.' His mouth smiled at his little taunt and his eyes kept watching me from their four-inch height advantage. I drank.

'Are you always as nice to new acquaintances?' I asked.

He leaned forward and down. 'You won't ever be an acquaintance of mine, son.'

I feigned deep disappointment, shaking my head. 'And after we'd started on such friendly terms.'

He leaned even closer. I could hear him breathe in his nostrils. 'And you won't ever be an acquaintance of this lady either, you randy little bastard.' The grey in his eyes was darkening like rainclouds and I felt like saying, I've got news for you, mate, but for Charmain's sake I didn't.

Charmain clutched his sleeve. 'Howard, please come and introduce me to some of your friends ...' He hesitated, glaring at me for another ten seconds, then he grabbed her arm and turned away. She didn't look at me as she followed him. I called after him, 'Very nice meeting you, Mr Stoke.'

He turned and snarled, 'Up yours.'

'Likewise.' I smiled. They went into the throng and I watched his head bob away across the room as he dragged Charmain behind him. Beauty and the Beast ... How the hell had she ever got tied up with him?

I looked around wondering if there were any other guests as nice as Howard Stoke. No one was watching me so I took it that the small altercation either hadn't been noticed or was accepted as normal practice when someone spoke to Charmain.

Taking another glass of champagne I went looking for Alan Harle. I saw him standing by the entrance door and started making my way across, but when I was half a dozen steps away he opened the door and went out. I followed him.

CHAPTER NINE

Six paces ahead and weaving unsteadily along the corridor Harle stopped halfway down and pushed carelessly against a door. It swung back and he went in. I reached the door; Gentlemen, the sign said. I was one of those.

It was all tiled, pale blue. There were three cubicles, two sinks with blue bars of soap and two blue containers of liquid soap.

The door of the middle cubicle was closed. Harle was behind it. I stood by the sink nearest the drier and waited. A minute went by. There had been no sound.

The door opened and Harle, fiddling with his jacket collar, took two paces out. He almost caught his breath in surprise when he saw me and turning back in he flushed the toilet. When he came out again he looked completely calm and so pleased to see me you'd have thought I was his dinner date.

He walked right up to me and shook hands. 'Eddie ... They told me you were back. Great news, eh? How've you been doing?'

I smiled back at him. He was small, even for a jumps jockey, about five three, but he had what bodybuilders called perfect symmetry though his face was far from symmetrical. He'd been a stablelads boxing champ in his younger days. Some said he was a hell of a lot better at boxing than jockeying.

He couldn't have been that good because his nose

was spread a fair bit and had been for as long as I'd known him. His face was chipped in one or two places from racing falls and a crescent-shaped thick pink scar showed through his dark thinning hair. I remembered that one.

He'd got it from a ragged racing plate attached to a flying hoof and it opened his head like a razor slicing a melon. I'd been in the ambulance room when they brought him back. There was enough blood to make a stone of black pudding. They stitched it and he was back riding next day.

'I've been doing all right,' I said, 'but not riding Champion Hurdle winners.'

'Magic, eh?' he beamed. He was drunk but looked lively.

'Fantastic,' I said, 'but no more than you deserve after all the dogs you've ridden in the past.'

He turned to the mirror, still smiling widely, and smoothly drew a comb from his back pocket. Only his head and shoulders showed in the mirror as he combed his sparse hair. 'Yeah, you can say that again. And you won't see me on no dogs in the future either, it's going to be all top quality stuff from here on in.'

'Yes, I heard you'd landed a good retainer with, eh, whaddyacall'im . . .?'

The comb still moved in useless sweeps. 'Roscoe,' he said, 'Basil Roscoe.'

'That's right. I couldn't remember the name. He's a newcomer, eh?'

'After your time anyway, Eddie.'

'Yes, I've been out of touch.'

The comb stopped. Harle admired its work then pushed it back into his pocket. He was still looking in the mirror so I turned too and our reflections carried on the conversation.

'Any more like Castle Douglas tucked away?' I asked.

'We've got a couple of cracking novices. One runs in the Triumph on Thursday, Tourist Attraction, he's called.'

'Fancy him?'

'He'll skate up. Don't miss him.'

'I won't. Who owns him?'

He hesitated a moment. 'He's the same owner as Castle Douglas.'

'Lucky man. Who is he?' I tried to appear open-faced and innocent. I don't know if he bought it because he paused again before answering and gave me a glance which said, Is this guy kidding?

'Mister Perlman, he's Roscoe's biggest owner.' He straightened his tie, leaving the top shirt button loose.

'Perlman? Never heard of him either,' I said.

'He's only been on the scene a couple of years.'

I shook my head slowly. 'Boy, I can't get moving for overnight success stories since I came back.'

Turning from the mirror he looked at me squarely, accusingly. I smiled in apology and grabbed his arm. 'Hell! I don't mean you, Alan. You deserve every winner you get, you've worked hard for your success.' He looked placated.

I followed up. 'But if you were honest, doesn't it make you sick when guys like Roscoe and Perlman flash a few quid around and suddenly they've got a Champion Hurdler when they haven't been in the game five minutes?'

He shrugged. 'That's the way it is, Eddie, money talks.'

'Where did Perlman get his hard-earned fortune?'

'Nobody knows.' He was fishing in his pockets but his hands came out empty. 'Any smokes?' he asked.

'Sorry.' I laughed. 'Go in and ask Perlman for a Havana, I'm sure he can afford it.'

'I would if I knew what he looked like.'

57

I looked puzzled. 'What are you talking about?'

He smiled.

I thought I heard the door open. Harle spoke. 'What I could tell you about Perlman . . .'

There was a slight squeak of the doorspring returning. I heard no footsteps on the tiled floor but Harle became alert. He gave a follow me nod and turned to leave. Whoever was inside the door was hidden from us by a dividing wall; he heard us move and began walking in. Turning at the end of the wall we almost collided with a small, neatly dressed and apparently stone-cold sober man with thick glasses.

He looked surprised. 'Oh sorry!' he said and stepped aside to let us pass. 'Have to be getting the old eyes tested again, Alan.'

Harle nodded at him and smiled. We went out into the corridor.

'Friend of yours?' I asked.

'I've seen him around the racecourse and he's in here with us tonight. Don't know who asked him.'

We began walking back towards the party. 'Anyway, what were you saying about Perlman?' I asked.

We reached the door of the Directors' Suite. 'Some other time, Eddie, eh?'

'Sure.'

He took my elbow. 'Come on in and have a few drinks.'

Not knowing who might be among the crowd in there I decided to leave it till I could get Harle alone. 'No, thanks.' I smiled. 'I'm riding out in Lambourn early tomorrow. First time back on the gallops . . . you know how it is.'

'Come on, it wouldn't be the first time you'd ridden out on five minutes' sleep. Remember that party at Welsh's, all Saturday night and most of Sunday?' He still gripped my arm.

I smiled. 'I remember it well, that's why I'm going home.'

He let me go. 'You've gone soft, Malloy.'

'Just out of training, Alan. I'll meet you after racing on Thursday and we'll make up for it.'

'Okay, you're on!' He stuck his hand out. I shook it. 'Enjoy what's left of the party.'

'Don't worry, I will,' he said, opening the door and pushing back in. I headed along the corridor to the lift, knowing Harle wouldn't see a bed before dawn and when he did he wouldn't be in it alone.

As I reached the toilet door our little friend came out and almost bumped into me again. 'Oh, sorry! I'm sure I'll have a serious accident before the night's out. Sorry.'

'That's all right.'

He waddled back towards the party scratching his head, trying to promote his bumbling image. I was not impressed.

When he'd gone I went back into the toilet. All three cubicle doors were open. Stepping through the centre one I closed it behind me. Although I had half an idea what I was looking for it didn't stop me being surprised when I found, taped to the base of the cistern, a plastic bag containing an empty glass phial and a syringe.

On the return journey I drove faster than was safe on those twisting roads. All the way back there was an old familiar feeling in every part of me.

For the first time since I'd last sat in a racing saddle everything was synchronising inside me: brain, blood, muscles, confidence, reflexes – everything was moving at racing pace.

I was in a new job and I'd just found out how good I was at it. The adrenalin was back.

I slept better that night than for years and next morning I bounced out of bed, dressed and made coffee.

59

Carrying the hot mug I went to the telephone and dialled McCarthy's number. He answered the phone himself.

'Can't you afford a secretary?' I asked.

'Who is this?'

'Malloy.'

He wasn't pleased. 'What do you want?'

'Some information.'

'On what? Is it important?'

'It is to me.'

'Look, Eddie, I'm under severe pressure over yesterday's Champion Hurdle. The Jockey Club want a report by noon today. There's no way . . .'

'What about the Champion Hurdle?'

'Well, nothing . . . Nothing about the race itself, anyway. But someone high up says heads will roll because the Queen Mum was embarrassed at the presentation by the absence of the owner. She didn't complain but the course executive look on it as a deliberate insult by this guy Perlman.'

'Go on.'

He hesitated. 'You know something about this?'

'Finish your side first.'

'Okay. We sent someone to interview Perlman this morning . . . He can't be found. His house, or at least the address we have registered, is completely empty and has been for a while according to the locals who also say they've never heard of Perlman.'

'Wasn't he checked through the normal procedures before you people accepted him as an owner?'

'Of course he was! Couldn't have been more impressive. A million quid's worth of country house in Wiltshire, a Rolls in the drive – we even sent the same guy this morning who interviewed him initially. The place is deserted.'

'What happens now?' I asked.

'Arses get kicked, we tighten up our clearance procedure and we keep looking for Perlman.'

'Have you spoken to Roscoe?'

'Yes. He claims he's never met Perlman nor spoken to him. He communicates with the stable by telex only and pays his bills prompt on the eighth of every month. Obviously we'll be looking further into that but time is what we don't have at the moment.'

Frayed as it was, I offered the lifeline. 'If Perlman actually exists then I know someone who might tell me a few things about him if I buy enough champagne.'

'Who? And what do you mean if he actually exists?'

'Oh, come on, Mac, how many owners do you know who don't turn up when they win the Champion? How many have never met their trainer? The name's got to be a front for someone, maybe somebody who's been warned off in the past.'

'For what?'

'How would I know? But whatever it was he might be doing it again in the name of Perlman.'

There was silence at the other end. I went on, 'Anyway, I'll see if I can find anything out from Alan Harle.'

'Roscoe's jockey?'

'More like this Perlman's jockey. Can you remember if Roscoe took Harle on around the same time that Perlman appeared on the scene?'

'Not off hand but I can find out. Ring me here this evening.'

'Listen,' I said. 'I'll see Harle at Cheltenham today and ask if he wants to go partying tonight. You find out what you can about him and Roscoe and I'll try and ring you around ten.'

'Right.'

'Mac – does nothing else about Harle ring a bell?'

'Like what?'

'Like the reported sighting of him with the men who probably killed Danny Gordon.'

There was silence for a few seconds then McCarthy said, 'I'll check it out.'

CHAPTER TEN

I missed the first three races that afternoon and despite the melancholy it had caused the previous day I decided to watch the fourth from out on the course. There wasn't a single space in the crowd lining the rails at the last fence so I wandered down to the starting gate as the big field of novices lined up ready to jump off when the starter raised the tape.

Harle was booked to ride Craven King for Roscoe and I tried to pick him out as the jockeys pulled their goggles down on tense faces. The horses pranced and pricked their ears and strained at their bits, some rolling their eyes back till the whites showed.

The starter was on his rostrum gripping the handle. 'Walk up!' he cried, his voice betraying his own nervousness and sense of urgency. 'Ready?' he called. The grey horse turned away from the tape and his jockey shouted, 'No, sir!'

This snapped another strand in the starter's nerves. 'Come on, Scott, turn him!' The jockey hauled at the grey's head and kicked him in the belly. He turned back to the tape. They were all facing the right way and standing completely still. There was a moment of almost eerie silence. I trained my binoculars on the packed stands and twenty thousand pairs of lenses looked back at me.

'Come on!' yelled the starter, breaking the spell. The tape snapped upwards, the riders let out an inch of rein and the ground shook as twenty-one novice 'chasers set off to prove who was champion.

I walked slowly away towards the centre of the course till the commentary was out of earshot and there were no people around. That feeling of desolation at not being involved was coming back again and I was trying to fight it.

I decided to concentrate on Harle and Craven King in Louis Perlman's rather sickly green colours. They travelled well for the first circuit but began to tire as they approached the top of the hill for the last time.

Harle wasn't hard on him but Craven King repaid him by taking a heavy fall at the third last. I kept my glasses on them waiting for Harle to rise but he didn't. Neither did the horse. I was only a couple of hundred yards from the fence and I hurried towards it.

Two St John's men stooped over him waiting for the ambulance which was speeding towards us along with the vet's Land-Rover and the horse ambulance. Craven King lay on his side breathing heavily as one of the groundsmen crouched by his head murmuring words of comfort.

I ducked under the rails. 'Is he okay?' I asked as I reached Harle. 'Just concussed, we think,' said one of the ambulancemen as the other undid the jockey's chinstrap and raised his goggles. I looked down at the unconscious figure.

It wasn't Alan Harle.

'That's not Harle,' I said rather stupidly. One of the St John's men glanced up at me but didn't reply. I looked across at the weightcloth on the prostrate horse, number 6. I checked my racecard, definitely Craven King, trained by Roscoe and due to be ridden by Alan Harle.

The doctor and the vet arrived at the same time and I watched the doctor as he eased the jockey's helmet off. Hunkering down beside him I asked, 'Is he going to be all right?'

His fingers explored the base of the skull as he lifted the boy's head and turned it gently. 'I think so. Just concussed.'

'Who is he?'

'Greene, Philip Greene,' the doctor said as he signalled for the stretcher. 'And he's just earned himself a short holiday.' I wondered what he was talking about till I remembered that every jockey suffering concussion had to take a compulsory break from race-riding.

They loaded Greene carefully into the ambulance and it trundled gently off towards the stands. I turned, hoping the horse was okay, only to see them erecting screens to protect the sensibilities of racegoers as the vet put a pistol to Craven King's head and pulled the trigger. The horse shuddered briefly and lay still.

A man in overalls pulled a length of chain from the interior of the horse ambulance and looped it round the horse's neck. Another man pressed a button to start the winch and the chain clattered and heaved as it hauled the body across the muddy hoofprints in the grass and up the ramp into the darkness.

The vet was starting back towards the Land-Rover followed closely by a man I recognised as Mr Skinner, still thermometer thin from smoking too much and eating too little. He was dark-haired, maybe forty-five and had the blue face of a twice-a-day shaver. He'd been renowned as a compulsive gambler when I'd been riding and by the expression on his face (he had a constant look of worry mixed with impatience, like a man who can't wait for a parcel to arrive even though he knows there's a bomb in it) he hadn't kicked the habit.

Gambling, I recalled, had cost him his job. He'd been a racecourse vet when I was riding but had been sacked when the Jockey Club decided his obsession with betting was not in their best interests. What the hell was he doing back on a racecourse?

I fell into step beside him and he looked up and nodded, not particularly pleased to see me. 'What was wrong with him?' I asked.

'Broken shoulder.'

'It's a tough business.'

'You should know,' he said sarcastically, still walking towards the Land-Rover.

'Wasn't Alan Harle down to ride him?' I asked.

'I'm not the bloody starter,' he said as he climbed into the passenger seat. The driver revved the engine.

'Any chance of a lift back?' I asked but the only acknowledgment was a cloud of blue smoke from the exhaust as they pulled away.

Back in the enclosure I made my way through the betting ring to where the reps for SIS stood. SIS is the racing news service which relays information and live pictures from the racecourse to all betting shops.

There was only one person in the booth as I approached, a pleasant looking bloke with brown hair and a moustache. He was speaking on the phone. When he finished I introduced myself.

'Grenville Riley,' he said, offering his hand. 'What can I do for you?'

'Do you know if Alan Harle has a mount today?'

He didn't have to consult any papers. 'No, he's not riding today or tomorrow. He was booked to ride two today and one tomorrow as far as I know but his trainer told me he wouldn't be riding for the rest of the meeting.'

'Roscoe?'

'That's right.'

'Did he say why?'

'Said he had a bad case of flu.'

Bad case of a hangover, I thought. 'When did he tell you?'

'About an hour before the first.'

'Did he say who'd be replacing him?'

'Young Phil Greene. The poor bugger just got buried in the last.' He looked genuinely sorry about the boy's fall.

'I know. He's all right. I've spoken to the doctor.'

He nodded. 'Didn't look too good for the horse though,' he said.

'No, he's been destroyed.'

He frowned and shook his head slowly.

'I don't suppose you know any of the vets?' I asked.

'Yeah, most of them.' He pulled a box of small cigars from his coat pocket.

'Skinner isn't back on the Jockey Club payroll, is he?'

'You kidding, with his reputation?'

'I know, but he was out there with the vet when he put Craven King down.'

'I heard he works for Roscoe now.'

'Skinner does?'

'Yeah, private vet to the stable so they say. If Roscoe's got any brains he'll be watching what Skinner jabs those horses with!'

I smiled. Many a true word . . .

'Smoke?' he offered.

'No, thanks.'

'My only vice.' He smiled, lighting one.

'You're lucky . . . Listen, is Greene Roscoe's usual standby?'

'Not really. I've noticed he's been riding one or two in the last few weeks for him but before that he's used anyone who was available.'

His mobile phone rang. I slapped his shoulder lightly. 'Thanks a lot, you've been very helpful.'

He smiled, 'Any time, Eddie, any time.'

I thought about going to the trainer's bar and asking Roscoe how my pal Alan was but I decided against it in case Roscoe was smarter than he looked. A phone call to Harle's hotel would pay better dividends. In the callbox below the main stand I rang Directory Inquiries and asked for the number of the Duke's Hotel. The pretty voice of the receptionist answered on the second ring.

'Can you put me through to Mr Alan Harle's room, please?'

'Do you know the room number, sir?'

'I'm sorry, I don't.'

'Hold on, please.'

I held on.

'Hallo, sir, I'm afraid Mr Harle left this morning.'

'When do you expect him back?'

'We don't, sir.'

I hesitated. 'Did you see him leave?' I realised as soon as I asked that it was a strange question from her point of view. She must have been asked stranger though, she was non-committal. 'I didn't start till two o'clock, sir.'

'Of course . . . Did he pay his bill?'

'I'm sorry, sir, we're not allowed to answer questions like that about guests.'

'I understand. Thanks for your help.'

I hung up and headed for the paddock.

Standing around by the weighing room I waited for a homeward bound jockey. It was late afternoon. The sky was clouding over and a cold wind flexed its muscles. There were only a few officials around the weighing room which virtually looked out onto the paddock. The race in progress on the other side of the stands had most people's attention.

A figure came out through the glass doors and started across the paddock. My height, my age, dark hair, fresh face, he wore a brown leather jacket and corduroy trousers and carried a black leather holdall. His hair was still wet and he smelled of soap. Falling into step beside him as he passed I said, 'Hallo, John.'

He glanced across at me but kept walking. He walked pretty fast. 'Hallo, Eddie. Heard you were back.'

Jockeys are a strange breed. When you're one of them it's like being a member of some élite heroic regiment in which your colleagues will do almost anything for you. It's a profession in which you put your life on the line every time you pull a coloured jersey over your head. Your next ride could always be your last and everyone knows it – but no one discusses it. In a company of men who are all taking the same risks there is a lot of comfort and camaraderie.

But as soon as you're outside that circle, unless through injury, you become a stranger again, a man in the street, a passer-by. It is nothing intentional or preconceived, it's just the way it is. The way I'd known it would be. But it still hurt.

I didn't feel like talking any small talk and I knew John didn't feel like listening. Quickening my pace to match his I asked, 'Where's Alan Harle staying now, is he still in Trowbridge?'

'As far as I know he's got digs with Roscoe.'

'He trains at Lambourn, doesn't he?'

'That's right, Benson's old place.'

That was all I'd wanted to know. 'Thanks, John.' I slowed down to let him walk on towards the car park. He stopped and turned towards me. 'Harle owe you money, too?'

I played along. 'Eh, yes, he does. You too?'

He shook his head. 'Not me, but he's had a few quid from some of the others.'

I nodded slowly, trying to look resigned.

'I wouldn't worry too much,' John said. 'He's paid

all of them off in the last month or so. You might be next.'

'I hope so. Thanks.'

'Okay, Eddie.' He smiled and I saw what looked like pity in his eyes and it made me sick.

I decided to go home.

CHAPTER ELEVEN

It was dusk when I got back. I cleared last night's ashes from the grate and brought the logs and firelighters from the kitchen.

Ten minutes later flames from the white cubes were licking the wood into life. I washed in cold water, closed the curtains and picked up a drink. Looking at the young flames through the liquid, I wondered if this was becoming too much of a habit, but I drank some anyway and it burned its way down and lay warm in my gut. Watching the flames and the shadows I pushed my brain back into operation to stave off the melancholy before it got a foothold.

Damn it to hell.

I finished the drink, poured another and went to the telephone. It was just after seven and I couldn't be sure if McCarthy would be back from Cheltenham.

I decided to give him another half-hour before ringing and spend the time trying to contact Harle.

A guy I knew in Lambourn told me Harle was staying in a cottage about a mile from Roscoe's stables and gave me his number. I tried it. Nobody answered. I hung up and suddenly felt hungry. There was little to eat in the kitchen and my limit as a cook was tinned food.

I decided to burden McCarthy's expense account further by eating out again. There were some good restaurants in Newbury, which was close to Lambourn and Harle's place.

Half an hour later I was heading south-east on the A40 with a ten-minute phone call to McCarthy under my belt. I had washed, shaved and changed into dark comfortable clothes topped with a flat cap.

It was a cloudless night, cold enough for frost and I pushed the heater up a notch to blow warm air round my ankles. The conversation with McCarthy played back in my mind.

Roscoe had been training Perlman's horses for just over a year. Before that he had trained under permit which meant he could train only horses owned by himself or his immediate family.

In Roscoe's case his father had provided the horses, two of which were still in training along with ten of Perlman's. No other owner had horses with him.

Harle had never ridden for Roscoe while he was a permit trainer. He'd been appointed stable jockey, much to the surprise of many, within a month of Perlman's horses joining the yard.

Some said Perlman was simply being philanthropic, others said Harle would be much easier to manipulate than a top jockey if the stable had any skulduggery in mind.

Harle appeared to be doing all right from the arrangement. McCarthy had checked the files and found Roscoe was paying him a retainer of ten grand on top of his normal percentage of winning prize money. He wasn't picking up any more outside rides than he'd done as a freelance, but McCarthy didn't know whether this was through choice on Harle's part. All jockeys would like to pick and choose, especially with novice 'chasers.

Anyway, whatever outside rides he was getting had dried to a trickle over the last three months; he was riding almost exclusively for Perlman now. As for Perlman himself McCarthy was no further forward in finding out where he was or indeed who he was.

The RSS man who'd screened Perlman could remember only that he was small and round with thick glasses and he didn't talk much.

I told McCarthy about Harle's sudden disappearance. It didn't make him happy. I told him I was going looking for him and if that made him any happier he didn't show it.

It was nine o'clock when I reached Newbury and my appetite had gone but I ate dinner anyway in a quiet hotel restaurant. I even remembered to get a receipt before tipping the waiter and leaving for Lambourn.

Most of the training yards in the village were set fairly close together, but Roscoe's was high on the downs about three miles from his nearest neighbour. The Rover moved smoothly along the recently resurfaced track which was barely wide enough for two cars to pass.

The moon was full now, silver and bright and high in the sky. You could almost have driven under it without lights. Somewhere along here was Harle's cottage; I kept my speed down and my eyes sharp.

It lay back from the road behind high trees. Turning off the new tarmac onto dirt I cut the engine and killed the lights as the car rolled to a halt. The cottage was small, fronted by a neat lawn. Between two chimneys the roof sparkled under a layer of frost. The building was in darkness.

Skirting the lawn I walked up the centre path to the front door which had a large brass knocker in the shape of a bull's head. Raising the heavy ring through the animal's nose I let it fall and it hammered and bounced twice on the brass plate . . . there was no sound from inside. I waited. High in the trees behind me an owl hooted.

I went to the window. Below it was a yard-wide strip of soil. Keeping my feet on the cement I leaned on the

73

windowsill. The moon was so bright I saw my reflection loom towards me as I peered through the glass. The curtains were open but I could see little.

I went back to the car for my torch and lockpicks then followed the path to the back of the house. There was one window and a door. I tried the handle – no luck. Taking a slim metal rod I bent to the keyhole, slid it into the lock and silently started counting. At seven it clicked open. Not bad for an amateur. The trouble with prisons is the inmates have nothing better to do than teach tricks to newcomers.

I shone the torch around. The room was fairly big. A heavy wooden bare table stood in the centre between a small fridge and a gas cooker. On the floor in the corner the beam glinted on a stainless steel pedal bin.

Hanging on a wall above the sink was a mirror the size of a bicycle wheel. Vanity begins at home.

The living-room looked cluttered and untidy in the sweep of the torchbeam. There were newspapers on the floor, a footstool on a rug in front of the fireplace, two fat fireside chairs and a short matching couch.

On the wall opposite the window was a glass display cabinet which held a dozen or so trophies. There were many framed photographs around the room; Harle on horses, Harle jumping, Harle galloping, Harle with friends – all Harle's pictures were here, but he wasn't.

I searched the two bedrooms but found only an unopened pack of condoms.

Going back to the living-room I considered switching on the lights but decided against it. It should have been safe but I was on edge.

Against the wall opposite the fire was a big rolltop desk. It was locked but the small brass catch took only a few seconds to click open. The top rolled up silently revealing a broad writing surface and eight pigeon-holes.

I sat in the big leather-seated revolving chair and started going through what papers there were. I found two foil-wrapped syringes but that didn't teach me anything new. Leaving by the back door I relocked it.

The moon was lower in the sky but still bright and a frost was forming on the lawn. The cottage sat staring at me in cold, composed silence, pleased that it hadn't given up any secrets. I started the engine and reversed slowly onto the tarmac. Time to go home.

Harle stayed stubbornly missing. I spent the next week looking for him, visiting racecourses, speaking to mutual friends or should I say acquaintances as it soon became apparent Harle didn't have any real friends.

Nor had he any family. I remembered he'd been an orphan but thought there might be a brother or sister somewhere. If there was, nobody knew where they were.

The Press had shown an interest initially but Roscoe told them Harle had walked out on him after an argument and he didn't know where he was and 'frankly, didn't care'.

Someone did not want Harle found. There was only one more thing I could think of to try and trace him, one last card. On the Saturday I went to Ascot and played it.

CHAPTER TWELVE

At Ascot it was raining. I heard someone describe the going on the course as 'dead' which was more than could be said for the chicken sandwich I was trying to eat in the bar. Next to me, munching her way contentedly through a smoked salmon sandwich, was a regular racegoer known among jockeys as Walk Over Wendy. She was what's known in the rock business as a groupie. In this case a racing groupie. And she was proud of it.

The reason she was enjoying the sandwich so much was that she was washing it down with champagne and I was paying for both. She was plumpish, fair-haired and pretty. No more than twenty, she didn't have the highest IQ in the world but she was always happy – and obliging. Ex-jockeys though were off her list. She liked to stay in fashion that way. Has-beens got nothing except information, for which they had to pay.

She finished the sandwich and wiped her hands and face with a paper napkin. Cocking her head to one side in what she imagined to be a coy pose her eyes sparkled as she said, 'What is it you're after?'

'I want to know if Alan Harle has a girlfriend at the moment.'

She frowned. 'Oh, I haven't seen Alan for ages, weeks; I'd forgotten all about him.' She talked like he was a sheep she was supposed to feed along with the rest of the herd.

'Do you know where he is?' I asked.

She shook her head slowly, still looking serious. 'I haven't seen him since . . . when was it? . . . yes, Haydock, Greenall Whitley day.'

The girl's life calendar didn't run on dates, it was big races she counted time by or certain race meetings.

'Didn't you see him at Cheltenham?' I asked.

The smile returned to her chubby cheeks. 'Afraid not, I had Gary all to myself at the Festival. I don't remember much else.'

She looked far away and grinned at the memory. 'Though he's the same as all you other jockeys, after sex,' she said. 'He just pats you on the neck and says, "Good girl! Good girl!"'

She grinned at me mischievously to see if I'd got the joke and I smiled and nodded, making her look very pleased with herself.

I pressed on. 'Do you know if Alan was seeing someone when you last spoke to him?'

She didn't hesitate. 'Yes, he was.'

'Did he tell you her name?'

'He didn't tell me anything.' She was trying to look coy again. I poured some more champagne into her glass and she emptied it. I waited.

'She told me,' Wendy said.

'Who's she?'

'Her name's Priscilla. Prissy by name but not by nature.'

For a moment I thought she was going to start giggling, but she resisted.

'Do you know where she lives?'

'London. She goes racing quite a lot – met Alan at Kempton, I think . . . Said he was a real modern guy.'

I knew what she meant. 'Is Priscilla a friend of yours?'

'Mmm, sort of. I've seen her around the tracks a few times.'

'Have you got her phone number?'

She lowered her head and puckered up her nose. 'I didn't think you were one for second-hand goods, Eddie.'

'Strictly business.'

'I'll bet. You want to take up where Alan left off, don't you?'

'How do you know he has left off?'

She sat up straight and looked serious. Maybe I was making it sound too much like interrogation.

'I don't, I was just thinking, if Alan hasn't been around for a few weeks . . . well . . .'

'Look, Wendy, I've got to get in touch with Alan. It's a business agreement we've got to tie up and time is pressing.'

'Okay. Let me think . . . I don't have her number but I could probably get it before racing's finished.'

'Can you meet me back here after the last then?'

'I'll be thirsty again by that time.'

I stood up and pushed the chair in. 'I'd better make sure I back a winner then, hadn't I?'

Resting her chin on her hands she smiled what was supposed to be a seductive smile. 'You know, Eddie, it really is a pity you're not riding any more.'

I walked away, the double entendre in her voice bouncing around in my head.

I bumped into Wendy again before the last race. She gave me the phone number and I gave her the price of another bottle of champagne, declining the invitation to share it with her. She didn't seem disappointed at losing my company.

'All the more for me then.' Gambling was probably the only vice she didn't have.

I called Priscilla from the racecourse. Her flatmate

answered. Priscilla was away. When would she be back? Haven't a clue.

It was almost a week before she turned up. Six frustrating days which I spent quizzing her flatmate, grilling Wendy trying to find out if Priscilla was with Harle (they'd disappeared around the same time), and visiting racecourses trying to pick up the trail. It was stone cold.

When I finally contacted her by phone Priscilla was not enthusiastic about discussing Alan Harle. Cold, would be a fair description.

When I said I had some good news for him her attitude changed. She agreed to meet me that evening in a pub near her flat.

'How will I know you?' she asked.

'What do you drink?' I said.

'Pernod and blackcurrant.'

'I'll order one, it'll be on the table beside me.'

The lounge was quiet. Three men and two women were drinking at the bar. I sat at a table in the corner. The girl saw me when she came through the door and walked over without hesitating. The barman nodded and smiled at her when she caught his eye.

She was tall, a head taller than me, with dyed black hair which swung at shoulder length. She wore little make-up and skin tight trousers as black as her hair. Her heels were three-inch spikes and her skinny torso supported a short red leather jacket. She was at least ten years older than Wendy.

I stood up as she reached the table and held out my hand. 'Eddie Malloy,' I said.

She touched my hand with her fingers like it was hanging by a piece of skin and she was scared it would fall off. Another girl with bad affectations. 'I'm

Priscilla,' she said. The accent wasn't hers. It wasn't anyone's. She'd made it up herself.

She sat down and I pushed the glass with the dark liquid towards her. She sipped, half-sucked, then opened her small handbag and took out a packet of cigarettes and a 'gold' lighter.

Opening the dark packet she took out an even darker cigarette which was long and slim with a thin purple band round the tip. She hesitated with it in her mouth for a second and glanced at me but I couldn't bring myself to be as corny as to take the lighter and click it on for her. There was a hint of a scowl in her eyes when she picked it up and pressed for a flame.

She drew deeply on the cigarette then rounded her lips and silently whistled the smoke out. It smelt spicy. The preliminaries over she turned her attention to me. 'You're looking for Alan?' she asked.

'That's right.'

'Does he owe you money?'

'No, but it'll cost him money if I don't find him.'

'How come?'

'A business deal we were working on. I need to see him to tie it up.'

'You're not the smartest guy in the world, are you?' She sucked in some more smoke and looked coldly at me.

'Why's that?' I asked.

'Taking Alan Harle on as a business partner.'

'What's wrong with him?'

'He's a lying, scheming, unreliable bastard.'

I shrugged. 'Nobody's perfect . . . Can I ask when you last saw him?'

'What kind of deal is it anyway?'

'I can't tell you. Ask Alan.'

'No, thanks, I'm finished with him.' She sipped her drink.

'What's he done to upset you?'

'More like what hasn't he done . . . He never turns up when he says he will, never rings, never buys you what he promises, screws around . . .' She hunched forward glaring at me as though it was my fault.

'So you'd fallen out?' I asked.

'Not as far as he was concerned, but as far as it goes with me we're finished.' She sat back folding her arms. I was beginning to feel like an agony aunt. pressed on.

'Can you remember when you last saw him?'

'I haven't seen him since before Cheltenham.' She sulked.

'And he hasn't phoned?'

She drew on the cigarette again and her eyes narrowed to slits as the smoke curled slowly upwards from her nostrils. 'What's it worth?'

'What's what worth?'

'To know where Alan is?'

'It's worth a hell of a lot to me . . . and to him.'

'What's it worth to me then?'

Wendy had obviously taught her well. 'I'm sure Alan will show his gratitude when he sees you.'

'Oh, you think so, do you? Well I'm sure he won't.'

'Look, if you can put me in touch with him I'll make sure you come out of it smiling.'

'What does that mean, you going to buy me a funny video? Hold me down while Alan tickles me?'

She was really beginning to wind me up. 'I mean financially.'

'And why should I believe you any more than Alan?'

I sat forward putting my elbows on the table. 'You'll just have to trust me. If you don't, then none of us will get anything.'

She stared at me, smoking in silence, weighing things up. Finally she said, 'He phoned two days ago.'

'From where?' I asked.

'I'm not sure.'

'What's he doing?'

'I don't know.'

She saw the frustration coming through on my face and her voice lost some of its harshness. 'I hung up on him . . . I thought he was just messing about.'

'Why?'

'He was always playing practical jokes, Alan. thought it was another one . . . It probably was.'

'Can you remember what he said?'

'Yes. He said, "Help me, Priss, I'm at Ruddock 2 . . ." Then I heard him laughing and hung up on the bastard.'

'You sure he was laughing?'

'That's what it sounded like to me and I'm nobody's fool, Mister Malloy, least of all Alan Harle's.' She beat her cigarette out in the big white ashtray and finished her drink.

'Why would he be laughing after asking you for help?'

'I'm telling you! That's what it sounded like to me. He was always taking the piss. Probably in bed with some bitch and thought he'd have a laugh at my expense.'

'Supposing he was in trouble?'

She looked uncomfortable. 'What kind of trouble?'

'I don't know . . . Was that a telephone number he was going to give you before you hung up?'

She shrugged. 'I suppose so.'

'Ruddock 2 something.'

She nodded.

'Does it ring a bell?'

'Very funny,' she said, but didn't smile.

'Unintentional,' I said. 'Does it mean anything to you?'

'Never heard of the place in my life.'

'Did he sound scared?'

'I told you! He sounded like he was taking the piss!'

'Try to imagine for a minute that he wasn't. Would you say there was fear in his voice?'

'If it was real, yes, but I'm telling you he was putting it on!'

I sighed and went to get her another drink.

She sipped and watched me warily. 'When you last saw Alan, did he say he had any plans to go away?'

'He was supposed to pick me up on the Friday evening.'

'Friday of Cheltenham week?'

'Yes, we were meant to be going to Jersey for a long weekend. He'd even called off two mounts at Lingfield on the Saturday.'

I doubted that.

'But he never turned up?'

'The bastard,' she said, and drank again.

'Would you mind telling me where you've been these last few weeks?' I asked, at the risk of upsetting her further.

She smiled. 'Think I done him in, do you?'

I smiled back. She went on. 'Nothing so romantic . . . I was looking after me mother in Devon, she's sick.'

'Oh . . . is she all right now?'

She swigged from her glass. 'All right as she'll ever be, I suppose.'

I finished my drink. 'If you hear from Alan, will you ring me?' I gave her a piece of paper with my number at the cottage.

She took it and pushed it inside her handbag. 'What are you going to do now?' she asked.

'Phone Directory Inquiries and find out where Ruddock is.'

'Then what? Dial all the twos?'

'Maybe, if I have to.'

'Jeez,' she said, staring at me.

'Want a lift home?' I asked.

She was staring at the opposite wall doing her impression of someone who could concentrate. 'Nah . . . no thanks, I'll walk.'

'I'll wait till you finish your drink then.'

She was still miles away, looking at the wall. 'It's all right. I'll stay here a while. I'll be okay.'

I didn't doubt she could take care of herself. 'Okay, thanks for your help. I'll be seeing you.' I got up and started for the door.

'Mister.'

I turned.

'If you find him, will you let me know?'

'Sure.'

She nodded slowly and went back to smoking and staring.

Heading home as the street lights came on I was glad to clear the city and hit the open road west. I switched the radio on and a saxophone blew some soft jazz around the car.

I had one digit of a phone number that might lead me to Harle. Whether he'd be alive or dead when I finally found him was a different matter.

Something in me guessed dead. Nothing in me argued.

CHAPTER THIRTEEN

Directory Inquiries were helpful but unproductive. They had no Ruddock telephone area on their lists. Could it be a subscriber's name? the girl asked. Maybe. She checked, it wasn't. At least not in my telephone area. Try your local library, she said, for access to directories from other parts of Britain. I said I would and thanked her.

Was it worth poring over a hundred telephone directories? How far away was Harle when he'd called? What was I going to do anyway, phone everyone in the country called Ruddock and ask what they'd done with Alan Harle?

I rang McCarthy on the off-chance Ruddock would strike a chord with him. It didn't. He asked how I was doing and I told him I was hitting brick walls at the moment but I was sure I was on the right track with Harle.

Cheltenham library had all the directories I needed. It had a table and chair and peace and quiet. I took off my jacket and sat down with the Berkshire area; no Ruddocks. Hampshire: none. Devon: Ruddockless.

It started cropping up in small doses as I moved North. After spending five hours on four shelves of books I had ninety-six phone numbers, sore eyes and a nasty taste from frequent finger-licking and page turning.

Ninety-six Ruddocks, all north of the Trent and none

starting with 2. Carefully folding the paper with the numbers on it I pushed it into my jacket pocket. As I stood up and stretched two of the library staff gave me funny looks. Pulling on my jacket and heading for the door I swore if I ever saw another telephone directory I'd tear it in half.

The evening was mild with a slight breeze which refreshed me after being stuck inside so long. I decided to stay in town to eat.

There was a nice place away from the town centre where the bill wouldn't make McCarthy cringe when he saw my expense sheet. It was a fine evening for walking so I left the car at the library and set off at strolling pace for the restaurant.

I had a list of numbers in my pocket and not the faintest idea of what to do with them. One of them might mean something but if it did the likelihood of the person at the other end wanting to tell me everything was a million to one. Still, it was all I had. If I didn't ring them all it would niggle at the back of my mind till I found something more solid to go on.

When I reached the restaurant it wasn't at all as I remembered it. An old type swinging sign outside said it was now called the Mail Coach Inn. On either side of the door two brass lamps protected a real flame from the night breeze.

I hesitated before going in. Modernisation in restaurants and pubs these days usually means half portions and double bills. Still, I'd walked up a good appetite and I didn't feel like walking all the way back on an empty stomach. And, McCarthy was paying.

I went in. It was very dull, almost dark. Wooden beams, brass lamps and candles on the table kept up the Olde Worlde atmosphere of the outside of the building. It was longer than it was broad and from the back a waiter approached, not hurrying but smiling pleasantly.

His accent was clipped, almost upper-class and I began to wonder if I should be offering him service.

'For one is it, sir?'

'Yes, thanks.'

'This way, please.'

He turned and I followed him to a table by the right side wall. He pulled back the chair. I sat down and he produced a menu from somewhere and drifted silently away. I went for the Royal Mail steak with peppercorn sauce.

While the chef was cooking it I looked around. There were two couples. The pair four tables from me on my side were involved in deep debate about the merits of the Government's education policy.

Across from them against the opposite wall sat a young couple who had finished eating and were now drinking wine and whispering and laughing and holding hands.

My gaze went to the wall above me. On it was a framed map of Gloucester in the eighteenth century, all done in deep colours and copperplate writing. A thick red line running through it traced the mail coach route to London. The route passed places with strangely spelled names, some recognisable today but many completely unfamiliar.

I followed the road. A cross on the red line showed where I was, the Mail Coach Inn. My eyes left the main route and roved along the byways while I waited for my steak to arrive. They passed something on their travels and raced on without remembering where it was. But it registered in my brain and set the alarm bells ringing.

My eyes searched frantically for the name that had triggered the response. It was happening too quickly for me to even know what I was looking for till my eyes found it again and fixed it like a cornered rabbit. It all happened in about two seconds. There, standing serenely among all the reds and browns of the countryside, was a place that had just saved me ninety-six phone calls.

Ruddock Farm.

Ruddock bloody Farm.

The waiter brought my steak and I smiled at him like the plate was made of gold which made him look a bit uneasy. The steak was perfect. The place was perfect.

In the cold light of the following morning logic reared its ugly head and argued that a farm that was there in the eighteenth century would be far from odds-on still to be there. I would need a more up-to-date map before following the route to Ruddock Farm.

I drove to Cheltenham and bought an Ordnance Survey map. Sitting smack in the middle of it was Ruddock Farm. I returned to the cottage to make plans.

Either the farmer's name was not Ruddock or he wasn't on the phone. I checked again with Directory Inquiries and gave her what details I had. Nothing listed.

But if Harle was there it had to be listed. He'd made a phone call from there to his girlfriend. Still, it made no difference. I'd be paying a personal visit anyway. The question was, should I go in daylight or under cover of darkness? The night offered cover and surprise but no alibi if I got caught. If I met someone there in daylight I could play the innocent traveller lost while touring the Cotswolds.

I chose daylight.

CHAPTER FOURTEEN

The map was on the seat beside me but I didn't have to look at it. I knew exactly where I was going.

It was just under an hour's drive south-west of Cheltenham. The closer I got to it the narrower grew the roads and the sparser the houses. Just after one o'clock I passed through the last village on the map and out into open country.

Twenty minutes later I was still driving. The road climbed and the surface worsened. Bushes on the overgrown verges scratched at the Rover as we sped along. In that twenty minutes a Mercedes passed me going in the opposite direction; that was the only vehicle I saw.

It began to rain.

I knew the farm was off the road and I estimated from the map that it was two or three miles down a track. I hoped it was signposted.

It was, but all that was legible on the rotted wood was '.. ock .. ar ..' It must have been the original sign from the eighteenth century. The track was off the road to the right and it dipped steeply like a ramp in the first fifty yards. It ran between trees and broken, rusted barbed wire fencing and I could hear the tyres slushing through the rain-softened surface.

The fields on either side were empty. The trees grew denser the further I went till I seemed to be driving in a tunnel. I broke out of it into daylight and a farmyard, so suddenly that I ran past and had to reverse to a point where I faced what looked like the main house.

I sat in the car and watched for some sign of life. The yard, rutted and puddled, was about the size of two tennis courts and seemed to envelop the house in a grasping semi-circle of black muck.

The dark grey stone walls were pitted and dirty. The front door was not in the centre of the building but well to the right side like it was trying to sneak around the back. Mustard coloured curtains sagged in tatters behind the two windows, one of which had a smashed pane. The other had a crack which spread each leg to touch a corner of the wooden frame. What was left of the glass was filthy.

Broken guttering hung from the roof and rainwater ran down over the green moss clinging to the end of it onto the earth below, drilling a small spreading mudhole.

Enough of the grey roof tiles were missing to make it look like a big wet crossword puzzle with no letters filled in.

As I got out of the car the wind snatched at my collar and rain peppered my face. I hurried towards the house, my hands buried in the pockets of my jacket gathering it close round me.

I stood at the door. The dark green paint was cracked and blistered and tiny pools gathered in the open paint bubbles till they overflowed and raced down the scarred surface.

I knocked hard with my left hand . . . Nobody came. I tried the handle. It turned half an inch, no further. Going to the window I squatted to look through the hole in the glass but the dirty curtains hid whatever was inside. In the glass I saw the reflection of something move quickly behind me. There was a slapping, rustling sound . . . I spun round to see a black plastic rubbish sack blowing across the yard.

I realised I was holding my breath.

My pulse was pounding.

The black muck sucked at my boots as I went round the side of the building, trying to be cautious. I'd decided to adopt the lost tourist routine if anyone was round the back but I realised it wouldn't wash the way I was creeping along, so I straightened up and strode out boldly till I reached the yard behind the house.

It stretched back towards a field with a broken fence which lay collapsed on ground that was charred by fire. Around the burned edges grass grew high.

To the right of this patch were the wrecks of an old grey van and a car. The car sat up, nose first, on the bonnet of the van like a dog begging.

A barn-type block with a huge brown door joined the house at the far side. The comparative newness of the stonework showed it had been added to the original building.

The big door was fixed on runners top and bottom and I grasped the handle and leaned back, pulling. It wouldn't budge. Using both hands I pulled hard – solid. For a derelict property things were kept pretty secure. I stepped away from it ready to turn towards the back door of the house when I heard a noise. I stopped and listened and it came again . . . Moaning, like an animal, long and low and guttural.

Whatever was making the noise was behind the sliding door. I looked up. There were two small windows, both too high to see through.

Against the opposite wall was an old upturned barrow and I went across to drag it back but the bottom was so rusted it wouldn't have taken the weight of a cat.

Along the wall beneath a broken drainpipe was a metal beer barrel lying on its side in the guttering.

I hauled it out. It was so heavy I thought it was full. Toppling it over I rolled it through the mud towards the big door.

The rain fell steadily and by the time I got the barrel across the yard I was mud-splattered and thoroughly soaked. My hair clung flat and rivers of water ran down my face and neck inside my collar.

My trousers and hands were filthy and though the jacket I wore was waterproof the rain ran from it onto my thighs till my trousers stuck to my skin.

I climbed onto the barrel with the thought that whatever was in here would probably get the fright of its life when it saw me. It also occurred to me that if anyone came out of the house now I was going to have a hard time convincing them from atop a barrel, filthy and drenched, that I was a lost tourist.

My hands clasped the ledge and I looked in. There were three stable boxes, each with its own door. Metal bars ran from the ceiling into the front wall of each box. The floor towards the rear, which was all I could see over the walls, was covered in dirty straw. From the bars of the middle box hung an empty hay net.

I heard the moan again. It was long and painful and, I decided, human. Trying to work out which of the boxes it came from was pointless, I had to get inside. I jumped down and two arcs of mud splashed away from my feet as I landed.

Going back to the door I looked more closely at the lock. The keyhole was large and empty. I went to the car and got the lockpicks. The mechanism, though heavy, was crude and it clicked open in a few seconds.

Leaning back on my heels I pulled at the handle and the door trundled on its runners, sounding noisy as a train in a tunnel. I took an anxious look round the yard before going inside.

The first thing I noticed was the smell. The only time

I could remember anything like it was years before on the Lambourn gallops, schooling a horse over fences. At the very first fence I put him to the horse barely rose at all. I went over his head still clutching the reins and landed heavily on my back. I heard the horse's neck crack and crunch as he came down behind me and rolled over to rest on my lower legs. I lay trapped, my feet under his belly as he shuddered into death. In his final throes his bowels and bladder opened and emptied six feet from my head – the smell was similar to what was in my nostrils now.

It grew worse as I left the fresh air. It was old and stale and dank and held more ingredients than any horse's bowels. I followed the stench to the end box where the door lay open. Stepping through onto dirty wet straw I found what was left of Alan Harle curled up against the inside of the wall below a torn hay net.

He was naked and his flesh was filthy with smeared faeces. He lay with his knees pulled up to his chin, his head in a foul patch of stale vomit which clung, along with short strands of dirty straw, to his face and hair. From the bars above him hung a heavy dog chain which was fastened around his neck. He moaned.

Kneeling in the straw beside him I tried to turn his face towards me. He felt my hands on his shoulders and tried to fight against me, drawing himself closer to the wall.

I eased his head up and he whimpered pathetically. Small islands of flaked whitewash from the wall stuck to his forehead and a stream of saliva ran from the corner of his mouth down his chin. His eyes stayed closed.

'Alan!' I whispered it and didn't know why. No response. I pushed my fingers inside the heavy chain links around his neck and he flinched. The flesh was a raw ring where the chain had sawed at him.

I stood up and examined the end that was fixed to the bars; it had simply been looped through its opposite end and shortened up. It had to lock together somewhere.

I knelt again and supported his head with my left hand while my fingers followed the chain round to the back of his neck. I found a small padlock just below his left ear.

Easing the chain round as best I could without hurting him further, I picked the lock. The chain end slid smoothly from his neck and lay in the straw.

I raised his eyelids and saw the eyes of a sick waxwork dummy. The pupils were pinheads and the whites were yellowish green. A sore festered in the corner of his right eye so I couldn't open it fully.

His knees were still drawn up and I turned him gently on his back to try to straighten his legs. I pushed down slowly on his knees and somewhere in his subconscious he tried to raise a struggle but he was too feeble and gradually his knees unbent.

His right thigh and lower left leg were badly scarred but they were old wounds from pin and plate insertions after leg-breaks. Shuffling through the straw I manipulated his legs and feet one by one, watching his face for signs of pain. There were none, his joints moved freely. I moved back up and checked his arms and wrists.

The bones were all right but the skin on the inside of his left arm at the elbow joint was black with bruising and punctured with needle marks, some of which were growing scabs.

His ribs were all in one piece, which was easy to see because they virtually showed through his skin individually. Harle had always been wiry but in a whipcord sort of way, now he looked emaciated. I doubted if he'd been fed anything but heroin since he'd disappeared.

So, no bones broken but he was in a bad way. The question was, what did I do now, call an ambulance? That would mean the police, too. Take him to hospital myself? That would mean concocting a story good enough to persuade the doctor not to call the police. Take him home? That was out of the question. Although I knew what was wrong with him there was no way I could treat it. If he was to survive it had to be hospital.

I decided to get him there and worry about the story I would tell on the journey. Going outside I checked the yard back and front to make sure no one was waiting. The last thing I wanted with my hands full of invalid was to walk into our two friends.

The place was still deserted. I opened the rear door of the car and went back for Harle.

Crouching low I scooped him up, my right hand under his arms and my left under his knees. I tried to support his head as I walked to the door but couldn't and it hung over the crook of my elbow.

His lower legs dangled and swung as we moved. I stopped and looked out again before going into the yard; the rain was heavier, coming straight down with force.

I carried him out and the big raindrops pelted his flesh and ran in rivers through the stinking brown smears. It streamed down the vee shape of his ribcage and gathered in his closed crotch till a pool rose to cover his pubic hair.

When I pulled up outside the Casualty Department of Cheltenham General Hospital steam was rising from my clothes and the smell from Harle filled the car.

I went inside and spoke to the nurse at the desk. Two orderlies came back out with me and slid Harle onto a stretcher, grimacing as they did so. They covered him with a blanket and hurried inside.

The nurse wanted particulars. I told her his name

was Jim Malloy and that he was my brother (I reckoned it would be a while before he was recognisable as Harle again), a registered heroin addict who'd been taking treatment at home but had disappeared two weeks ago.

I said I'd been searching for him and had just found him in a filthy squat, deserted by his friends.

She gave me sympathetic looks and said they'd do their best for him, but they'd have to inform the police of his condition. I told her to save herself a call as I was going to the police station next to update them as I'd originally reported him missing. She believed me.

I left, promising to return and visit him next day, and I assured the nurse I would bathe and change, as she suggested, as soon as I got home. Which was exactly what I did.

I stood on the bathroom floor letting the sodden clothes slide from my body. Then I stepped out of the dirty soaking pile and lowered myself into the hot water. Beautiful . . . I wished immediately I'd poured a drink and brought it with me.

Promising myself a double when I got out, I lay back to think about what had happened and what was about to happen.

I had no doubt our two friends were responsible for Harle's abduction and subsequent treatment. Did that mean Roscoe was implicated? At the start he'd claimed Harle was ill, then he said he'd walked out. Harle's unexpected disappearance could have been looked on by Roscoe as voluntary but I had a feeling the trainer knew all about it.

If so did he know what Harle had been involved in before they'd caught up with him?

And what the hell was Harle involved in? The whole Perlman/Roscoe/Harle thing stunk of something illegal and with Skinner the vet involved it looked odds-on to be horse-doping.

But where did the heroin come in? Was it just a personal habit of Harle's? Was he dealing in it?

Who had abducted him, Kruger's men? The same two he'd been seen talking to? The same two who'd visited Odin, Elrick and Danny Gordon? If I could tie Kruger into it more solidly it seemed certain I was on the trail of the people we wanted.

What it came down to was where did I go next? Where did Kruger's men go next? Could Roscoe help me track them down or should I put my name about as the one who rescued Harle and let them come straight for me?

I felt distinctly cool about that even in the warm water. These were imaginative guys, not your straight-forward hit men. They liked a bit of variety in their work: cut-throats in running brooks, pulped ankles, chained-up jockeys. I wondered what page of their cookery book I'd turn up on.

The prospect of being the fox to their hounds didn't enthral me that much but it didn't petrify me either. They'd had the advantage of surprise over their past victims but I would know they were coming for me. I was also angry that those two could go around maiming and killing without fear of retribution. They were due back a little of what they'd been dishing out.

I decided to let them know through the grapevine what I'd done and take my chances when they came looking. A visit to Roscoe's still might prove fruitful though, especially if I called when he wasn't at home. I would have to plan it.

But firstly, I decided, a chat with Danny Gordon's widow might throw up something. I'd go and see her next morning.

I was warm throughout now and my body felt light in the water. Outside it was daylight but I closed my eyes and fell asleep.

CHAPTER FIFTEEN

I was in Newmarket for ten o'clock on a fine morning and I rang McCarthy and updated him. He seemed considerably cheered that we looked on the right track and managed to find Mrs Gordon's address for me.

She lived in an upstairs flat just off the High Street but either she wasn't in or she wasn't answering the door to strangers. I turned to go back down the stairs just as a plain, tired looking woman started climbing them.

She stopped and stared up at me, pulling her coat closed over what looked like a track suit. 'Morning,' I said, 'I'm looking for Mrs Gordon.'

'I'm Mrs Gordon.'

I walked down to where she stood and held out my hand. 'My name's Eddie Malloy. I wondered if you'd mind answering a few questions about Danny . . .?'

She stared, frowning, unsure. I continued. 'I think the people who killed him are trying to do the same to a friend of mine.'

Still holding her coat closed with one hand she reached out tentatively with the other and shook mine. 'Did you say your name was Malloy?'

I nodded. 'Eddie Malloy.'

'Are you the man that found Danny?'

My mind went back to that freezing morning on the Heath. 'That's right.'

The frown disappeared but she seemed to stoop as a long sigh deflated her. She looked very weary.

'Come upstairs.'

The flat was dark, depressing and untidy. Mrs Gordon put the kettle on then moved around silently and steadily picking up kids' clothes and toys and sweet wrappers from the floor. I sat in a chair by the unlit gas fire on top of which was a half-empty bottle of Valium tablets.

'Milk and sugar?' she called from the kitchen.

'Just milk, please.'

She brought two mugs. Mine had a greasy smudge on the rim and I turned it and drank from the other side. Mrs Gordon sat down opposite me, still in her coat, and pushed the light brown hair back from her face. She wore no make-up and sipped her coffee carefully to avoid a large cold-sore on her top lip. Her hazel eyes should have been her best feature but they looked dull and lifeless.

'I'm sorry about Danny,' I said quietly.

She nodded slowly but said nothing. 'It takes a lot of getting over . . .' I offered.

'What was he like when you found him?'

I shifted awkwardly.

'You see, I never went to see him . . . to see his body . . . I wanted to, but they said it would be best if his father identified him. I lie awake now knowing I should have seen him . . . to say goodbye . . . I miss him.'

'I'm sorry,' I said, feeling helpless.

'Tell me what he was like . . .' She persisted. Her eyes were vacant. I didn't know whether her thoughts were back on the Heath or the Valium had dulled her mind. And I didn't know how to answer.

'He was . . .' I began. 'It was very cold that morning . . . He was . . . white. The frost made him look . . . peaceful.' I waited. She stared, but looked less tense. 'There wasn't much blood, was there?' she asked.

I didn't know which way to go. If I painted too bland a picture she might berate herself more for not going to see the body. But I couldn't bring myself to describe to her anything like the real horror of it. 'No, there was very little,' I said, which was no lie as virtually all the blood had drained from him.

She shook her head slowly, still miles away. 'I think you did the right thing,' I said. 'He wouldn't have wanted you to see him . . . He looked very calm, as though he'd made his peace with the world.'

'You think so?'

'I'm sure he did.'

She pursed her lips. 'You didn't find any letters in his pockets or anything?'

I shook my head, reluctant to tell her I hadn't looked.

'I thought he might have written one to me . . . you know, to say goodbye.'

I nodded, desperately sorry for her. All the more so because the Valium seemed to have killed the emotion she should have been showing as she spoke. The drugs just channelled her feelings into a monotone. God only knew how long she'd take to get over this.

'I asked the police,' she went on, 'but they said they didn't find anything either . . . They're fucking useless.'

The curse, completely lacking in vehemence, took me by surprise. She continued in that flat voice. 'I told them who killed him but they did nothing.'

'Who killed him?' I asked.

'I don't know exactly who did it but I know who had him killed.'

'Who?'

'Two men called Odin and Elrick.'

I concentrated on keeping the excitement out of my voice. 'Do you know why?'

'They'd been trying to blackmail him and Danny got his friends to beat them up.'

'Which friends?'

'I don't know. Danny didn't tell me their names.'

'Why were Elrick and Odin trying to blackmail Danny?'

She sipped coffee. 'They said Danny had been sacked from the Tote in Sweden for trying to steal money. They said they'd tell his boss at the Lab.'

'What did they want from him?'

'They wanted him to cover up samples from doped horses.'

'Why?'

'They were doping them with a trainer . . . betting them.'

She reached in her coat pocket, brought out a packet of cigarettes and lit one.

'Do you know who the trainer was . . .?' She shook her head and drew on the cigarette.

'You told the police all this?'

She nodded. 'They asked me for evidence, blackmail notes. I didn't have any. They told me they took Odin and Elrick in for questioning but had to let them go. Useless bastards.' She flicked ash onto the carpet.

'You definitely don't know the trainer who was involved with Elrick and Odin?'

She shook her head. 'No.'

'And you've no idea who Danny's friends were, the ones who beat up Elrick and Odin?'

She shook her head.

'Did you know Odin was dead?' I offered by way of some compensation.

'Good. How did he die?'

'The police say he hung himself.'

I saw the first trace of a smile. 'Is there anything else you can tell me?' I asked.

'I've told you everything I know the same as I told the police, only they didn't do anything about it.'

I scribbled my phone number on her cigarette packet. 'Would you get in touch with me if anything else comes up?'

She took the packet and looked at the number. 'Where is that?'

'Gloucestershire.'

She nodded. 'Okay.'

I stood up, leaving the half-finished coffee on the floor. She pushed herself out of the chair. 'Who's the friend you're trying to help?' she asked.

'He's a jockey.'

'Did he know Odin and Elrick too?'

'I don't think so . . . I'm not really able to question him just now.'

'You talk like a policeman.'

I smiled. 'I'm not, but I know what you mean.'

She led the way to the door and opened it. 'If you find who killed Danny will you come back and tell me?'

'Sure.'

'Do you have anyone to help you?'

'One or two people.'

'Do you think you will catch them?'

I shrugged and tried to look sympathetic. 'I'll try.'

She stared up at me and I started to see the first real signs of despair as tears welled in her eyes. Reaching with one hand I gently squeezed her arm then turned and left.

It was a relief to be back out in the sun.

On the long drive home I tried to analyse the new information. When she'd started talking I'd thought I had struck a rich seam, but trying to sift the nuggets from the dirt didn't clarify things a hell of a lot.

Ignoring the fact for the moment that she wasn't completely stable and assuming everything she said was true, the same two men who killed her husband couldn't be, as McCarthy thought, the ones who'd maimed Odin and Elrick. Then again, after Gordon was murdered, I suppose it was only natural for her to blame Elrick and Odin.

McCarthy had said the pair weren't really major leaguers and if Gordon had been responsible for setting the two men on them I would have thought they'd have been so terrified revenge would have been the last thing on their minds.

Let's assume the men were Kruger's and Gordon had persuaded Kruger to send them to sort out the Swedes. Why would Kruger have arranged it for Gordon? What did he owe him or what did he want from him in return? Some of the secrets from the Forensic Lab? That had to be a distinct possibility.

But if McCarthy's assumption was correct then it was Kruger's men who killed Gordon . . . Why? Why almost kill for a man one week then kill him the next? Had Gordon double-crossed Kruger? Had Kruger got what he wanted from Gordon and murdered a potential witness?

Who was the trainer involved with Elrick and Odin in the dope cover-up plot? Roscoe? If he was tied up with Kruger in developing the perfect dope then there'd be no need for an accomplice in the Forensic Lab since it would be pointless covering up what was already undetectable.

A visit to Roscoe's had to be next but I decided in the meantime to throw my hat visibly into the ring by letting it be known on the racecourse that Harle was back in circulation. That was sure to flush out Kruger's boys.

CHAPTER SIXTEEN

I phoned McCarthy and told him what Mrs Gordon had said. He said he'd check with the police on her blackmail story. When I told him I planned to make it known on the racecourse that Harle was out and 'Malloy had seen him' to urge the hit men to come looking for me he didn't like it.

Apart from thinking I was tempting fate he said the Press would pick up on Harle's story and start digging dirt he wanted to keep undisturbed till the case was over.

I persuaded him it was a chance we had to take. After McCarthy I phoned Priscilla in London.

'Hallo?'

I recognised her voice. 'Priscilla, it's Eddie Malloy.' She thought for a few seconds and I prompted her. 'Remember? I was looking for Alan.'

'Oh, yes, did you find him?'

'He's in Cyprus.'

'Cyprus! What the hell is he doing there?' She didn't sound pleased.

'He says he's sick of the British weather and he's going to ride there for the rest of the season . . . Don't be upset, he's thinking about you. He sends his regards.'

'I'll regards the bastard when he gets back. He could at least have sent me some money.'

'I think he's a bit skint just at the moment.' Which was telling no lie.

'Have you got an address for him?'

Her womanly wiles were moving into top gear.

'No, I'm sorry, I haven't.' I heard a grunt of anger and frustration and guessed that things were about to start getting thrown around her flat. 'I thought you'd appreciate the call anyway, Priscilla. If you do bump into Alan in the future remember to mention my name. Goodbye.'

I hung up on one sore lady who was guaranteed to blab around the racecourse how Alan had done her wrong and how Eddie Malloy had found him in Cyprus. After that it was only a matter of time till I received a visit.

I made dinner from tins and enjoyed it more than I thought I would. Then I settled down in front of the fire with two inches of whisky and the *Racing Calendar* to see where Roscoe planned to have runners the following week. It seemed he always liked to go racing with his horses and invariably took his wife with him.

Wetherby had a two-day meeting the following Tuesday and Wednesday and Roscoe had horses entered on both days, which meant he'd be away for at least one night and possibly two.

There had to be a chance his house would be deserted on the Tuesday night, just ripe for a visit with the lockpicks.

That evening I went to see Harle in hospital. He was in the intensive-care ward heavily sedated and a doctor told me it would be days before he'd be well enough to talk sensibly. I said I'd come back next day anyway.

Driving home it occurred to me how vulnerable Harle was lying virtually comatose in a hospital bed. If the heavies found out where he was they wouldn't have too much trouble finishing him off . . . But they'd have to find him first.

The smug smile was still on my face when I realised

how stupid I'd been. Pulling in to the side I stopped and switched off the engine. There had been racing at Ascot that afternoon, a London track. Chances were Priscilla had been there and if so she'd have been mouthing off about Harle being in Cyprus. As soon as our friends tagged onto this they'd be hotfooting it down to Ruddock Farm to check on Harle.

They knew his condition and they knew he was beyond escape. If he wasn't there he'd been rescued and if he'd been rescued there was only one place for him: hospital.

And not just any hospital, the nearest hospital, which was the one I'd just left.

I started the engine and turned the car back towards Cheltenham. If Harle stayed in that bed another twenty-four hours I was pretty sure he'd leave it in a box. I'd put him in hospital, in danger, now I had to get him out.

I told the ward sister I felt bad about leaving my brother alone and could I stay with him till nightfall at least. 'Absolutely not,' she said, leaving me in no doubt that she meant it. I pleaded with her, told her our mother was desperately worried about him, but she wouldn't budge.

Despite this formidable character in charge of the ward I didn't doubt that Kruger's men had sufficient ingenuity to gain access and kill him where he lay or abduct him again.

As from now his life was in danger and it was my fault for being so stupid as to make that call to Priscilla. I should never have done it without ensuring he was protected and much as I hated the idea the only way to make amends was to call in the police.

I'd been so used to going it alone, so determined to get the evidence needed to regain my licence that I didn't want anyone else involved in case they queered my pitch. Especially the police. I was an ex-jailbird, they were hardly likely to treat me with anything but suspicion. I didn't need them blocking my way.

I tried to think of some way out of it, some way of not involving them but with the exception of sitting outside the hospital with a gun there wasn't one. Getting back in the car I headed for the police station.

They showed me into a small brightly lit room and said there would be someone along soon to interview me. Ten minutes later he came in with his notebook. About forty years old, five seven, twenty pounds overweight, reddish-fair hair, bad acne and an attitude that said he'd rather be doing something else.

He approached the desk. 'Mister Malloy?'

'That's right.' I offered my hand and he shook it reluctantly as he sat down opposite me. 'Detective Sergeant Cranley.'

'Pleased to meet you.'

He grunted and in world-weary tones said, 'Now what's this about some friend of yours in trouble?'

'Alan Harle. He's a jockey. At the moment he's lying comatose in hospital. Somebody's trying to kill him.'

He pursed his lips and stared at me and his look said time-waster but he managed to keep it to himself. 'Who's this somebody?'

'I'm not sure.'

'Well, who do you think it is, Mister Malloy?'

This was going to be a long haul. 'I think a man called Gerard Kruger is behind it.'

'And why would this Mister Kruger want to kill your friend?'

'I don't know. That's what I was trying to discover when I found Harle.'

'Found him where?' He was making notes now. I told him what happened at Ruddock Farm.

'Why didn't you call us?'

'My first thought was to get him to hospital.'

'Well, what was your second thought?'

I bit back a sarcastic reply. 'Look, it only happened yesterday. I'm here now telling you about it and telling you he needs some protection.'

'That's hardly for you to decide.'

'Well, who the hell is it for, then? Harle's life is in danger.'

He stared at me, frowning so hard his acne joined up. 'Keep your voice down, Mister Malloy, you're getting yourself all upset.'

'Look, sergeant . . .'

'Detective Sergeant . . .'

'Look, the guys who are after Harle . . .'

'I thought you said it was one man, a Mister Kruger?'

'He uses two hit men.' He raised his eyebrows as if to say, oh is that so? 'And they've already killed one man and maimed two others.'

'You've got evidence of this, I suppose.'

'No, I haven't.'

He held the pen about two feet above his notepad and stared at me as though I'd crawled from some hole. Then he dropped the pen and crossed his arms. 'You're sitting there naming names, accusing people of murder without any evidence . . .? What are you all about, Mister Malloy?'

'If I had evidence I'd be talking to somebody higher up than you,' I said foolishly.

Unfolding his arms he clasped his hands. 'Is that right? And just who would you be talking to?'

I sighed in frustration. 'Look, I'm sorry, I shouldn't have said that. I'm worried about my friend. Everything I've told you is true, I'm just trying to convince you that he's in grave danger, that he needs some protection until he's well again . . . Send one of your men to see what sort of state he's in if you don't believe me.'

'And you don't know why these people are after him?'

'No.'

'How did you know where to find him?'

'His girlfriend had an idea where he was.'

'Does she know who's trying to kill him?'

'She doesn't even know he's been injured.'

'A very secretive fellow this Mister Harle.'

I put my elbows on the desk and leaned towards him. 'Detective Sergeant Cranley, the two men I told you about may very well be walking through the door of the hospital right now. I've signed Harle in under a false name, but they're clever and they won't take long to find him and when they do they'll probably finish what they started at Ruddock Farm.'

He clenched his jaw and his nostrils flared.

'If Harle dies before your men get there I will kick up the biggest stink in the Press that you have ever smelt. My visit here is logged at your main desk. You yourself have made notes of what I'm here to ask for. Now, it's your choice. If I turn out to be wrong on this at least it won't cost a life. If you're wrong it will.'

His face reddened with anger and his next words came through almost gritted teeth. 'Which hospital is he in?'

'Cheltenham General.'

'Ward?'

'Intensive care, under the name James Malloy.'

He got up almost kicking the chair aside. 'Wait here,' he growled.

Twenty minutes later he came back looking no calmer. He didn't bother sitting down. 'Have you given your address and phone number to the desk sergeant?' he asked. I nodded. 'You can go,' he said.

'But don't leave the country . . . I've a feeling I'll want to see you again.'

I stood up. 'What about Harle?'

'What about him?'

'Are you going to give him protection?'

'I don't discuss my plans with members of the public.' He baited me with a little cold smile.

'Only because they talk more sense than you do.'

His smile disappeared. He was being a bastard because I'd scared him into protecting Harle. We both knew it. I walked past him and headed home with the definite feeling that DS Cranley was the type of man to bear a grudge.

Sometimes I wished I could keep my big mouth shut.

CHAPTER SEVENTEEN

Nine the next morning found me pulling into the hospital car park. I wanted to see what Cranley's idea of protection was and I nursed a faint hope that Harle might be fit enough to talk.

The ward sister told me a policeman had been with the man she now understood was called Harle, all night, though the patient had not yet regained consciousness. I asked if I could spend five minutes with him and though she 'didn't see the point' she agreed.

The young constable sitting by the door of the small ward looked weary and bored. When he saw I intended to stop by the door he stood up.

'Good morning,' I said.

'Morning, sir.'

'I'm Eddie Malloy . . .'

'Uhuh.'

'I brought Mister Harle in.' He wasn't impressed. 'It was me that arranged protection for him . . . I spoke to DS Cranley last night.'

'That's right, sir, he told me.'

I put my hand on the door. He gripped my wrist. 'I'm afraid you can't go in there, sir.'

I looked up at him. The grip stayed tight. 'I've cleared it with sister, don't worry.'

'It's nothing to do with sister, sir, with respect.'

I let go the handle and he let go my wrist. 'Who is it to do with then?' As if I didn't know.

'DS Cranley, sir. No one is to see Mister Harle until we have a chance to take a statement from him.'

'But . . .'

'DS Cranley did mention your name in particular, Mister Malloy,' he said with finality.

I took a couple of steps back, trying to conceal my anger. I didn't want Cranley to have the pleasure of hearing I'd blown my top at the first obstacle. 'Okay. Do you know if Cranley's on duty just now?'

The constable looked at his watch. 'Shouldn't think so, sir. You'd get him around two this afternoon.'

'Thanks for your help, constable.' I turned and started down the corridor.

'Don't mention it, sir. That's what we're here for.'

Very funny.

I stayed in town and rang McCarthy. He was at a meeting, try again in an hour, his secretary said. I had a feeling this wasn't going to be my day.

McCarthy was free when I rang back. 'Mac, things are starting to get complicated.'

He read my tone immediately. 'What's happened, Eddie?'

'I've had to bring the police in.'

'Oh shit!' This was the strongest word I'd heard him use. 'You didn't mention us, did you?' he asked.

'Who's us?'

'RSS . . . The Jockey Club!'

'No . . . Not yet.'

'What do you mean, not yet? Why did you involve them in the first place?'

'To give Harle protection. You were right. It was a bad idea to drop it on the racecourse that he was out. Even an idiot would know he had to be in the nearest hospital. There was no way I could stay with him day and night, so I had to go to the police.'

'Who did you speak to? Maybe I know him.'

'God help you if you do . . . Detective Sergeant Cranley.'

'Never heard of him.'

'Lucky you, he's a major pain in the arse. He's already stopped me from seeing Harle. The police want a statement as soon as he's conscious . . . God knows what he'll tell them.'

'Eddie, listen . . . you will have to keep us out of this.' The stress he was feeling came through in each word.

'I'll do my best, Mac.'

'If you do anything to embarrass us . . .'

'Mac! I'm having a bad day and it's just started. Don't wind me up. I've told you, the very last thing I would do is involve you. Now take my word for it and let's leave it at that.'

'Look, keep me fully informed, Eddie, will you?'

'As and when I can, Mac . . . Did you find anything out about Mrs Gordon's claims?'

'Not yet. I haven't had time. I'll speak to Newmarket police today and you can ring me tonight.'

'I might be at Roscoe's place tonight. I'll check tomorrow's declared runners at noon. Roscoe's got two entered at Wetherby, if they run he'll travel up this evening and . . .'

'Don't tell me any more, Eddie . . . Just keep in touch and don't mention RSS to the police. Goodbye.' He hung up. I banged the phone down and swore.

Several coffees and a car wash later I went into a quiet little betting shop and checked next day's runners: Roscoe's were in. I felt a short unexpected thrill in my stomach – tonight's visit was on.

But first, much as I knew I was probably stirring up trouble, I was determined to confront Cranley. At five past two I was tapping on the inquiries desk at the police station. The desk sergeant returned. 'I'm

113

afraid Detective Sergeant Cranley can't see you jus
now, Mister Malloy, he's rather busy.'

'When will he be free?'

'He said if you'd like to take a seat for an hour or s
he'd try to fit you in but he can't promise anything.'

Bastard. 'I'll come back at three.'

Cranley himself was standing at the inquiries des
when I returned. He looked up, smiling sarcastically
'It's Mister Malloy! To what do we owe the pleasure o
today's visit, Mister Malloy? Don't tell me . . . you'v
caught all those villains you were after, haven't you
Are they outside in the car? Would you like me to sen
some men?'

'What I would like is five minutes of your time
Detective Sergeant.' I was determined to keep calm.

'Five minutes! For a famous crime-buster like you
Certainly . . . No problem. Come this way.'

He led me into the same room we'd used last night
We both sat down. His smile had gone and the snee
was back.

'I'm not here for a shouting match,' I said. 'All I wan
is reasonable access to Alan Harle.'

'What for?'

'Because he's my friend. I'm entitled to see him.'

'Why would you want to see him?'

'Because I'm interested in his welfare.'

'Oh don't worry about that, we're taking good car
of him. That was what you marched in here demandin
last night, was it not? That we take care of him?'

I stared at him. 'Why are you making things difficul
for me?' I asked.

He smiled his cold little smile again. 'Becaus
I don't like you, Mister Malloy. Because I doub
your motives. Because you think you're a real cleve
bastard.'

I fought back the rising anger.

'Would I be right to doubt your motives?' he asked. 'Why were you trying to find Alan Harle?'

'I told you, he's my friend, I was worried about him.'

'Very noble. Was that the only reason?'

'Yes.'

'What were you doing in Newmarket yesterday morning?'

I hesitated. 'I had business there.'

'What kind of business?'

'Personal.'

'Did you visit anyone there?'

'Yes.'

'A Mrs Gordon, by any chance?'

'What if I did?'

'What did you talk about?'

'Nothing that would interest you.'

He smiled. 'You're lying again, Mister Malloy. See, that's another thing I don't like about you, you're a liar.'

Once again I was beginning to regret my haste in coming here. 'It was me who found Mrs Gordon's husband after he'd been killed. I was as much entitled to go and see her as I am to see Harle.'

'You're not entitled to interfere with police business and that's what you were doing in Newmarket and that's what you're trying to do here and I am not having any of it.'

'How am I interfering?'

'Because you told Mrs Gordon you'd catch her husband's killer and Mrs Gordon passed that on to my colleague in Newmarket in no uncertain fashion. In fact, she raved and ranted so much at them in the station yesterday afternoon that she almost got herself locked up.'

'Maybe if they'd done their job properly . . .'

'Don't get yourself in deeper than you already are, Mister Malloy. I am looking at this whole case and if I can find anything at all to nail you with, it will give me great pleasure.'

'You're in charge of it personally, are you?'

'That's right.'

'Well, I haven't got much to worry about then, have I?'

His acne got redder. 'Listen, Malloy . . .'

'I'm finished listening.'

We both got up. 'And you're finished with this stupid personal crusade or whatever the hell it is,' he said. 'What is it, Malloy, all this amateur detective stuff? Because you found Gordon's body and the police haven't caught anyone yet? Is it some personal vendetta to embarrass the police?'

'They don't need me to do that, they manage fine themselves.'

I walked past him to the door and out along the hall. He followed, calling after me. 'Listen, Malloy, stay out of this from now on! If you don't you'll end up *back* in prison, believe me, that's a personal guarantee!'

The doors swung closed behind me on his whining voice.

When I reached Roscoe's place the house was in darkness. I had parked the car in a lay-by half a mile away and cut across fields and fences to reach the stables. The house stood separate from the stable block and the lads' hostel.

Dressed in my best housebreaking clothes and wearing soft silent boots I crept towards the front of the house and stopped at the main entrance. It was like a porch with an American-type screen entrance guarding the main door.

The housefront was quite long with three windows

116

either side of the porch. Stopping, I leaned against the wall and listened. The wind rustled the hedges and pushed clouds across the moon. Away in the stableyard at the back a dog barked; another answered, louder and longer. Then they were quiet. Turning to the porch I was through both doors and in Roscoe's hallway in less than a minute.

I stood and waited for my eyes to adjust, though it wasn't completely dark inside. Shafts of half-light came through the windows when the clouds passed the moon and I caught shadowy glimpses of the decor in the hall.

The floor was highly polished wood, the walls wood-panelled to about eight feet up and painted white between that and the high ceiling.

It was wide enough for half a set of starting stalls and long enough to put the door at the far end in complete darkness.

Although I had a torch I only wanted to use it when absolutely necessary and even then in short bursts. I started walking towards the far end but the crepe soles on my shoes came off the floor at each step with the sound of sticky tape being peeled. I stopped, took off the shoes and carried them.

Passing the dark shapes of furniture against the walls as I went I was ten steps from the door at the bottom when I froze in mid-stride. I stood completely still, the breath I'd just taken locked in my lungs.

Someone was standing in the corner by the door. He was small, narrow and motionless. I waited, letting the breath trickle slowly through my nostrils, hearing my heart beat, feeling the adrenalin racing ... I was aware of my eyes straining, staring in complete concentration.

More than a minute passed. Neither of us moved. I could not hear him even breathe. The doubts crept in.

Bringing the torch up quickly I pointed it at his eyes and pressed the button. A shiny painted face smiled back at me. A life-size statue of a jockey wearing red and blue silks. When the tension rushed out of me I almost laughed.

I looked round all of the rooms, paying more attention to the study and the library than the others, but I found nothing you wouldn't expect to find in a trainer's house.

Trophies, photographs, paintings and bronzes of horses, copies of the *Racing Calendar*, entry forms, bills, vet's certificates for two new horses, expensive writing paper and a gold pen. On his desk, ironically, was a glossy brochure showing burglar alarms. Two separate systems had been ringed in ink and marked 'cottage' and 'house'. I wondered which cottage he meant.

I searched the other rooms but found nothing that linked Roscoe to anything other than training racehorses. I sat down at his desk for one final check through his papers in case I missed anything and that's when the phone rang and scared me half to death.

It was on the desk in front of me and after three rings an answering machine clicked on setting off Roscoe's rather monotonous voice asking callers to leave a message after the tone. The tone bleeped. I waited. An accented voice, the anger barely subdued, said, 'Roscoe! Who the fuck is running this show? I want a meeting and I want it fast!'

He hung up. The machine clicked and the tape rewound. I sat there in the darkness smiling as I wondered what had upset the caller, the normally calm Gerard Kruger.

Standing by the porch door I let the night air cool my face. Sweat ran from my armpits down my ribs. Moving along the wall to the corner of the building I listened before cutting across the narrow road. All was quiet. The wind had dropped and the sky was clear.

Crossing the road quickly I vaulted the wooden fence into a small apple orchard waking a pair of wood pigeons who flew in panic from the tree above me, their wings slapping like rifle-fire, and I quickened my pace through the orchard into the fields.

They were grazing fields and empty of livestock though the grass was fairly short. I jogged in the direction of the car, casting a short bobbing moonshadow as I went.

My mind was buzzing. Just when it had looked like I'd get nothing on Roscoe, Kruger's phone call had implicated him ... Roscoe had to know something about Harle's abduction.

Slowing to a walk as I reached the lay-by I was breathing quite heavily – I needed more exercise.

An owl hooted as I opened the car door. And good night to you too I thought as I slid into the seat. Leaning over I opened the glove compartment and put the torch inside. When I straightened up someone in the back seat pushed a cold metal tube under my ear. It pressed against my jawbone and my heart almost burst through my shirt in shock.

CHAPTER EIGHTEEN

I looked in the mirror; he was wearing a black balaclava helmet with two eyeholes and no mouth-hole. Someone sat silent beside him.

'Reverse,' he said. The voice was even, calm. I started the engine, switched on the lights and as I turned to look through the rear window he moved the gun from behind my right ear to the same position behind my left. My heart was still beating fast but I'd handled the initial shock. I reversed the car into the road, facing the way I had come.

Sliding the gearstick to neutral I waited for directions. He moved the gun back to its original position.

'Drive.'

I slipped into gear and drove, trying to force my mind to work on the problem, to analyse it, suggest a solution. But it kept veering off. How did they know I was here? Had they followed me? How long have they been watching me?

I tried to be conversational. 'Where are we going?'

No answer.

We were less than a mile from the main road when a warning light showed on the dashboard. The temperature gauge was in the red section and climbing. I clutched at the straw. 'We're overheating badly,' I said. 'We'll have to stop.'

'Stop,' he said in the same level voice. Pulling in to the side I switched off the engine.

The back door clicked open and he began sliding out, but the gun stayed in contact with my skin. He stood outside now, though his hand was still inside holding the gun against my neck.

'Get out.'

He stayed behind my door so I couldn't bump him as I opened it. I stepped out. His friend got out the other side. The gun went to the nape of my neck. 'Open the bonnet,' he said. I thought I detected a West Midlands accent but couldn't be sure.

'The catch is inside the car,' I said. He nodded to the other one who got in the driver's door and fumbled under the dash till he sprung the lock. I walked to the front, released the catch and opened the bonnet.

'Prop it up,' he said.

I felt for the metal supporting rod and fitted it. The radiator hissed steam from tiny openings.

'Put a hand on each wing,' he said.

I did so slowly, wondering what the hell he was up to. He changed position behind me, moving slightly to the right. I sensed him switching the gun to his left hand but it never lost contact with the upright hair on the back of my neck. I could just see him reach inside his army style jacket and bring something out. I couldn't see what it was.

'Spread your legs.'

I did. I was now half bent over the radiator, arms and legs spreadeagled. He started pushing down on the back of my head with the gun. 'Bend.'

When I realised what he was going to do I felt nauseous.

A man must have instincts to help him survive, especially when the brain is caught by surprise or unable to function and as my face was forced nearer and nearer to the boiling radiator surface, Instinct tried to take over from Brain. But although my ears were clanging every alarm bell in my body as they listened to the bubbling, spitting water Brain knew the consequence of resistance was a bullet in the head.

The gun barrel pressed against the protruding bone at the base of my skull now, hurting. My face was ten inches from the hot grey metal.

A heavy bead of sweat fell from my forehead onto the radiator surface and I watched from six inches as it sizzled into vapour. I felt my fingers grip the wings of the car as my feet slid wider on the loose gravel.

My eyes were three inches away. They were already burning. I closed them. Gritting my teeth I tried to turn my head sideways so my left cheek would make contact first. He stopped pressing down. He held steady. I was looking at the radiator cap an inch away. The steam inside was under terrible pressure, hissing and bubbling, it seemed deafening.

He spoke. 'Stay away from Harle and Roscoe.' His voice was still calm. I had not heard mine for a minute. Mine would not be calm. I thanked God or whoever was up there that they were settling for a warning and not frying my face. I thought of Harle and how far away from him I'd be staying in future. I wondered when he would let me straighten up, things were pretty uncomfortable.

Then I saw a hand. The other guy's hand.

It was moving slowly, very slowly towards my face at eye-level. It was inside a thick grey industrial glove and it crept over the top of the radiator and came to rest on the cap. The sickness returned quickly.

An inch from my eyes the hand pressed down on the cap. I watched as it slowly unscrewed it. The captive steam sensed freedom and the hiss became a roar in my left ear. I was a rabbit. The hand was a snake. I was transfixed with horror.

The final seconds were a blur. On the last turn of the cap the hand disappeared. The cap burst off and steam and boiling water rushed upwards as my face was pushed over the scalding eruption. I opened my mouth to scream but I don't remember hearing any sound. I don't remember anything else except the moments of searing pain before I blacked out.

Consciousness returned as dawn broke. I came to lying on the road. It was cold. I lay there staring at the tyre a foot from my face. Small pips of gravel were stuck in the tread. I didn't move. Just my eyes. I became aware I was lying on my side under the front bumper, my right arm beneath my body. My eyes moved again and I saw under the car the frosted spiky grass at the roadside. It was higher than my head.

Funny.

It was cold.

I tried to remember the season. It was spring. I was sure. Must be a cold snap.

The pain came back to my face. My eyelids felt like dried, wrinkled leaves. My left cheek and nose throbbed and stung like someone had shaved my face with a dry razor after my skin had been cooked in the desert.

My lips felt puffed. I prodded them with my tongue and regretted it immediately. They were tender, raw-flesh tender. Painful . . . very very painful.

The sky was getting lighter. I lay still. It wasn't the first time I'd lain injured on the ground. I had fallen from horses at speed more times than I could count.

I'd seen the green earth coming at me fast, felt it pound the wind from my body. I'd heard the crack of my own bones at impact. I'd shut my eyes and rolled my head on a pillow of mud and wet grass counting out the pain with each turn of the head till the ambulance arrived.

And they always had arrived. Sometimes they took longer than others but they had always come. I wished they were coming to get me now.

Pick me up from this road. Wrap me in warm blankets. Morphine the pain away.

Help me.

Cold. God it was cold.

I moved. I lifted my right cheek and felt the gravel stick to my skin. Rolling onto my back I looked at the sky. It was still grey but getting bluer. Slowly I tried to flex my arms and legs. A crow sat in the tree above me, watching as I moved like a dying spider.

My limbs were stiff and though they weren't sore the slightest movement anywhere in my body seemed to increase the pain in my face.

Very slowly I sat up. My eyes reached the level of the radiator grille. Gripping the bumper I pulled myself up very very slowly, trying to keep my head perfectly still.

Every movement seemed to send shock waves into my skull to bounce around on the inside walls of my face like some kid's computer game. Direct hits every time. No electronic beeps, just agony. Agony. Agony. Agony.

I held on to the front of the car for a long while. I stared down at last night's instrument of torture . . . the cap was nowhere to be seen. Just a dark hole rimmed on the inside by, of all things, ice.

The journey from the front of the car to the driving seat must have taken half an hour. Moving in tiny steps, stopping till the pain was bearable for the next few inches, I heard the crow fly off. Bored, I suppose. If he'd been a vulture I think he might have stayed.

The final small movements had to be done in bursts of held breath – squatting slowly to sit on the side edge of the seat, sliding backwards, hauling my legs in and turning round to face the front. Each an individual stage. Each, like a dive from high cliffs, preceded by a deep breath. Each breath held till the stage was complete.

Finally I sat. On the softness, the warm velour. No more gravel. No more cold.

I was sweating now. The drops ran out of my hair and carved paths down the burned skin. More and more of them. A big field. Many runners. Racing down my face ... cutting it up ...

I passed out again.

The sound of an engine woke me, a big engine. My eyes came open slowly. It was a horsebox, coming to a halt in front of my car. It stopped. The engine stayed on. I heard a door slam shut and boots hitting gravel. I began to panic and I was ashamed of my terror. If they'd come back for another session over the radiator ... I suddenly felt very badly in need of a toilet.

I saw the boots running alongside the box. They were small boots. They were beautiful small undangerous boots. Their owner came into view . . . it was a girl. A loud involuntary sigh of relief groaned out of my body.

She came to the door which still lay open and she bent and looked in. 'Have you broken down?' she asked in a lovely soft Irish accent.

I turned slowly to look at her and when she saw the full frontal her brown eyes seemed to double in size in her beautiful freckled face. Her head went back with the speed of a rifle recoil. 'Holy Mary Mother o' God!'

'Hallo,' I said. Moving my lips was a big mistake. I resolved not to do it again.

'What in the name of God happened to you?' she asked.

'Accident,' I said without moving my lips.

'How, what happened?'

'Later,' I said, again through still lips.

'Will I fetch a doctor?'

There was nothing in the world I wanted more but doctors meant police and police meant, eventually, Cranley who would gloat and taunt.

'No,' I said.

'But why? . . . You're in an awful state. Have you seen your face?'

I hadn't. If it looked as bad as it felt I didn't want to see it.

'You'll have to have a doctor.' She was pleading now.

'Please . . . no,' I managed to say. If I'd been able to use my facial muscles to help express how much I didn't want a doctor perhaps she would have been more easily convinced. I could see she wasn't. She was getting angry, maternal.

'Not here.' The pain was in my voice now. She softened and moved in closer, squatting down. 'I see how sore it is for you to talk.' She puzzled for a few seconds then looked at my hands in my lap.

'Can you move your fingers?'

A cinch. I drummed on my thigh.

'Good,' she said. 'I'll just ask you questions and you can answer with your fingers. Right hand for yes, left for no.'

I raised my right forefinger.

'Are you hurt anywhere else except your face?'

All the other hurt was not physical. Left hand.

'Can you move?'

I hesitated.

'With my help?'

Deep breath. Right hand.

'Can your car be driven?'

Left hand.

'If we go very slowly can you make it to the horse-box?'

126

Right hand.

'Okay, I'll take you back with me, then we'll get a doctor.'

After a million years we reached the door of the horsebox. It was high, offering only two steel footholds. I looked at them. She looked at me. I was sweating again.

She climbed up and opened the door then jumped down. 'Wait,' she told me. Running round the front of the box she climbed in the other side. Appearing above me in the doorway she reached down to help me up. Breath-holding time again.

As it turned out it wasn't a hell of a lot worse than the walking; the pain level had come down or my tolerance had increased. I reached the seat without blacking out again.

'I'll drive slowly,' she said. And she did, but the road was bad in places with ruts and holes. Every time we bounced I sensed her glancing across at me and felt her grimace for both of us. I wondered how far we had to go and she read my mind.

'It's not far, another two miles or so.'

We rumbled on, slower than an old carthorse.

'The family are away just now though they may be back the morra,' she said. 'So you can have a bed till the doctor comes and maybe even stay overnight if he doesn't want to put you in hospital.'

It wasn't the doctor that wanted to put me in hospital but I knew what she meant.

'Even if you're still here when the guv'nor gets back, he won't mind. He's a decent sort, so he is.'

I was glad of that.

'And Mrs Roscoe's nice too.'

If she'd only known there was nothing in this world she could have said that would have made me feel sicker in my gut.

The little straw-clutcher inside said maybe it wasn't the same Roscoe, but cold logic laughed him down. How common was the name? How many had horseboxes? How many had stables within two miles of where I'd been last night? Not many. Just one . . . Basil.

CHAPTER NINETEEN

I wondered if Roscoe knew yet that I'd been to his house last night. The hit men must have reported in to somebody and if that somebody was Roscoe there had to be a chance he was hammering down the A1 right now to find out how much damage had been caused.

I tried to imagine the look on his face when he walked in and found me being sympathetically tended to by his stable staff. It didn't make for a pretty picture.

The girl chatted on beside me, something about this not being their horsebox and how she'd have to take it back later that day, while I tried to figure out what I was going to do.

My main fear was passing out again and finding Roscoe there when I woke up.

When we reached the stables the girl drove round to the back of the buildings and turned into the yard. She stopped, switched off the engine and looked across at me. 'I'll get help,' she said, and, opening the door, she jumped to the ground. I watched her go into the house I'd crept out of less than twelve hours before.

My vision was limited by the ground my swivelling eyes could cover without moving my head, but I could see that the yard was cobbled though many of the stones were worn almost flat. Some were missing and had been replaced by cement which had been painted the same slate grey colour.

The house was L-shaped, standing away from the

main stableyard. The small windows had lace curtains with pink bows drawing them in at the waist. Under a window was an old wheelbarrow full of soil through which new shoots were poking their heads.

The girl reappeared and ran towards the stables behind me. Seconds later I saw her in the side mirror hurrying back to the horsebox. Following her was a lanky teenage boy whose arms hung like a gorilla's. His lime-green sweater stopped halfway down his forearms and as he walked his hands dangled and swung as though his wrists were broken. His face was long and pointed and looked like it hadn't seen soap and water since Christmas.

The girl climbed up and opened the door and I turned slowly and painfully and came out backwards. They guided my feet to the rungs and took most of my weight on the last big step to the ground.

Inside, they helped me to a chair in the kitchen, straight and high-backed, much easier to stand up from.

The girl went to the sink and tore two yards of pale blue tissue from a roll fixed to the wall.

She soaked the tissue under the cold running tap and came towards me, water dripping through her fingers as she cradled the soggy mass in both hands.

'If I can dab some of this on your face it should soothe it,' she said.

'No,' I said, fearing unconsciousness again if anything touched the skin. If it had to be done it would have to be somewhere else.

'But you need something on it till a doctor gets here . . .' I could see she was beginning to get frustrated with this invalid with the poached face. Each time she'd offered constructive help like calling doctors or bathing wounds I'd stopped her. Wondering how long her patience would hold I decided to try one more request which I knew would not be popular but would at least go some way towards getting me out of her hair. I prepared myself for another session of talking through still lips.

'Have you called the doctor?' I asked.

'Not yet,' she said. The water still dripped, making a pool on the tiled floor. I looked at the boy. He was staring at my face with his mouth hanging open like someone had removed the bolt from his jaw. The girl saw me look at him and turned.

'Thanks, Bobby. You'd better get back to the feed room and finish off that mash.' It was an order and Bobby looked used to taking them.

He started drifting slowly sideways towards the door, still staring at my face. I lost sight of him when he moved out of eye-swivelling range but I heard him speak for the first time.

'What you gonna do with 'im, Jackie?'

'Don't worry, I'll get him a doctor, he'll be all right,' she said.

He didn't reply and I didn't hear him move. 'Bobby,' the girl said sternly, 'go back and finish the feed. I'll make sure he's all right.'

I'm sure Bobby would rather I stayed the way I was so that when he got bored he could come and stare at my face for an hour or two. I heard the door close as he left.

The girl turned back to me. By the look of her she was approaching the border of anger. 'Don't tell me now you don't want a doctor!'

I didn't say anything but she could see from my look that that was exactly what I was about to tell her and she turned, strode back to the sink and dumped the saturated handful of tissue. It splodged and stuck by the sound of it. Back she came to me.

'Maybe I should just let you sit there till you die!

Maybe you'd be happier then!' A flush spread under her freckles and her eyes sparkled. She was very attractive.

'Jackie . . .' I said. The use of her name puzzled her till she remembered Bobby had used it.

'Don't you Jackie me with any soft talk.'

I tried to make my eyes look apologetic. 'Just do one more thing for me.' The m's were not coming out, but she understood.

'What?' Hands on hips now, she was ready for an argument.

'Call an ambulance,' I said. Her eyes went up to heaven. 'Thank God! You're coming to your senses.'

On a shelf by the window was a white telephone and, picking up the receiver, she looked back at me over her shoulder. She was lovely as the sun caught her through the glass. Pity about my face. If they ever repaired it sufficiently I'd take her or at least ask her to dinner.

'999?' she asked.

'Yes.'

She began dialling. 'Tell them I had an accident in the boiler room.'

She stopped dialling and turned, still holding the receiver to her ear. 'We don't have a boiler room.'

'They don't know that.'

Shaking her head slowly she dialled the last digit. Pacing the kitchen in silence while we waited, she asked again what happened to me, but I persuaded her to wait till some other time to hear the story.

I heard the siren in the distance, but when the ambulance came within clear hearing range of the stables the noise stopped.

It took me a few seconds to figure out they'd switched the siren off deliberately in case we ended up with terrified horses kicking down their box doors and careering all over Lambourn.

There were two ambulancemen and they breezed in cheery and efficient looking. Onc had a beautifully kept beard and when he saw me he whistled low and said, 'Nice one.'

The other man gazed studiously at my face from about a foot away as though he were looking in an aquarium for a lost fish. 'You won't be shaving for a while, old son,' he said. 'What happened?'

Jackie answered. 'The boiler blew.'

He straightened and looked at her. 'These burns aren't fresh.'

I watched her. She didn't turn a hair. 'It happened last night when he was here alone. I found him this morning when I came back from the races.'

He looked at me again. 'Not the comfiest night you've ever spent, I'll bet,' he said. Then the bearded one said, 'I'll get the stretcher, John.'

'Okay,' John said. He smiled at me. 'We'll have you sorted out in no time, old son.'

He turned to Jackie. 'What's his name?' He was blocking my view but I could imagine the look on her face. 'Eddie Malloy,' I said, using my lips so he wouldn't ask for a repeat. It was very painful.

He turned his attention back to me. 'You used to be a jockey, didn't you?'

'Yes.' Back to still lips. I saw him reflect briefly on his use of the past tense. He must have remembered the circumstances of my warning-off because he looked uncomfortable. I wished I felt well enough to say something consolatory to fill the embarrassed silence.

His friend barged in with the stretcher and saved further blushes.

They stood, one at either end, holding the stretcher and Jackie helped me lie down on it. The bearded one was facing me and John was at my head. 'All right, Eddie?' he asked.

133

'Yes.'

'Will you open the door, love?' he asked Jackie.

'Do you want to come with him?' the bearded one asked her.

'Not now, I'm expecting Mr Roscoe back soon. I'll telephone the hospital to find out how he is. Newbury General, is that right?'

'That's it, love,' John said. 'The number's in the book.'

'Thanks,' she said.

They carried me past her and when she looked down I tried to smile, but it hurt too much.

CHAPTER TWENTY

They sedated me heavily and I remember little of the first couple of days in hospital. On the third day the pain had eased enough to move me from pain-killing injections onto tablets. On day four I asked if I could have a bath and they took so long deciding they must have assembled the whole area health board to discuss it.

They said Yes, I could have a bath in warm not hot water and that I must not lie down in it or let the water touch any area above my collarbone. And I must also leave the door unlocked in case I needed the assistance of a nurse. They stopped just short of a signed agreement and I made my way to the bathroom.

When I closed the door behind me the first thing I saw was a stranger in the mirror staring back at me.

The image you carry of yourself in your mind's eye is so solid that even age seems to change it only imperceptibly. To see someone you don't recognise using your body is a hell of a shock. The first reaction is one of panic and my brain took some time bringing things under control again.

I stood there for a long time, staring. The mirror was five feet away. After minutes rather than seconds I moved closer. I stopped and looked at myself from six inches.

The damage was bad. There was nothing on my

face that looked like skin in either colour or texture.

It was made up of patches: livid pink, blood red and colours in between. There were large areas of tiny blisters and smaller areas of egg-size blisters. My forehead and cheekbone on the right side were badly grazed and my nose and lips under the blistering were swollen to twice their normal size.

On the remote islands of skin that had survived grew a week's stubble. It flourished on the large sections of uninjured skin on my neck, making me even uglier.

I ran a warm bath and lay a long time in it thinking. I thought about damage. Permanent damage . . . temporary damage . . . ? I wondered. Damage to my face, my ego, my spirit, my supply of courage . . . Well, I could hardly claim to have used any of that which, in the normal way of things, would be good because I would have plenty left.

But I didn't have. I was frightened. My memory kept taking me back to the pain. I tried to make myself think of other things, but I couldn't because that cold logical section of my mind kept making me face reality.

It wasn't a game. It had never been, I had only thought it was. I'd planned to be the hero, the one who'd get justice for himself and other victims. Too many movies, Eddie . . . You've seen too many.

In real life you were like a child. Helpless, pathetic. They just took you and did what they wanted and you never raised a finger. You're out of your league, Eddie. They'll kill you next time. Give it up. Go back to breaking horses.

Conscience speaking. Logic. The Real Me. Whoever . . . I knew he was right. Knew I'd never go back. Never try to find the men who did this, never find Kruger.

No licence. No career.

But I'd be alive. I'd be breathing. Nobody would be coming looking for me to burn my face again. A deep groaning sigh came out of my body, taking me by surprise. Tears welled in my eyes and a terrible heavy weariness came over me ... I had never felt so vulnerable in my life.

I was conscious of lying completely still in the water, staring. Staring unblinking with dead eyes.

The nurse forgot about me and I lay there lost for so long in my miserable world that only my shivers in the cold water brought me back to reality.

I dragged myself out to face a long depressing sleepless night.

Over the next couple of days I came as close as I ever have to total despair. There was a lot of pain – and a lot of self-hatred.

I spoke little and ignored those who spoke to me. I criticised the nurses, wouldn't eat the food, was sullen with doctors; when most patients were in bed I'd go to the day room to be alone. If anyone came in there I'd leave and lock myself in a toilet cubicle, staying there for hours.

At night I lay awake trying not to think of how much of a bastard I was being, how much of a coward. I knew I should have phoned McCarthy, found out if Harle was okay. I knew the longer I delayed the call the harder it would be to make.

Finally I couldn't live with it any longer. I rang McCarthy and told him where I was.

Two hours later he was sitting by my bed trying to hide the initial shock at seeing my face. 'You don't look too good.'

'Don't feel too good.'

He stared. 'How long've you been in here?'

'A week.' I avoided his eyes.

'A week!' The whole ward heard it. I glared at him. 'For God's sake stop shouting.'

He leaned forward, lowering his head and whispering harshly, 'Don't tell me to stop shouting! I get a call from the hire company that the police have found your car abandoned in Lambourn, I'm wondering whether you're dead or alive and now you tell me you've been here a week and you haven't rung me before now . . . Why?'

I looked away again. 'I'll tell you sometime.'

'You'll tell me now!'

Slowly I turned back to face him. 'Mac, sometime, if I ever feel human again, I'll tell you why I didn't contact you . . . I've spent a hellish time in here, it doesn't look like getting any better and I don't need you making me feel worse than I already do.'

He shook his head and sighed, 'Okay.' He said, sitting back and crossing his legs, 'Can you tell me what happened then?'

I told him, though when it came to the scalding I felt my voice go and had to stop and compose myself. McCarthy listened in complete silence.

When I finished I couldn't look him in the eye but I had to tell him, forcing it past a lump in my throat, 'Mac, I'm finished . . . I'm sorry . . . I'm sorry, but it's not there . . . I can't cut it . . .'

He leaned forward and squeezed my arm. 'This isn't the time to decide, Eddie. I know that's the way you feel just now but you'll get better, then you'll want to come back . . . You'll want revenge.'

I shook my head in silence, still avoiding his eyes. Harle was in my mind and I wanted to ask Mac to find out if he was still okay but I knew that would be me getting involved again, so I kept quiet.

McCarthy persevered with the pep talk but soon saw it was pointless.

The weight of the whole business settled so heavily on me it felt almost physical. I couldn't talk any more. McCarthy, who'd just started one of his nosebleeds, went home.

I had a bad night and didn't get to sleep till dawn. The nurse left me undisturbed through the morning and when I woke around noon I felt better.

Much of the pain in my face had subsided and I felt altogether brighter. I wondered if that was due to me telling Mac I was pulling out, but as soon as I considered it my conscience niggled and I began wondering if I'd done the right thing.

Thoughts of Harle still crowded me and I decided to get him out of my mind by ringing Cranley. His voice snapped down the line, 'Malloy! Where are you?'

'In a call box and I don't have much change so . . .'

'Where are you, Malloy?'

'Never mind that, just tell me Harle's all right.'

'Harle is not all right! And you're the man I want to talk to about it.'

'Where is he?'

'That's what I want to ask you. Now get to this station or tell me where you are!'

I felt a sinking in my gut. 'You took that guard off him, didn't you?' I asked quietly.

'Listen, Malloy . . .'

'You took the guard off him, Cranley, didn't you, you stupid arrogant bastard . . .'

'Malloy!' He was almost screaming. 'I'll have you for this!'

I hung up, then rang McCarthy and asked him to come and get me. I told the nurse I would be discharging myself and started getting my things together.

McCarthy looked tidier than usual when he arrived. His tie was straight and clean, he hadn't missed any

139

patches when shaving and there were no breakfast crumbs around his mouth, though he'd definitely eaten because he burped loudly as he sat down.

Excusing himself with his customary 'Pa'n me,' he took off his hat, slung it carelessly on the bottom of the bed and combed his hair back with his open chubby fingers. 'How goes it?' he said. 'You look better.'

'Thanks, I feel a lot better.'

'And you're coming back for another go?'

I nodded.

'Knew you would,' he said smugly.

'How's that?'

'I just knew.' He smiled and tapped his nose. 'You're a born rebel. Angry young man. You'll always bounce back, always want something to fight against, it's your nature.'

'Good at summing people up, are you?'

He smiled again. 'Never been wrong yet.'

'I'm glad you're in such a positive mood, Mac, because I want to ask a favour.'

'Ask. I can only say no.'

'Let's talk in the car. I've spent enough time in here.'

I strapped on the seat belt and opened the window. The breeze cooled my face as McCarthy pulled away.

'Mac, what would you say to a gun?'

He frowned. 'What do you mean?'

'If I wanted one.'

'No way.'

'Why not?'

'No way, Eddie, it's not on.'

'Why?'

'Because it's going too far. It's illegal.'

'So's murder.'

'What do you mean?'

'You know what I mean, for God's sake! The two

140

guys who attacked me, who killed Danny Gordon and probably Alan Harle, it's called murder.'

'That's their problem. They'll have to face the consequences.'

'When? After they've killed me or somebody else, maybe even you?'

He was getting excited, shaking his head and rubbing the steering wheel with his left hand.

'No, Eddie, no. I'll get you anything else I can but no gun . . . I'd rather you chucked it altogether.'

'Mac, listen!' I clutched his arm but he jerked it free and kept staring at the road ahead muttering, 'No gun, Eddie, no gun.'

I'd been pretty sure he wouldn't wear it anyway but felt I had to try. At least it made him a bit more amenable to my other requests: a faster car, more money and a renewal of the promise to help me get my licence back.

After half an hour without me mentioning guns I think a trace of suspicion that he'd been conned into the other concessions was creeping up on him.

Searching for something to take his mind off the subject I suddenly remembered that the last time I'd spoken to Harle he'd given me a tip for the Triumph Hurdle.

'Mac, did Roscoe's horse win the Triumph?'

I watched his memory rewind the weeks. 'No, thank God, it didn't.'

'Why thank God?'

'Because it would have been another embarrassment for us with Perlman.'

'You don't honestly still believe this guy exists?'

'Maybe I don't, but what do I tell the Senior Steward, that we're dealing with a ghost?'

'You can tell him that Perlman is Kruger. If he has trouble remembering the guy just remind him he took my licence away because he couldn't nail Kruger. Then you can tell him that Kruger and Roscoe are running some major scam, probably from Roscoe's place. Whether it involves heroin, horse-doping or both I don't know yet but I'm sure as hell going to find out.'

He smiled. 'You've changed your tune from yesterday.'

'Blame it on that silly bastard Cranley. I get my face cooked for saving Harle and he goes and lets Kruger's men get him. Wouldn't that wind you up?'

McCarthy shrugged. 'Suppose it would.'

'Damn right it would!'

'Anyway, you're back in the game, that's the main thing. Back in pitching.'

We drove along in silence for a minute then I thought back to Cheltenham. 'Mac, I take it the dope test on Roscoe's Champion Hurdle winner was okay?'

'Yes, why?'

'It would have been a hell of a race to pull off if Kruger had perfected his dope.'

McCarthy's foot eased involuntarily off the gas pedal. 'Don't say that, Eddie, for God's sake.'

'There's got to be a possibility. What would the chances be of having tests done on every one of Roscoe's runners from now on?'

He shook his head. 'Virtually impossible. We'd be openly declaring our suspicion without any real evidence to justify it.'

'Okay then, couldn't you have one of your men visit Roscoe's? They must have something set up there. Did you know Skinner was Roscoe's private vet?'

He nodded, pondering. 'Maybe we should arrange a visit, maybe we should . . .'

It was late afternoon when Mac dropped me at the cottage. He came inside just to make sure I had no unwelcome guests, then left me with the address of one of his friends in Cheltenham and told me to call there next morning and pick up my 'new' car.

The furniture was dusty. Mooching around, half-heartedly I cleaned up and opened windows. I felt claustrophobic. I'd been cooped up in hospital too long. I needed fresh air and exercise.

Outside in the failing light I chopped wood till I was tired, which was quickly after lying around so long. Sitting on a pile of logs I breathed hard and waited to recover energy enough to chop some more.

But the longer I sat the weaker grew my arms and legs and I accepted it would take a few days to get back to full strength. I put away the axe and went inside. When the water was warm enough I ran a bath and eased myself into it.

Lying back in the hot water, sweat quickly started breaking on my body. My face didn't hurt but I got steadily weaker. I ran the cold tap till it was cooler and lay back again. My palms stung from gripping the axe shaft. I stretched. My body relaxed, my mind drifted and I slept.

CHAPTER TWENTY-ONE

Next morning I took a taxi to Mac's friend's house on the outskirts of Cheltenham. He gave me the keys to a black 2-litre injection Cavalier which was parked, hidden by trees from the house, on a concrete standing at the bottom of his long drive.

When I reached the car I started practising a routine I intended to make habitual.

Cupping my hands around my eyes to block out reflection I looked inside the car, at the seats, back and front, and the floor. Going to the opposite side I did the same.

I went to the rear passenger door, then thought again and turned to the boot. Opening it, I took out the floor rug and put it on the ground, then I knelt down and bent low so I could see the underside of the body.

Where I couldn't see I ran my hands over. I moved the mat around and covered the whole car.

I was congratulating myself on thinking ahead and being clever when it dawned on me that while I was poking my head under cars someone could be aiming at it with ten inches of lead pipe.

Still, I would have to learn as I went along and hope my next mistake didn't prove costlier than my first. When I was sure no one had stuck fifty pounds of gelignite on the chassis I replaced the mat and closed the boot.

I got in to the driver's seat and shut the door. It

was quiet. Thinking of the last time I had driven a car memories of the pain came back and scared me a little. But I shook them off. My mood was bright, positive. I was out, doing something, ready to hunt this time, ready for trouble.

Taped to the steering wheel was a note from McCarthy: 'Eddie, this is a Jockey Club vehicle, for God's sake take care of it.' Smiling, I peeled it off and folded it into my pocket.

Slanting the rear-view mirror round I looked in. Still bad but getting better – even my face couldn't depress me today.

Pulling out onto the road I headed for the police station to find out exactly how much damage Cranley had done.

After much of his usual bluster he admitted he'd ordered the removal of the guard after the third day, planning to 'review the situation' daily. He didn't get a chance. By noon the same day Harle had disappeared.

Fellow patients reported he'd been wheeled away on a trolley by two male nurses wearing surgical masks. Cranley said he was now pursuing a 'certain line of inquiry'.

He took a statement about the attack on me then told me I deserved all I got for playing amateur detective. He seemed to take an evil delight in meeting someone at last whose skin was worse than his.

I spent an hour with him. He would have liked it to be longer, he would have liked to have me there for days, locked in a cell, he told me. And he repeated his promise to 'get me'. I told him he'd be better off trying to 'get' Harle or, rather, his corpse.

The meeting ended in the usual shouting match. I walked away with another warning to stay out of it ringing in my ears.

Though I held out little hope of him talking I drove

to Nottingham next to try to see Elrick. He was in the same spot by the door in his wheelchair wearing the same clothes, almost as if he'd never moved since I'd last been there. There was no sign of the sister.

I had to remind him who I was and he started into the same spiel about me being a good jockey, but as soon as I mentioned Danny Gordon's name he clammed up and sat staring straight ahead.

'You and Odin were blackmailing him, weren't you?' Silence. 'Answer a few questions and I'll leave you alone . . . I promise not to involve the police.' Nothing. 'The men who did this to you, were they working for Kruger?' No response. I even tried a veiled threat, 'Odin's dead now . . .' But his expression was blank.

I gave up. It was late afternoon. I set off on the two-hour drive home.

*

Halfway down the track to the cottage I pulled over and parked in a small clearing. Locking the car I crept through the trees towards the cottage.

From the front it looked to be as I'd left it. Staying in the trees I circled to the back – nothing. All the windows and doors looked secure.

Moving to the front again I hid behind a thick oak for fifteen minutes, watching and listening. Nothing . . . My mind told me there was nobody there, but my heart pounded as I crouched and hurried across the track for a close-up check of the whole building.

There were no signs of entry, no footprints in soft soil, nothing amateur. Turning the key in the lock I hoped there was nothing professional waiting inside.

I opened the door into the living-room and immediately, instinctively, pulled it closed again as my brain registered someone sitting in the chair by the fireplace. In the time it took my heart to miss a beat, recognition followed and I opened the door again. Jackie, the girl

146

who'd 'saved' me and taken me to Roscoe's, was slumped in the chair.

Resisting the temptation to rush to her in case it was a set-up I cautiously pushed the door slowly all the way in till it touched the wall. No one was hiding behind it. I could see the whole room. There was no sign of anyone else. The only sound was Jackie's steady breathing.

Moving silently through the house I checked all the rooms and cupboards. None concealed any threat. I hurried back to Jackie.

Holding her wrist in a pulse-taking grip I gently raised her chin. Slowly she opened her eyes and smiled. 'Hallo,' she said, 'I must have fallen asleep . . . I've been waiting ages.'

'Holy Mary Mother o' God,' I said in an Irish accent while slumping back to sit on the floor. 'You had me scared half to death. How the hell did you get in?'

'Don't you mock me!' she said, trying not to laugh. 'The back door was open.'

'You're kidding.'

'I'm not; it wasn't lying open but it wasn't locked. I just turned the handle.'

'Jeez!' I couldn't believe it. All those precautions I'd been taking with the car and creeping through the woods and I'd gone out and left a door unlocked.

'At least you're okay,' I said. 'I thought they'd done you in and dumped you here.'

'Who?' She was still smiling.

'The same people who did this to my face.'

'It's better than it was when I last saw you.'

'Not much.'

She stared at me, the smile fading. 'Does it still hurt?'

'A bit, but I'll survive. Listen, I hate to seem inhospitable, but what exactly are you doing here?'

'I went to see you at the hospital last night but they

said you'd gone home. They gave me your address and I hitched a lift this morning.'

'Does Mr Roscoe know you're here?'

She shook her head. 'I had a few days off coming so I told him me mother was ill and I had to go home and see her.'

'Where's home?'

'Killarney.'

'He thinks you're in Ireland?'

She smiled mischievously. 'Well, that's where Killarney was the last time I looked!'

I smiled. 'So instead, you've come all the way up here to see me?'

'It's hardly all the way, it only takes about an hour and a half in a motor.'

'That's long enough, especially to see somebody who caused you nothing but hassle and wouldn't let you phone doctors when you wanted to.'

'Well, you're right, but I'd spent money on a present for you and I'm not one for waste.' She reached into a baggy rucksack and presented me with a book.

Short stories. I looked at her. 'You didn't seem the type to read anything that would take long,' she said.

'I don't know how to take that, but thanks.' She blushed slightly but held my gaze. We looked at each other in silence. There was a definite attraction between us, though God knows what she saw in me through raw blistered skin. She read my thoughts.

'Will you be badly scarred?'

'Does it matter?'

'Only for your sake.'

'The doctor said he didn't think so. The liquid that forms inside the blisters can do more damage than anything if it seeps out but he said we're over that problem, though they weren't exactly delighted when I discharged myself.'

She nodded slowly and after a few moments of silence said quietly, 'Why didn't you tell me you were in trouble with Mr Roscoe?'

I shrugged. 'Well, firstly, I didn't know I was in trouble with Mr Roscoe till somebody tried to boil my face and secondly there was no reason to suppose you would take my side. You've worked for him for a while, haven't you?'

'About two years.'

'And you hadn't known me two minutes. Besides, by the time I knew where you were taking me it was too late to do anything about it. Not that I was in a fit state to.'

'You should have said something.'

'There was no point, especially since Bobby would have talked anyway.'

'How did you know?' She seemed surprised.

'Because he thought I was a one-man travelling freak show, there was no way he was going to keep quiet.' I had thought at the time about asking her not to mention me to Roscoe but she would have been compromised when Bobby talked. It wasn't a responsibility I was entitled to put on her.

'I knew there was something wrong when you didn't want to stay in the house even long enough for a doctor to get there, so I decided not to say anything about you when Mr Roscoe came home.'

'But Bobby blabbed anyway?'

She nodded. 'Then he asked me why I hadn't told him and I had to say I was going to only Bobby didn't give me time.'

'Did he believe you?'

'I think so but I knew right off there was something funny because he knew who you were even though nobody told him your name.'

'Does he know where I am now?'

'I don't know.' She stared at me, hesitant, real concern in her eyes. 'I heard him talking about you on the phone yesterday afternoon and he was in a fierce temper. Whoever was at the other end was trying to calm him down but he said you'd just cause more trouble and that they should have done more than just try to scare you off.'

'They came pretty close to it.'

'And he said the man was now deciding if he wanted it done properly.'

'Who's the man?'

She shrugged. 'I thought you might know.'

I shook my head slowly. 'Did he say when the next time would be?'

'No. What is it they're doing?' she asked. 'Why do they want to kill you?'

I didn't want to tell her. The more she knew the more danger she'd be in. I had to decide how much I wanted her tied up in this.

'I've half an idea, but that's all it is. And anyway, the less you know the better. For your own sake.'

'What about you?'

'I'll put some sort of plan together. Don't worry.'

'Is there anyone helping you?'

'Sort of . . . Look, don't worry, I'll be okay.'

She gazed at me again with those beautiful brown eyes. 'Let me help you, Eddie . . .'

I stood up. 'Jackie, you don't even know me! I could be a crook or a murderer for all you know.'

She smiled at me and wrinkled her nose. 'What a crap line! What gangster movie did you get that from?'

I laughed. 'I give up,' I said and headed for the kitchen. 'Want some coffee?' I asked.

'I'll take some coffee if you let me help you.'

'Okay, you can wash the cups.'

'Very funny. You know what I mean.'

'I know what you mean and it's a crazy idea.'

She followed me through to the kitchen. 'How can it be crazy? I'm in the perfect place to spy for you.'

'That's what bothers me. You're also in the perfect place to have your face ending up like mine and then how would I feel, especially since yours is a damn sight prettier to start with?'

'Flattery won't put me off, Eddie.'

'I was already getting that impression.'

'Well . . .?'

'Well, let's have a cup of coffee and talk about something else like how we're going to get you back to Roscoe's.'

'I can't go back till Sunday, remember, I'm in Ireland.'

I turned to her and put my hands on her shoulders. 'When I opened the door and saw you in that chair my first thought was, big trouble. Then I recognised you and said, Thank God, it's only Jackie. I'm beginning to think the first impression was right.'

She smiled her crazy, soft warm smile again then, leaning forward, she closed her eyes and kissed me.

Maybe if I'd been physically and emotionally stronger, maybe if I'd been in a serious relationship during the last couple of years rather than the odd tacky drunken one-night stand, I would have succumbed less easily to Jackie's determined seduction.

But I, or rather we, ended up doing nothing for the next three days but making love, indoors and out, walking in the woods, eating, drinking, sleeping, laughing, talking (the only taboo subject was Roscoe, Harle and associates).

At twenty she was seven years my junior but she cooked for me, tended my blisters, bathed me, made me

151

laugh, made me feel better than I could ever remember and made me fall in love with her.

When McCarthy rang me on Saturday to ask if Harle had turned up I was sorely tempted to tell him I was packing it in. It just didn't seem to matter any more. I was totally infatuated with Jackie, as she was, I think, with me.

She was due back at Roscoe's on Sunday morning. I told her we'd rise before dawn and I'd drive her there. On Saturday night I took her to the Mail Coach Inn for dinner. In the previous three days Jackie had made me forget all about my face and we breezed in to the restaurant laughing, only for some of the ruder diners to stare almost open-mouthed at this Beauty and the Beast.

She gazed at me through the candle flame. 'Never mind, when your face is better we'll come back and show them!'

'They'll probably get a bigger shock than they just did.'

'What do you actually look like under all that, anyway?'

'A cross between Mel Gibson and Tom Cruise. It won't be my fault, of course, if I don't return completely to my former glory.'

She smiled and squeezed my hand. 'I'll never forget seeing your face that first morning in the car; I almost fainted.'

'I was doing enough fainting for both of us, thanks.'

The waiter appeared and we ordered champagne while we waited for our food. I reached for her hand. 'I'll miss you . . .' I said.

'I won't go then.'

'Seriously?'

'Why not? It's not exactly the best job in the world. I'll miss the horses, but you would just about make up for that.'

I thought about it. 'We could leave here,' she said. 'Go to Ireland. I know places where they'd never find us.'

'They . . . That's the trouble, that's what it would always come back to. They . . . Them . . . Looking over our shoulders all the time.'

'Why would it come to that? What have you done that would make them come after you?'

'I don't want to talk about it, Jackie. I don't want you involved.'

'Okay, so I won't get involved, I promise. I'm only asking you what you've done so far which means you can't stop now?'

I thought about it . . . 'Nothing, I suppose.' It was the easy way out, the way Kruger wanted me to take. To clear the field and let him run riot.

'Well, then,' Jackie said, 'why don't you forget it? You don't have any family ties, there's nothing to keep us here . . .'

Us . . . me and Jackie, tucked away in some little village in Southern Ireland. No more villains, no more scaldings, no more stupid policemen.

'. . . I could ring Mr Roscoe in the morning,' Jackie said. 'Tell him I'm not coming back because me mother's worse than I thought. We could leave tomorrow.'

I looked at her and saw the happiness in her eyes at the thought of it. Leaning across the table, holding both my hands, every ounce of her was saying, Please, let's go, and most of me was agreeing. She reached forward and gently touched my cheek, and I thought back on what had happened to me.

I thought of the two bastards who'd done it and what they'd done to others. I thought how happy they'd feel if they knew they'd had another success and frightened me away. Then there was Kruger – how satisfying it would be for him if I dropped out, he'd have cost me my licence twice.

And Harle who, although I knew he must be mixed up with the crooks, I'd begun to feel some real responsibility for . . . I'd certainly suffered for him. McCarthy too, he was a pain in the arse at times, but he'd stood by me. God knows how much fighting he'd had to do to keep me on the case.

Then there was the matter of a certain racecourse less than a mile from where I sat. A course where they ran the Gold Cup and the Champion Hurdle, where the best steeplechasers in the country soared over big black fences, a course which tested jockeys' skills more than any other . . . skills and courage . . . Courage.

She saw it in my eyes. 'I think I've lost this one, Eddie, haven't I?'

'Don't count it as a loss. We'll think back sometime and we'll be glad we didn't run.'

'We will or you will?'

'Both of us. I know I could never live with it and I'd take it out on you.'

'I'm strong, I can stand it.'

I smiled at her youthful optimism. 'Maybe for a month or a year, but not for ever.'

'Try me.'

'Listen to the wisdom of an older man.'

'But . . .'

I squeezed her hand and shook my head. 'It's our last night, let's not argue.'

Pursing her lips she lowered her head and nodded almost imperceptibly. Right on cue the waiter brought the champagne.

All through dinner she worked on me to let her help. I was dead against it for her sake, but she persisted. I knew she would make a valuable ally, the best I could

154

wish for, a spy in the camp. On the drive home we reached a compromise.

'Okay, we're agreed,' I said. 'You take no chances whatsoever. You don't go prowling around, you don't ask anybody any questions, and I mean anybody, even someone you think you can trust. All you do is listen and observe as you go about your normal daily business. All right?'

'Yes, sir.'

'Come on, Jackie, this is serious.'

'Okay! Okay! But I'm not some kid, you know!'

'I know you're not. You're twenty and I want you to live till you're thirty, and then forty and so on. That's why I'm going to keep drilling into you how serious this is . . . These people are killers and maimers. The two guys who do the dirty work positively enjoy it, to the extent that they like to think of imaginative ways to assault new people on their lists. Think about it!'

She was silent for a minute as we drove through the darkness, then she said, 'Tell me the story so far.' By the time we reached the cottage I'd told her everything.

I didn't really learn much that was new from Jackie about the people at Roscoe's, though the fact that Roscoe ran a couple of horses regularly at the small tracks in France was interesting. The runners were always accompanied on their travels by either Skinner or Harle. I'd have bet they weren't there just for the racing.

Lying together on the rug in the firelight, clutching whisky glasses, we finalised plans. 'I'm particularly interested in what Skinner's doing at the yard,' I said. I felt her shiver.

'Yugh!'

'Not your favourite person, I guess?'

'He's a dirty old bastard. Always trying to touch me up or making filthy suggestions.'

'He does look the part.'

'If I'm grooming or mucking out he'll wait till my back's turned and, preferably, till I'm bending over, then he sneaks into the box under some silly pretext and tries it on.'

'You'd be amazed how much he'd probably respond to a well-aimed prod with a pitchfork.'

'I thought of that but up till now I've needed the job too much. Once this is over I'll think of some way to get him back.'

'Let me know, I'd like to be there.'

'I will.'

'How long has he been at the yard?'

'Almost a year. I remember him first trying to grope me on Derby day.'

'Just doing normal vet-type things, apart from the groping, that is?'

'Yes, as far as I can see. He takes blood tests, checks legs, gives injections, that sort of stuff.'

'Ever seen him injecting what you thought was a healthy horse?'

'No, definitely not. I'd have noticed. Then again I don't see everything he does.'

'I bet you don't. Where does he live?'

'Mr Roscoe moved him into the Head Lad's cottage when he arrived.'

'Must have pleased the Head Lad.'

'He left shortly afterwards.'

'Does he have a lab to analyse the blood tests?'

'Mr Roscoe converted part of the office. I wouldn't call it a lab exactly, but it's all right.'

'Ever been in his cottage?'

'What kind of a girl do you think I am?'

I smiled. 'Come on, Jackie, stop messing about.'

'No, I haven't. Nobody goes up there 'cause he keeps this big bloody Rottweiler and lets it roam around the house.'

'Does he spend much time in the cottage?'

'Can't say I've really noticed.'

'That's one thing you could start looking out for then, but for God's sake don't take any chances.'

'Okay, okay, I won't!' She leaned forward and kissed me. 'You're a terrible nag, Edward Malloy!'

'I've ridden some terrible nags, too, in my time.'

She grimaced. 'Your jokes are worse than your face!'

I grabbed her around the waist. 'But you love it anyway.'

'Oh, do I now?'

And we kissed. Then, in the glow of the dying embers, we made love, but not with the passion and energy of the last three days. Though the thoughts remained unspoken we knew the next time might be weeks or months away or, depending on the coming days, depending on Kruger and his men, maybe never.

Our moods and our thoughts and feelings meshed and our lovemaking was a slow, tender, caring and beautifully sad goodbye.

On the drive to Roscoe's next morning we went over the things she was to watch out for: any sign or mention of Harle or Kruger or the two men, any hint of what Skinner did on a daily basis. She was to ring me from the pub each night if she could at ten o'clock, though I told her not to worry if I wasn't there. I stressed again she was to take no chances.

'What about you?' she asked. 'What are your plans? How do I get in touch?'

'Tomorrow I'm going to Kempton in the hope of seeing Harle's girlfriend. She hangs around the London tracks and there's a faint chance if he's still alive that he's tried to contact her. Where I go from there I don't know yet but I'll keep you up-to-date each time we talk. Remember, if you can't get me or if anything happens to me, you've got McCarthy's number. I'll speak to him tomorrow and tell him what we've planned.'

We stopped a mile from Roscoe's knowing it was safer if she walked the rest of the way. As dawn broke we stood holding each other tightly, then we parted in silence.

CHAPTER TWENTY-TWO

At Kempton I saw people I knew but either they didn't recognise me because of my face or didn't want to be seen talking to me. Not that it bothered me much any more.

I saw Mac standing alone by a racecard kiosk. He didn't want to be seen with me, I knew that, but there was nobody around. He saw me approach and looked nervous.

'I told you not to speak to me on the racecourse.'

'Relax. As far as everyone's concerned I'm the invisible man anyway.'

'What do you mean?'

'It doesn't matter.'

He still looked worried. 'Mac, there's a race going on, everyone is on the other side of the stand.'

Looking more resigned than relieved he said, 'Okay, what is it?'

I told him about Jackie. 'That's a bad decision, Eddie.'

'How the hell is it a bad decision? She won't take any risks, she's just observing! She's an insider, for God's sake! It's the best break we've had.'

He stood shaking his head. 'What else can we do?' I asked.

Glaring at me he said, 'Look, Eddie, do what you want, just start getting me some results!'

I stared at him. 'What the hell's that supposed to mean?'

'It means I need some results from you! I'm under pressure!'

'Results? Pressure? I just came out of the fucking hospital after getting my face fried for you and you talk to me about pressure!'

He looked around nervously. 'Calm down, Eddie, for God's sake. I'm sorry ... Look, I'm getting calls from my boss virtually every time there's a major form upset. We're well into the flat season, there could be a drugged horse in every damn race and we wouldn't know about it.'

'That's way over the top, Mac, and you know it.'

'Okay, maybe it is, but everybody's feeling it, not just you. Now look, I'll have to go. We'll talk soon when we've both calmed down a bit.'

The way I felt, that would take a while.

The paddock bar was full of babbling people with newspapers under arms and racecards protruding from pockets. As more punters pushed through the door those already inside scowled and moved aside reluctantly to let them pass. When I got to pulling my toes out of the way of trampling feet every five seconds I decided it was time to leave.

I excused my way across half the floor and when that stopped working, elbowed my way across the rest. As I stepped out, two tight-trousered girls, deep in conversation, were trying to get in.

'Hallo, Wendy,' I said to the smaller one. She stopped and stared but didn't recognise me immediately. When she did her eyebrows went up and her hand clapped her open mouth. 'Eddie! What the hell happened to you?'

'It's a long story, as they say.'

'You look like you've had skin grafts from an old saddle.'

'I wish it were as tough.'

Wendy stepped to the side to see how far round the scarring went. I turned to her friend. 'Hallo, Priscilla, remember me?' Priscilla looked more bored than shocked. 'Not like that I don't.'

'Heard anything from Alan?' I asked.

She gave me a bitter look and shook her head. 'You told me he was in Cyprus.'

'I think he may be back.'

'He'd be riding if he was back.'

'Yes, I suppose he would.'

She sneered. 'Tell him when he does come back I hope he falls off his first ride and it kicks his balls up into his belly before he hits the ground.'

'Painful.'

'Not half enough for the slimy little sod.'

Wendy had completed her inspection and was back facing me. She knitted her brows in a half-quizzical smile. 'You got scars anywhere else then, Eddie?'

'Nowhere you haven't seen before,' I said. She giggled, uninsulted.

'You coming in to buy us a drink?' she asked.

'Sorry, Wendy, not today. But if you hear anything of Alan Harle, ring me. There'll be a bottle in it for you.'

'Make it a magnum.'

'Give me a break.'

Her smile said it was worth a try. Priscilla's frown said let's get away from this freak. I said goodbye and went to see a couple of guys I knew in the Press bar.

The rest of the day was spent drifting, listening, trying to pick up any snippet leading to Harle, but I came up with nothing. I left before the last race.

As I approached my car in the car park I knew something was wrong but couldn't pinpoint what it was. Slowing down I started looking around.

From what I could see there was nobody but me in the car park, though the high sides of the numerous horseboxes could be hiding any number of potential attackers.

Ten paces from the car I realised what was wrong, it was parked nose up to a horsebox. I had reversed into the space when I'd arrived. Someone, in the previous two hours, had been driving my car.

As I reached it I looked through the windows. No unwanted passengers. I walked to the front and checked the bonnet-catch to see if it had been tampered with. There were no signs.

Squatting, I ran my hand along the underside of the car then decided that wasn't thorough enough. Lying down I dug my heels in and pushed myself under the car for a proper look. I found nothing.

Sliding back out I got to my feet and dusted myself down. Close behind me someone spoke. 'Looking for something?'

I took a large step, almost a jump away from the voice and turned very quickly. My hand was raised to punch when my brain recognised the uniform of the Metropolitan Police. It cancelled the message to my fist and began whirring through the plausible excuse file. The policeman was tall, thin and patiently waiting.

I tried playing for time since I didn't think he'd quite believe I was looking to see if someone had stuck twenty pounds of explosive on my exhaust pipe. 'Do you always creep up so quietly on people?'

'Only suspects, sir.'

I looked suitably flustered. 'Suspect? Me? What of? This is my car.'

'What were you doing lying under it?'

'I thought I saw a cat.' Jeez, I thought, what a lame excuse. 'A big black one. It was under the back wheel. I saw it as I came up and I didn't want to risk running it over if it was trapped.'

'Animal lover, are you, sir?'

'Honestly . . .'

Unclipping the radio from his lapel he asked HQ to run a computer check on the licence number. That's when it dawned on me the car wasn't registered in my name. I thought about trying to explain while he waited for an answer but since I didn't know who the car was registered under I decided to stay quiet and explain later.

The tinny voice of the controller came back through. The constable had his notebook out. 'The car is registered in the name of the Jockey Club, Portman Square, London.'

'Roger,' he said, pressing a full-stop from his pencil into the book. I waited for him to speak. He looked at me. 'You a member of the Jockey Club, sir?'

Very droll.

'I have the use of the car for a while.'

'Do you have the keys?'

I pulled them from my pocket. 'Open the car, please,' he said.

I pushed the key in, the lock clicked and I opened the door.

'Close it now, please.'

I closed it.

Walking to the back of the car he looked again at the registration plate. He still had his notebook and pencil in hand.

'Will you open the boot, please, sir?'

'Sure.'

I pushed the key in and turned it. The boot lid came smoothly up and I stared inside and wondered if the day was going to get any worse. There was someone in the boot. It was Alan Harle. He was dead.

CHAPTER TWENTY-THREE

They took me to a small square room with a table and two chairs and a vase of daffodils on the windowsill and kept me waiting with only a silent constable for company.

Under the circumstances it didn't take Detective Sergeant Cranley all that long to get there and the evil glee which had no doubt shone on his face throughout the journey was still obvious as he came through the door.

One of the London CID boys who looked a bit like Michael Caine, though his suit was three sizes too big, was with him. He couldn't have failed to be impressed by Cranley's completely unbiased opening line. 'Well, well, well, Malloy . . . got you by the bollocks at last!'

I saved my reply. This already had the makings of a long night. Cranley didn't disappoint me. He kept referring back to my previous jail term on the basis that the leopard never changes its spots. He claimed I'd almost killed Harle the first time and that my taking him to the hospital had been a front to give myself an alibi.

So I'd boiled my own face, I asked, to give me another alibi for Harle's abduction from the hospital? Cranley said he wouldn't put it past me.

'You haven't asked for a lawyer yet, Malloy. I'm surprised.'

'Why would I want a lawyer? I've done nothing, Cranley, and you know it.'

But he persevered, all night he persevered, trying to extract a confession, screaming at me, pushing his sweaty pock-marked face into mine, breathing his garlic breath. At one point he raised his fist, but then he looked in my eyes and what he saw told him better than words could have that if he even tried it I would one day beat the shit out of him.

As dawn broke they took my belt and tie and shoelaces and threw me in a cell. I'd had no food or drink and my head pounded from Cranley's screaming. I lay down and tried to clear my mind, tried to analyse what had happened.

Who the hell were these guys of Kruger's? I'd been at Kempton no more than two hours. You don't just happen across a car and dump a body in it. How had they known I'd be there? How could they know which car I was driving? They began to seem, somehow, superhuman.

If they were that good I thought I'd better tell Jackie to forget what we'd arranged. She wouldn't be safe doing even that. Jackie . . . I thought about holding her . . . the way I had on Sunday morning when we'd parted. Trying to comfort myself, I replayed in my head our final conversation.

What are your immediate plans, Eddie? Well, tomorrow I'll be at Kempton . . .

Jackie . . . Surely not?

The more I thought about it the more my suspicion deepened, though I desperately didn't want to believe that she'd betrayed me, set me up. Surely everything we'd had during those three days couldn't have been false? There wasn't a woman alive who could put on such an act.

In the end I convinced myself it was just tiredness and mental bruising that made me suspicious of Jackie.

After all, hadn't Kruger's men traced me before, followed me to Roscoe's place?

Or had they? Maybe they'd been on their way to Roscoe's and just happened upon my car. If they'd followed me there, why hadn't they stopped me entering Roscoe's house?

My weary, battered mind tumbled the thoughts over almost in slow motion. I didn't know what to think any more, couldn't trust myself to be logical. Attempts at sleep resulted in a fitful two hours punctuated by snatches of the same nightmare.

At ten o'clock a policeman brought me breakfast, soap and a towel. 'Get that eaten, then get cleaned up. There's somebody here to see you.'

I ate but didn't bother cleaning up as I knew it was for their cosmetic purposes rather than mine. Then I was led to a room where McCarthy waited.

'You look awful,' he said.

'Thanks.'

'Have you been up all night?'

'Almost. Cranley was conducting one of his special interviews. You know, one of those where they tell you what you did rather than ask you.'

'Yes, he looks the type, I've just spent fifteen minutes with him. He is not your biggest fan, Eddie, I can tell you that. What the hell have you done to upset him so much?'

'Nothing, let's just say we took an instant dislike to each other. He's obsessed with my supposed involvement in all this, keeps saying he's going to get me . . .'

'Not this time he isn't. He's just had the results of some of the forensic tests – Harle's been dead at least a week, which gives you the perfect alibi, since you were lying in a bed in Newbury Hospital when he was killed.'

166

'What was the cause of death?'

'Still to be confirmed, but they've detected Hepatitis B along with a massive quantity of heroin. Either he injected himself with an infected needle or somebody else did.'

'I think we can safely say it was somebody else, don't you? They'll be claiming he dumped his own body in my car next.'

He smiled.

'I guess that's how they got you involved, through the car,' I said. He nodded. 'I'm sorry, Mac, I know that's really dropped you in it.'

'Forget it, it turned out to be a sort of blessing in disguise. It's made my people realise just how serious this is. There were a lot of heads in the sand, Eddie, a lot of people who didn't want to face the reality of what was going on – didn't want to face the fact that you were in there on our side. Harle's body in the boot of a Jockey Club car at Kempton sort of brought matters to a head. We had a very interesting meeting last night. If you still want to carry on with this, I can tell you that you now have everybody's support. And I mean everybody.'

He sounded like he was knighting me. 'What do you want me to do, Mac, get down on my knees and thank the Lord?'

He shrugged and looked hurt. 'We've been skulking around in back alleys so long I thought you'd appreciate being . . . accepted.'

'Well, how gratifying. I'm so pleased to know that Jockey Club members have now voted not to hold their noses and cross the street when they see me approach. I'm honoured, but did they say anything in passing about returning my licence?'

'I'm afraid that wasn't discussed, Eddie. And I'm not going to bullshit you, that is still going to depend very heavily on getting a confession out of Kruger.'

'Well, surprise, surprise.'

He looked tentatively at me. 'Are you sticking with it?'

'Can you get me out of here today?'

'This morning.'

'Can you get Cranley off my back?'

'I've told him you are now officially employed by the Jockey Club, temporarily, of course . . .'

'Of course!'

'. . . to work on this case on the basis that the police, good as they are at their job, do not have enough time to dedicate exclusively to this particular problem.'

'And how did Detective Sergeant Cranley take that little speech?'

'Let's say he didn't applaud. I then told him that you would give the police all the help and information you could and that you'd expect the same from them.'

'Fat chance. What have the Press got to say about it this morning?'

'Not that much in the racing papers who are closing ranks as usual, thank God, but a couple of the tabloids are featuring it, though that should soon blow over since Cranley intends to keep it low-profile.'

'Now, I wonder why that is? Could it be anything to do with the fact that so far he's made a complete balls of the whole thing?'

'Probably . . .' McCarthy looked at me expectantly.

'Well?' I asked.

'Well . . . ? Are you still in?'

I nodded. 'Either until they get me or the Jockey Club runs out of cars.'

McCarthy got me another car, a white Granada ('It'll make you feel like a cop'), and I went back to the cottage to bathe and change.

Mac had underplayed the Press reports. It turned out

168

that Harle had accomplished something in death that he seldom had in life: he made the front pages of *The Sporting Life* and the *Racing Post*. Most of the tabloids carried the story too.

There was much speculation over his killer or killers and the motive behind the murder. The police 'would not release the official cause of death but confirmed there were suspicious circumstances' which prompted them to appeal to racegoers at Kempton who may have seen anyone driving or acting suspiciously around a black Cavalier in the car park to come forward.

Roscoe was quoted as being 'devastated' by the news and repeated his story about Harle running out on him back in March and never contacting him since. Quotes from fellow jockeys were suitably gracious, urging one hack over the top with the 'tributes poured in' cliché. Never speak ill of the dead . . .

I slept for a while then prepared myself for another trip to Roscoe's. On the drive down thoughts of Jackie occupied my mind. I was missing her already, regretting I wouldn't be there for her ten o'clock call. I'd virtually discounted my suspicions of the previous night, though some dregs obstinately remained, making me feel guilty about harbouring them.

The gathering dusk found me perched halfway up a tree about three hundred yards from Roscoe's front door. In a small back-pack were a flask of tea and some sandwiches and around my neck hung a pair of 10×50 binoculars.

Things were bound to be stirred up by Harle's murder and I thought there was a reasonable chance that Roscoe might be entertaining some interesting visitors. I was prepared for a long evening.

It was almost midnight when I shimmied down to the ground, stiff, sore and cold. I could still smell the exhaust fumes of the car which had left Roscoe's and passed below me a minute before. The two men inside had been with Roscoe since 9.30. One was my little bumbling friend from the toilet of the Duke's Hotel and the other was a young man I'd last seen lying unconscious on the Cheltenham turf – Phil Greene, Harle's stand-in. Somehow, I didn't think they'd been on a social call.

Resisting a brief crazy temptation to break into the lads' quarters and find Jackie, I jogged to where I'd hidden the car and headed home.

CHAPTER TWENTY-FOUR

I was in Cheltenham by nine next morning, drinking smooth coffee in a restaurant overlooking the broad boulevard in the centre of town. Roscoe had announced to the Press the appointment of his new stable jockey, twenty-one-year-old Phil Greene. I very much doubted that all he was doing at Roscoe's last night was signing his contract.

And who was the little man who'd been with him, the same one who'd been shadowing Harle at the Duke's Hotel? The difference this time was that Greene obviously knew who he was. Harle hadn't, or so he'd claimed at the time.

There was a call box in the corner. I rang McCarthy's office and his secretary said sorry he wasn't in and who was calling.

'Eddie Malloy.'

'Oh, Mister Malloy, Mister McCarthy did leave a message that he'd be at Salisbury races this afternoon.'

'Fine, I'll see him there.'

It was the warmest day of the year so far and by the time I reached the racecourse I was hot and thirsty. I decided to have a beer before seeking out McCarthy. As I drank I noticed two men talking in the corner. One nodded towards me and pointed. The other came over, smiling, and ordered a bottle of champagne and two glasses.

Putting one in front of me and filling it with a regal gesture he announced himself as a reporter, Pile of the *Argus*. It turned out he was trying to make a name for himself by investigating Harle's death.

'They tell me he was found in the boot of your car, Ed.'

I don't like people calling me Ed, especially people I've just met and even more so when they're doing it to try to make it sound like they've known me all my life.

Pile was persistent. He was the most aptly named guy I ever met, a very large pain in the arse.

I liked him even less for thinking the champagne bought him into whatever I knew. I don't like to get too uppity because every man has his price but mine was not £38.50.

I ignored him and asked the barman for another beer. Pile looked shocked. 'But what about the bubbly I just bought you?'

'You drink it,' I said and paid for the beer.

Carrying the drink to the corner I tucked myself in to watch the world go by.

Funny places, racecourses, social melting-pots with ingredients off every shelf from Royalty to Villainy. It occurred to me that most people who recognised me probably placed me in the latter category.

You'll always see beautiful women at the races and that afternoon was no exception, but none looked half as good as Jackie. It occurred to me that I didn't even know her second name and I smiled to myself.

Watching by the running rails as they came out for the next race I'd almost forgotten how finely made and clean limbed these flat-race horses were compared to the jumpers. Delicate, pampered, . . . so were some of their tiny, highly paid jockeys. The jumpers were the real heroes, the real warriors, horses and jockeys.

I stayed by the rails to watch the race, a decent Class 6 furlong handicap. I was half a furlong from the winning post and as they charged past me the whips cracking on rumps sounded like a busy rifle range. They had speed all right; biased as I was I couldn't deny them that.

All around me the crowds were bawling their horses on to run faster, their jockeys to hit harder. As the winner passed the post the roar collapsed to a murmur in seconds. I decided to walk back to the winner's enclosure and watch them come in.

Walking steadily on the outside of the crowd flow I recognised a lady coming towards me. Elegantly dressed and beautiful as ever, moving smartly and staring straight ahead, Charmain marched past looking, for some reason, pretty pleased with herself. Stepping out of the shuffling line I turned and watched her walk away and thought about the last time I'd seen her – the Champion Hurdle night party at the Duke's Hotel.

A fine party that. One for reflecting on. Charmain had been there, so had Roscoe, so had Harle and our little bumbling friend who'd visited Roscoe's with Greene the other night. Maybe Skinner had been at the party too, and Phil Greene.

I remembered her ill-mannered husband, though I couldn't recall his name. How had she escaped him today? I doubted he knew she was parading about at Salisbury races drawing lustful glances from every heterosexual man she passed.

His name came to me, Stoke, and I recollected he was a bookmaker. Maybe he was betting here today. I headed for the ring to find out.

Scouting among the blackboards and satchels on my way towards the rails bookies, I exchanged the occasional silent nod with any bookmaker I knew. Bookmakers were something common to Flat and National

Hunt racing, they were completely unbiased as to who they took money from and in what weather they took it. Nice guys, most of them.

There was the odd bastard among them same as there is everywhere. Stoke was one of those. He was here, standing on his stool but deep in conversation with someone else I knew, young Phil Greene, Roscoe's replacement for Harle. Well, well, well, another ingredient. The pot was bubbling nicely.

Stoke was leaning over, his head close to Greene's mouth. His lips weren't moving so I guessed Greene's were. He talked with Stoke a few minutes more then they started getting interruptions from people wanting a bet.

Greene finished his conversation and headed towards the stands. Stoke bent over his book and went back to business. I followed Greene. He stopped at a bank of phones and skulked into the one in the corner.

Greene dialled and as he waited for an answer he turned, with the phone at his ear, and looked to see if anyone was watching him. I raised my *Sporting Life* – casually, I hoped – and pretended to study form. I was about twenty-five yards away from him. Glancing over the top of the paper I saw him trying to force money into the slot.

The coin wouldn't go in at first and each time he pressed he'd rise on his toes as though it would make a difference.

The money finally dropped into the box and Greene moved so far inside the booth you'd have thought he was touch reading the STD codes on the wall with his nose. The call lasted a couple of minutes on the one coin so it was probably local.

When the time did run out he scrambled in his pocket for another coin but when he found it he probably remembered the trouble he'd had with the box. He dropped it back in his pocket and said a hurried goodbye.

Raising my newspaper again as he walked past I watched him head back to the ring. I was pretty sure he was returning to Stoke and that's where I found him.

Stoke was taking his last few bets on the final race of the day and Greene wandered around near him, kicking at torn betting tickets.

A twenty-five-to-one chance won the race. The bookies smiled and got off their stools and the punters grimaced and headed for the exits, dropping crumpled tickets on the way.

Stoke forcibly jammed a wad of notes into the inside pocket of his jacket, peeled a few from another bundle to pay off his clerk then walked, with Greene, back towards the stands.

I followed them to the car park where they stopped beside a big sky-blue Mercedes. Charmain was in the back seat, though neither of the men seemed to acknowledge her presence. Stoke opened the driver's door, took off his jacket and slung it in beside his wife.

He got in and looked in the mirror, fingering his too long hair and his too thin tie. Greene got in quickly and closed the door. As they strapped on their seat belts I made for my own car which was parked near the exit.

Starting the engine I sat waiting for them but they didn't move and after five minutes I switched off. As soon as I did the Merc's reversing lights glowed and Stoke backed it out, swung it round slowly and headed for the exit. I followed.

The Merc went a sensible speed, heading North initially on the A34 past Oxford. I found myself dropping further behind as we got deeper into the countryside. The roads were getting narrower and other cars scarce. Stoke wouldn't have to be a mastermind to realise I was following him. I tried to keep him just in view but it was a tricky game; the hedgerows were high in places and if Stoke took a turn off while he was out of view I'd lose him.

Just after seven they stopped about a mile through a small village called Shipton-on-Cherwell. Stoke pulled up by a bridge near a lock-keeper's white cottage on the Oxford canal and Greene got out. He turned and bowed to speak to Stoke who was revving the engine sending puffs of grey smoke from the tailpipe. Greene straightened up and slammed the door and the Merc took off over the narrow bridge. He watched it go and was rewarded with a glance and a small secretive wave from Charmain.

I drove on down the road slowing to a crawl as I approached the bridge. Greene was walking along the canal bank by a line of four barges moored in the muddy water.

Two of the boats were completely covered by tarpaulins, another was a shiny varnished brown with brass fittings and a black chimney three feet high.

Greene jumped onto the deck of the third barge in line. It was yellow and light green, though the paint was faded and cracked. On the roof were a lifebelt, two old tyres and a TV aerial. At the far end was a small chimney. The name on the side was faded, it could have been Lickety Split.

Getting out of the car I ambled as casually as I could to the lock-keeper's cottage. There was still enough warmth in the evening sun for shirt sleeves but the man sitting on an old wrought-iron bench by the door of the cottage had a sweater on.

A thick silver-grey fringe hung over his tanned face as he stared down in concentration through a half-moon pair of gold-rimmed specs. On a wooden block at his feet was a squat threaded length of brass with various cogs and wheels and he was cleaning it with a light grease which glistened on his finger-nails.

'Hallo,' I said.

He looked up for just long enough to see if he knew me. 'Evenin','' he said and went back to work.

'Do you know if any of the boats on the canal are for sale?' I asked.

'Everythin's for sale, son, if you've got enough money.'

A philosopher was what I didn't need. 'Any idea about those particular boats then? I quite liked the green and yellow one.'

'Brassy as a two-bob whore.'

I wasn't sure if he meant me or the boat. I pressed on.

'Do you know who owns it?'

'The doctor.'

'Doctor who?'

This time there was a glint in his eyes as he looked up. 'No, not Doctor Who, son, he lives in a phone box.'

I laughed and smiled trying to sweeten him up a bit. 'Is it the local GP?'

'No, never see the fella in fact. He used to live in the house just up the road before you come to the farm.'

'Does he use the boat much?'

'Never seen him on it in all the time I've been here. There's a young fella been usin' it these last couple of months. He just stepped out of a big fancy car on the bridge. Maybe you should go and talk to him.'

'Maybe I should. Thanks for your help.'

He grunted. I turned and walked to the bridge and had a last look at Greene's boat before getting into the car.

Driving through the long evening shadows into the village of Shipton I found the shop (it was the only one I could see) still open. Two ladies, twins in their mid-fifties, stood behind the counter. They wore white blouses with a frill at the neck under black woollen cardigans.

Taking turn about, they both told me they knew the young man who lived on the boat by sight, though not by name, but they hadn't seen him for a week or so.

'I was actually interested in buying his boat but I can't seem to catch him at home.'

'Oh it's not his boat. It belongs to another man, the man who used to live in Fleming's cottage,' said Number One.

'Ah,' I said. 'Someone mentioned him. Would that be the doctor?'

'He's not a doctor, he's a vet,' Number Two said.

'Are you sure?' I asked.

Number One looked at her sister with some doubt in her eyes. 'I think so. Someone said he thought he was a doctor but I'm sure he's a vet. He works on the racecourse, you know.'

I smiled. 'How do you know that?'

She seemed slightly offended at me appearing to doubt her word and she tilted her head back slowly before looking down her nose as she answered, 'Because Walter the postman has seen him at Newbury races, a number of times! And he says his letters are addressed Mister and not Doctor.'

'Did Walter say what his actual name was?' I asked.

Number Two looked at Number One and they exchanged knowing smiles. 'We remember it, don't we, Dora? We thought it was quite an apt name for a vet . . .'

I waited.

'Skinner,' they said together.

Most apt.

I thanked the twins for their help, bought the biggest

box of chocolates in the shop, headed for the nearest public telephone and rang McCarthy at home.

'Mac?'

'Eddie.' He didn't sound delighted to hear from me.

'Sorry I missed you at Salisbury today, I got kind of side-tracked.'

'Anything worthwhile?'

'Could well be. What are your plans for tomorrow?'

'I'm seeing a trainer near Marlborough, around two-thirty.'

'Meet me for lunch at the Castle and Ball in Marlborough High Street at one.'

There was silence for a few seconds. 'Okay, I'll be there at one.'

'See you.'

My mind and body buzzing, I headed home and slept that night as well as I had for months.

In the lounge of the Castle and Ball McCarthy moodily chose a salad. I guessed he was on a diet and made him feel worse by ordering a fat croissant stuffed with chicken and mushrooms and spicy sauce.

I told him about yesterday's episodes with Greene and the Stokes and that Greene was staying in Skinner's boat.

'What do you make of it?' he asked, rounding up a maverick piece of lettuce.

'I don't know, but it set me thinking about Skinner. Can you remember him when he worked on the racecourse?'

He nodded, crunching noisily. 'Remember him well – it was one of my lads who had to tell him his services would no longer be required.'

'For betting, wasn't it?'

'Yep. They reckoned he was a compulsive gambler.'

'How long ago did he lose his job?'

'Must be a couple of years now.'

'Do you know if Howard Stoke was around at the time – making a book, I mean?'

He shook his head. 'I honestly can't remember, but I could find out. What's the connection?'

'I don't know that there is one, yet. But it would be interesting to know if Skinner bet with Stoke and if so, how much. There's obviously some tie-up between Stoke and Greene and with Greene using Skinner's boat, well, there could just be a little niche in Roscoe's set-up where we'll find Stoke fits nicely. Also, I saw Greene the other night leaving Roscoe's with the same little man who was trailing Harle in the Duke's Hotel after the Champion Hurdle.'

'Are you sure it was the same man?'

'Positive. Small, tubby, very thick round glasses – unmistakable.'

McCarthy stopped chewing and stared at me. 'Remember I told you we interviewed Perlman before accepting his registration as an owner?'

'Uhuh. At his big house in Wiltshire, wasn't it?'

'That's right. Did I tell you the physical description as far as my man could recall?'

'Let me guess – small and tubby with very thick round glasses.'

'Got it in one.'

'Well, well, well,' I smiled. 'The plot, as they say thickens.'

'So it looks like there is a Perlman after all,' Mac said.

'No chance, the little guy has got to be a decoy Kruger's the man, believe me.'

'Don't get too stuck on Kruger, Eddie; you're too single-minded with him, you've got to allow for other possibilities.'

'Come on, Mac! I told you about the call Kruger left on

Roscoe's answering machine, I heard it in person, live. Let me remind you what he said: "Who is running this ffing show, Roscoe?" '

'Well, let me ask you, who do you think Kruger was complaining about in that call? Who's trying to take over the show?'

I shrugged. 'Roscoe . . . That's what it sounded like.'

'That depends how you interpret it, doesn't it?'

That made me think. 'I suppose it does.'

'You shouldn't jump to conclusions, Eddie. Don't discount that little guy.'

'Okay, I'll keep him in mind.'

'I mean it!'

'Okay, okay.'

'God, I hate this rabbit food.' He threw down his fork and, like a hungry dog, watched me eat. 'What's that like?' he asked.

I smiled. 'Absolutely mouth-watering.'

After casting a few furtive glances around to see if anyone knew him he went to the bar and ordered a stuffed croissant. The anticipation of its arrival mellowed him considerably.

'So, what's next?' he asked.

'Well, Greene seems a brash little bastard who likes shooting his mouth off. I think I'll pay him a visit under the guise of a journalist and butter him up a bit.'

'I'd say you were a hundred-to-one against, Eddie. Roscoe or Kruger or whoever is bound to have him well briefed to give you a wide berth.'

'We'll see. Remember, officially he's just signed with Roscoe so they may not yet have pulled him into whatever racket they're running. Why, for instance, hasn't Roscoe moved him out of the boat and into Harle's old place?'

'Maybe he's afraid of ghosts.'

'Maybe he is, Mac, maybe he is.' I smiled.

McCarthy's croissant arrived and he wolfed it down before I'd even finished mine. 'That's better,' he said wiping his mouth. 'Well, Eddie, some of us have work to do, I'd better be off.'

As he stood up a loud burp escaped him, startling everyone in the bar. 'Pa'n me,' he said, unfazed, then hitched up his trousers and waddled out.

CHAPTER TWENTY-FIVE

At seven that evening I was back at the lock-keeper's cottage where I parked and walked across the small bridge down onto the footpath. The canal was so still I could see insects hopping on the surface. The boat with the brass fittings and polished wood had gone, leaving Skinner's and the other tarpaulin-covered boats. They were completely motionless as though the green slime surrounding them had anchored them to the bank.

I stepped onto Skinner's boat and it ducked slightly under my weight. A small tattered red flag hung limp from a thin six-inch pole on the roof.

Next to the flag lay a TV aerial with cable leading through a window on the side of the boat. On the wall at the front, above a small entrance door, was a Lucas headlamp. It was dirty and a hole had been shot through the C with an airgun pellet which lay flattened behind the glass.

I tried the door. It was locked. There was no window at the front. Jumping back to the towpath I moved along the side looking through the windows, but dingy green curtains blocked my view.

As I walked towards the back of the boat a man came along the towpath about a hundred yards away and ran towards me, accelerating as he came. I stopped and waited.

He came faster, sprinting. Reaching me he ran past and slowed down to stop at the front of the boat. He

bent forward, hands on his knees, and I walked towards
him. He wore a black tracksuit of heavy cotton. Sweat
dripped from his forehead and cheekbones and shone
on the back of his neck. His face was red and he was
panting hard. His name was Phil Greene.

I sat on the edge of his boat. He didn't look up. All he
would see from there would be my knees and shoes. 'In
training for the new season, Phil?' I asked.

He nodded and pearls of sweat bounced and swung
from his curly hair.

'Tough going,' I said.

He looked at me. 'I can handle it.'

I smiled. 'I'm sure you can.'

He straightened till he was looking down at me.
'What can I do for you, Mister . . . ?'

I could see from his face he knew exactly who I was.
'Malloy,' I said. 'Eddie Malloy.'

'I thought I'd seen your face somewhere.' His breathing was almost back to normal. Squatting down he
reached to the side of the path and plucked some of
the longer blades of grass. 'You used to be a jockey
didn't you?' he said.

Used to be . . . It always struck home, made me feel
bad. I wondered when I'd grow out of it.

'A long time ago,' I said.

'Couldn't have been that long ago.'

'Long enough. You can be a has-been in this game in
six months.'

'If you're a mug you can.' He darted a childish little
smile at me.

'Or if you get your neck broken.' I smiled back.

He didn't read the tone or if he did he ignored it.
'That's for mugs too, riding dodgy novices. No more of
that for me.' He smiled his smile again. I was beginning
to dislike it. 'That's right,' I said. 'A cushy number for
you this season, riding for Roscoe.'

'And for a few seasons after that if I've got anything to do with it.'

'Which is exactly what I came here to talk to you about.'

He looked up from where he was squatting like a three-year-old kid, absent-mindedly rolling the blades of grass he'd plucked between his palms.

'How do you mean?' he asked.

'Ever read the full page profiles of racing personalities in *The Sporting Life*?'

'Uhuh.'

'How'd you like to be a subject?'

'Who'd want to read about me?' he asked in a silly, boy, girl-like manner that made me want to throw him in the canal. Especially when he followed it up with his stupid smile.

'People are always interested in the young hopefuls,' I said through gritted teeth.

He stopped rubbing the crumpled grass between his hands, opened them and let the small green cigar come to rest in his right palm. Raising his hand to his lips he blew a short hard breath and the cigar disappeared. Only his eyes moved to stare at me. The little smile was still on his face but there was a sudden hardness, a greedily protective element now. 'I'm no hopeful, Malloy, I've arrived.'

I didn't like the look and I didn't like him calling me Malloy. He was a punk who wouldn't normally last five minutes in the business. I felt like slapping him around a bit but I needed to keep him sweet.

'Okay, you've arrived, I'm not arguing. But you must be thinking already of your first championship, riding a Gold Cup or a National winner . . .'

'That's only a matter of time.'

'One thing you need in this game is confidence and you're not short of that.'

185

'You bet I'm not. There's only one way I'm going and that's to the top.'

As if to reinforce it he stood up. I stayed sitting while he walked up and down the towpath, ten paces each way.

'A full page in the *Life* isn't going to do your career prospects any harm, is it?'

'I know it isn't. That's why I'm going to let you do it.'

'Good. When suits you?'

'Now, if you like.' He was still pacing.

'Fine. Why don't you get changed and we'll go and have a few drinks and outline the structure of the piece.'

'Okay,' he said and sprung past me onto the deck. Fishing inside the elastic waistband of his trousers he pulled out a small brass key. I stayed sitting, though I'd now swung my legs over to rest on the deck, letting me face the other way.

He opened the door, stooped and went in. I got up to follow him. He looked back at me from the doorway with his silly smile. 'Malloy, I'm shy. Wait outside and top up your sun tan, will you?'

'Sure,' I said and closed the door. This kid was hiding more than his modesty. In under five minutes he was back out dressed in cream-coloured trousers, open-toed sandals and a sweatshirt displaying a cartoon of a jockey with a wild smile and crossed eyes. The slogan read, 'Jockeys do it at the gallop'.

Bags of style, eh?

Swinging loosely from his right hand was what I would have called a leather jerkin but which I later heard Greene call a blouson.

You win some, you lose some.

The pub he chose was only ten minutes' drive away, though it was a long ten minutes for me. He didn't stop talking about how well he was going to do in the new season, how much his riding had matured, how good horses would let him show his real worth. Modest he wasn't.

Still, it had its benefits. If Roscoe had indeed warned him to avoid me it was just as likely, judging by his character, that he'd ignore him and go by his own opinions. And he'd already decided I was a nobody.

I followed his directions and we pulled in at a white-walled building with a thickly thatched roof. It was surrounded by a big well-kept lawn, a section of which was marked off and spiked at intervals with croquet hoops. On other parts of the lawn stood white wrought-iron chairs and tables, some with parasols sprouting from the centre.

The folks around the tables and the half-dozen or so inside the pub looked very much the country weekend set with not a ruddy face or a hard-skinned hand in sight. God only knew what the beer would be like. As we walked to the bar I thought how typical it was of Greene to bring me here. Soon to be one of the élite, he no doubt thought.

'What would you like?'

'Canadian Club on the rocks.'

'I'll have a bottle of beer, please.'

'Certainly, gentlemen,' said the barman who was all dickied up with a nice white shirt and black bow tie.

He brought the drinks and I paid.

'Let's go out in the last of the sunshine,' Greene said.

'A bit noisy for interviewing.'

'Break your concentration?' he said snidely.

I sat at a table by the window and took out a mini tape-recorder. 'No, just might drown out your highly intelligent and interesting answers.'

He took it as a compliment, smiled and sat down opposite me.

187

It wasn't hard to fill a tape. A one-ounce question brought a five-pound answer. It got to the stage where he was happy to keep talking, knowing the machine would pick it up, while I got us another drink.

He stayed with the clear-coloured whisky and the more he drank the more he talked. The more he talked the more obvious it was how big a hit the guy was for himself.

Calling a halt around 9.30 I switched off the tape. He seemed disappointed.

'Are you sure that'll be enough?' he asked.

'Could write a book from that, never mind a profile.'

He smiled, linked his hands behind his head and lay back in the corner of the sofa-type seat. 'Maybe some day I will write a book,' he said. 'Might even let you ghost it for me.' He nodded towards his empty glass. 'If you buy me another drink, that is.'

'My pleasure,' I said. It was far from it. He'd already drunk more than a camel at an oasis. Still, it was suiting my purpose. I brought the drinks back and steered him onto a general discussion about racing.

When the barman finally called time Greene objected, shouting for more whisky. The barman ignored him and moved around clearing up glasses, putting towels over beer pumps and empty bottles in crates.

Greene decided to abuse the barman along the lines of 'You take all our money when it suits you (he hadn't bought a drink all night), then think you can sling us out . . . I wouldn't put a dog out on a night like this.' (The drink had addled his brain, it was a beautiful night outside.)

Standing up I reached across the table with my right hand. 'Come on, Phil, we can go back to my place for a drink.'

He stared a while longer, or tried to, at the barman. His eyes were rolling slightly and his speech sounded like it had come through a contraflow and two chicanes on the way out of his mouth.

Still looking at the barman he took my hand, and I helped him up. 'Your place, Eddie! Good lad. No problem!' As he stood up and gained his balance he suddenly looked at me very seriously. 'Got any Canadian Club at home?'

'Some,' I lied. I knew by the time we'd reached my place that either the notion would have worn off him completely or he would drink anything.

He was surprisingly quiet for the first few miles and I glanced across occasionally to make sure he was okay. His eyes were half shut and his head nodded slowly and unevenly like one of those toy dogs in the backs of cars.

We must have been halfway there when he said, unprompted and staring straight ahead, 'I've got a mistress, you know.'

I slowed involuntarily but didn't respond. My first thought was that 'mistress' was an odd word for him to use.

'She's beautiful and I love her and when I'm champion jockey she's going to marry me.'

'What's her name?' I asked. I saw his finger go to the side of his nose and try to tap it but it was more like stroking.

'Secret,' he said. 'Big secret.'

I didn't answer. There was nothing for ten seconds or so then he said, 'Her husband's a bastard, a real bastard.' He turned towards me. 'She married him for money, see, she never really loved him.'

'Sure.'

'Sure . . . Sure's right . . . Sure is absolutely right . . . She never did.'

I wondered if he looked on marriage for money as a virtue when he was sober.

'Can you take me to her now?' he asked in a pathetic, begging tone. 'Please?' he added.

'Where does she live?'

'Suffolk. Somewhere in Suffolk.'

'Where in Suffolk?'

'Somewhere, okay? . . . Somewhere . . . None of your business anyway.'

'I thought you wanted me to take you there?'

'I do want it but I can't. Her husband's home tonight. I am not allowed to go when he's there.'

'Back to my place then, you can have another drink and forget all about her.'

'I'll never forget her . . . Never!'

I thought I heard a sob but couldn't be sure. He dozed off two minutes later and didn't wake till I leaned in and shook him, having already stopped further back in the trees and checked the cottage for unwanted visitors.

I helped him inside and sat him down by the dead ashes of yesterday's fire. Taking off my jacket I pulled on an old sweater and poured Greene a drink. His hand came up for it automatically. 'Is it Canadian Club?'

'Sure it is. On the rocks.'

'That's all I drink, you know.'

'So they tell me.'

'Sure,' he said.

I cleared the grate, dropped in a couple of firelighters and some logs and set it burning. I washed my hands, poured myself a whisky and sat in the chair opposite Greene.

I switched the lights off and shadows flickered on the walls as flames circled the logs.

I watched him. He sat in that loose way drunk men do in easy chairs, as though his bones were all an inch long and they'd folded and settled on one another.

Staring into the fire he held the glass in his right hand, though he seemed to be barely touching it.

'Take a drink,' I said.

IIis arm moved automatically to bring the glass to his lips, his head ducked forward noticeably to drink but his eyes never strayed from the flames. He gulped some whisky and settled back to his previous position.

'Romantic, isn't it?' I said.

He nodded slowly. 'I miss her, you know ... I miss her badly ... She's the only woman I ever loved ... and she's in trouble.'

I let it ride for half a minute, but he wasn't adding to it. 'What kind of trouble?' I asked.

'Deep,' he said. 'Deep, deep trouble.'

'With the police?'

'Maybe.'

'Why don't you tell me about it? Maybe I can help.'

He shook his head. 'I'll help her, I'm the only one.'

He went silent again for a while.

'Drink up,' I said and he did, raising the glass and pouring what was left down his throat. His arm came down again and the empty glass swung into position between his thumb and fingers. I reached and took it from him. 'One more?' I asked. He nodded. I refilled the glass and slotted it back into his hand.

'We're gonna buy a cottage by the sea when I'm champion.'

'You and Charmain?' I asked.

'Yes, just the two of us.' I watched his face as his memory tried to plough through the forty per cent proof haze in his brain. His eyes moved from the flames and he looked quizzical, but the best he could do was, 'You know Charmain?'

'Sure. Met her a few times. She's a beautiful woman.'

'Beautiful ... Beautiful ...' He seemed happy with that. I played on. 'How's Howard, her husband?'

191

'A bastard's her husband, she married him for money
. . . she didn't love him . . . understand?'

'Sure.'

A weak smirk (he probably thought it was very
strong) crept onto his face. 'He's lousy in bed, you
know . . . she told me that . . . Charmain told me . . .
he's a lousy lover.' He tried to raise his voice but it came
out in peaks and troughs of sound. He started giggling
and his head swayed back and forth though his body
stayed relaxed and as settled as a bag of loose sand.

'I thought Stoke was a big shot,' I said.

He stopped laughing and tried to stare at me. 'Big
shot! Big shot! . . .' He paused, considering. 'Who cares?
Who gives a toss about the big shot?'

'Aren't you scared of what he'll do when he finds out
you've been seeing his wife?'

'Me? Scared? . . . Of him? You don't know me, mate
. . . You don't know me!'

He was scared all right, even drunk you could tell. He
drank, almost emptying the glass, and I reached for the
bottle and poured him a double hangover.

'Do you plan to keep living on the boat when you
start your new job?'

His eyes were closed now, his head resting on the
chairback, the point of his chin aimed in my direction.
'Dunno . . .' he said, quietly.

'It's a nice boat, when did you buy it?'

'Not mine,' he mumbled.

'Whose is it?'

'Skinner's.'

'The vet?'

'Mmm.'

His lower jaw sagged and his mouth opened a
thumb's width.

'How well does Skinner know Stoke?' I asked.

He showed no sign of hearing me. I raised my

voice. 'Phil, how well does Skinner know Howard Stoke?'

He answered with what was to be the first snore of many on the way to a kingsize headache.

I waited five minutes till he was snoring long and deep, then I moved across and eased him out of his jacket. He didn't stir. I rolled his sleeves up to look for needlemarks but both arms were clean.

I'd have bet reasonable money that he was up to the same games as Harle with heroin but it looked like I was wrong. Still there was the culmination of my little plan to look forward to.

Greene snored on. 'You enjoy your sleep, pal,' I said. 'To go with your hangover in the morning I'm going to give you a hell of a hard time.'

I locked both doors and took the keys with me to bed.

CHAPTER TWENTY-SIX

By dawn I was awake and back in my chair facing Greene who was still asleep. Slumped much lower in the seat than when I'd left him, he was almost lying on the fat square cushion. His legs were splayed out and bent so that his knees were on the same level as his face which was at right angles with his chest. A very stiff neck awaited him.

It was cold now in the room. The grate held only ashes and I had no intention of lighting a fire; I wanted Greene to feel as uncomfortable as possible when he woke. Heating my fingers round a mug of coffee, I watched him.

He was so pale he looked almost grey in the early light. His lips were colourless. Whatever blood was flowing round his body was giving his face a miss. His beard growth was barely noticeable.

He moaned again. There was a frown with it this time. Hold tight, young Phil, the hangover's just about to begin.

'You awake?' I asked.

He didn't answer.

'Phil . . . time to get up.'

He frowned again but didn't answer. I kicked the soles of his shoes lightly and the frown deepened. Slowly, he pulled his foot away. I started kicking the other one. 'Rise 'n shine, Mister Greene, we've got visitors.'

He opened his eyes and stared at the ceiling trying to work out where he was and how he'd got there. I stopped kicking and stood up to look down at him.

'Some party, huh?' I said.

'Any water?' he croaked.

I got him some and he pushed himself onto his elbow and drank all but a mouthful. I took the glass from him.

'What were you feeding me?' His voiced still sounded coarse, probably from talking too much about himself.

'Firewater,' I said.

'Shit,' he said, and tried to get up. 'My neck's killing me.' I helped him into the chair.

'Want some coffee?'

'Mmm.'

I filled two mugs. He sipped his. It didn't seem to help.

'Your brain working yet?' I asked.

'No.'

'How many people do you know who carry guns and are built like brick shithouses?'

His eyelids opened fully revealing badly bloodshot eyes. He stared at me. 'What are you asking?'

I repeated the question.

'Know anyone who fits the description?' I asked. He looked away.

'No.'

'You sure?'

He stared into his coffee. 'Yes.'

'That's funny, they seem to know you.'

He stared at me again. 'Who? What are you talking about?'

'The two guys who paid us a visit during the night.'

'Here? . . . They came here?'

I nodded. He tried to smile but couldn't manage. 'You're kidding . . . You're just winding me up.'

'I've got better things to do. They asked for you in person.'

He sat forward. 'Just knocked the door and asked?'

'Not exactly. I heard them prowling around outside trying the doors and windows, trying to get in.'

'What did you do?'

'I stuck a shotgun out the window and pointed it at the big one's head.'

He slurped some coffee but didn't take his eye off me.

'I asked what he wanted and he said he wanted you. No trouble for me, just to send you out.'

Resting the coffee mug on his knee he rubbed his bowed forehead with his free hand. I shrugged. 'Never mind, if you don't know these guys then obviously they've made a mistake and you can go right on out there.'

He looked up sharply. 'Are they still there?' There was an edge of panic.

I nodded. 'They're in the woods . . . Waiting.'

'Oh, Jesus!' He bowed his head again and rubbed his eyes. I thought for a minute he was going to cry.

I got up and went to the window. Standing off to the side I pushed open an inch of curtain and looked out. I think Greene was holding his breath. I couldn't hear him breathing but could sense him watching my back intently. After a minute I turned towards him.

'They still there?'

'It might not be as bad as you thought,' I said.

The relief started creeping across his face.

'I can only see one of them . . . having said that, it is the one with the gun . . . I suppose his sidekick could be anywhere.'

He slumped back in the chair and some coffee slopped over and wet his trousers. I went back and sat down across from him. 'Want to tell me who they are?'

'I don't know who they are, not their names anyway.
But they are bad news.'

'How bad?'

'Ask Alan Harle.'

'Did they kill Alan?'

'I don't know!' His voice was growing panicky again.
'Shit! . . . What am I into here? I'm not saying
any more.' He sat forward again. 'Do you hear me?
Forget what I said about those blokes, I'm not saying
any more.'

'Suit yourself.'

We sat in silence for a minute while he grimaced
and fidgeted and sipped at his coffee. He would stare
without blinking for a while, lost in thought, then his
eyes would be moving everywhere like a trapped animal
looking for an escape route.

'Come on,' I said. 'I'll drive you home.'

'No way! I'm not leaving here. Not till they've
gone.'

'You can't stay.'

'I'm staying!' he almost shouted.

'Okay, but you're staying on your own. I've got business to attend to and I'm not sitting nursemaid to you.'

His head snapped up and he looked at me again. 'You
can't leave me by myself! They'll be through that door
as soon as you go.'

'Too bad, Phil. Until I know what I'm up against I'm
staying out of it.' I stood up and reached for my jacket,
pulled it on and felt for the car keys.

Greene got out of the chair and made to stand up
before realising it put him in direct line with the
window. He dropped quickly onto all fours and crawled
across to where I stood. Safely out of the window line
he got up.

His face was close to mine but not close enough for
him to start whispering, which is what he did. 'Look,

197

go out and tell them I've gone. Tell them I left by the
back door while it was still dark.'

'They don't look the type to believe it. In fact the
reason I can't see the other one out there is probably
because he's covering the back of the house.'

He stood just staring at me, expressionless. I waited
it out.

'How the hell am I going to get out of here?'

'I can get you out but I want to know who those two
guys are. You tell me that and I'll get you out.'

'Look, I'll pay you. I'll waive the fee for the article,
you can keep it.'

'There wasn't going to be any fee. You were doing it
for the glory, kid.'

'Don't call me kid.'

'I'd have thought you've got more things to worry
about just now than your ego.'

I started moving towards the window again. He
stepped quickly round me and stood with his back
almost to the wall. Going to the curtain I squinted out
of the corner.

'Is he still there?' Greene asked.

'Yep, come and see so you can be sure it is who you
think it is.'

'No, thanks. God only knows what kind of sights he's
got on that gun.'

'It was only a pistol I saw in his hand. There was no
rifle. None that I could see anyway.'

He was quiet again. I watched him as his mind
searched for answers. 'How much do you want?' he
asked.

'I'm not bargaining. I don't want paid. Just tell me
who the hell Butch Cassidy and the Sundance Kid are,
that's all I want to know.'

'Why are you interested in who they are? What's it
to you?'

'What it is to me is that Alan Harle was a friend of mine and I want to know why he was killed and who killed him. If I don't know in exactly two minutes I'm going out that door, you're staying here and you can take what's coming from your visitors.' Greene's legs buckled slowly and his back slid down the wall, like he was attached to a rail, till he squatted on the floor then, finally, sat. He stared at the ash-filled grate. 'Harle was killed dealing in drugs.'

'What kind?'

'Heroin.'

'What kind of deals?'

'Not the kind he wanted. He thought he was the big shot, moving among the internationals, the heavyweights. Some big shot.'

'You still didn't tell me what kind of deals.'

'He was trying to set something up with those two guys but he tried to screw them and they found out . . . Goodbye, Alan.'

'What was he trying to set up?'

'I don't know, some deal or other.'

I was getting frustrated. 'Look, you keep talking about deals, do you have any details? Was he supplying heroin or smuggling it into the country or out of the country or what?'

'How the hell should I know?'

'You must have some evidence.'

'Look, give me a break, Malloy! I'm telling you what I think was happening – my opinion, right?'

'But without any evidence to back it up . . . Your opinion's not worth shit, Greene. I think you're making this up to try and get yourself out of trouble.'

'I don't have to sit here and listen to this garbage from you,' he said.

'Sure you don't.'

I moved to the curtain and looked out again. The sky

was darkening. I walked through to the bedroom and heard Greene scramble to his feet and call after me, 'Where are you going?'

I came back into the living-room, zipping up my jacket. 'I told you, I've got business,' I said, turning towards the door. 'Good luck, Phil.'

He grabbed my arm. 'Wait!' I turned back to face him and his wrist twisted slightly. He loosened his grip. His eyes were tired, desperate. There was some white matter in the corners of his mouth. We were close. His breath smelled bad. 'I'll tell you all I know. It may not be any good to you but I promise I'll tell you what I know.'

I made coffee. We sat down and Greene talked. 'It was a kind of accident how I found out Alan was into drugs. I was still doing my two at Roscoe's at the time. I was stacking bales in the hayloft one afternoon when I saw Alan come out of the house and cross the yard to his car. He always parked it behind the top block, out of sight of anyone in the yard. Anyway, I could see him from the hayloft. He couldn't, or at least didn't, see me.'

Greene rambled on at great length filling in every detail down to how easily the veins showed in Harle's arms as he pumped up before an injection, but all it amounted to was that he knew Harle was a junkie. He tried to embellish the dealing side.

'One day I had a ride at Uttoxeter. Alan had three so we travelled up together. Alan, as usual, hardly spoke a word on the journey. Anyway, he had a fall on his last ride and came back in the ambulance.

'I rushed down to meet it and make sure he was okay. Not that I was worried about him, I just wanted to make sure he could drive so I could get back home okay. Anyway, he was all right. He'd just bummed a lift in the ambulance to save him trekking back in the rain.

200

That was in the second last race. My ride was in the last so he said to meet him in the car park afterwards.

'Mine ran like a dog. When I'd showered and changed I was one of the last out of the weighing room. It was getting dark but the rain had stopped. I walked to the car park. Alan had a green Saab at the time and he was standing beside it talking to two blokes, big guys. I mean, most jockeys look small even next to your Mister Average but these guys dwarfed Harle, both of them. Alan nodded towards me as I approached and they turned and looked at me. Then they said their last words to Alan, walked over to a black Merc and got in.

'Alan was in the Saab by the time I reached it. I got in but he didn't speak. He looked kinda pale but his eyes were bright. He set off, driving fast. I didn't ask who the guys were. I knew he wouldn't tell me.

'Back on the motorway he pulled in at the first services and told me to get myself a coffee as he was just going to the toilet. I got out and walked towards the cafeteria, but when I looked back I saw Alan rummaging in the boot. He took something out and slipped it under his jacket then he headed for the toilet.

'As we drove back he started talking. He said he'd be retiring from the saddle soon. "No more burials by horses that couldn't jump, no more sliding around in the mud at these gaffs in the middle of nowhere . . ." He was going places, going into business with his "Associates".'

'So you assumed he was dealing in drugs with these two guys?'

'Of course he was, what else could it be?'

'It could have been a million things. Did you hear the conversation with the two blokes?'

'I didn't but . . .'

'Did Harle ever say anything about dealing?'

'Well, no, but . . .'

'Supposing he was dealing in heroin, that might not have been why he was killed.'

'Look, Mister, you asked me what I thought and I told you, so gimme a break!'

He hadn't told me everything, I was sure of that, and I considered questioning him to try to catch him out. I considered asking him about Roscoe and Kruger and Skinner but it was highly unlikely that he'd tell me anything and it would only alert them further. If they believed I was only interested in Harle's murder it might make things a bit easier. 'So you think the two guys in the car park killed him?' I asked.

'Sure, they must have.'

'What was the motive?'

Greene shrugged. 'He must have double-crossed them.'

'How?'

'How the hell should I know? I'm only telling you what I think happened.' He finished his coffee. It didn't look like he wanted to hear any more questions. Leaning forward he put the empty mug on top of the old ceramic mantelpiece and held his head again. 'You got an aspirin?' he asked.

I brought four from the kitchen with a glass of water. He took them all at once and managed to keep them down. I squatted to his level and took the glass off him. He looked at me, waiting for me to speak. Spreading his palms upwards in an open 'honest' gesture he said, 'Look, I've told you everything I know. Can you get rid of those guys outside?'

'You haven't told me why they're after you. You say you don't know them. You say they killed Harle because he double-crossed them . . . what would they want with you?'

'I don't know, maybe they're scared I'll talk, just like I've done to you.'

'But if you didn't actually see them kill Alan then, as far as they're concerned, you'd have nothing to talk about, would you?'

He shrugged and tried the 'honest' gesture again. 'Look, I don't know why they're here, maybe they think Alan told me something about the deal they were setting up. Maybe they think I'll go to the police.'

I sat back and stared at him for a while. 'Okay,' I said. 'Okay.' I went to the window again and looked out from the side through a gap in the curtains. I turned away and started pacing slowly up and down the worn rug behind the sofa, trying to look like I was thinking hard. Greene was convinced. His anxious gaze followed me up and down the rug. I let him stew a while then, still pacing, told him the plan.

'My car's parked right outside the door. Now, as I walk out I'm within two paces of the driver's door, though I can be seen clearly from the woods. In the back seat I've got a long coat. Here's what happens. I go out, open the back door and pull out the coat. You'll be standing just inside this front door out of sight. As I straighten up, holding the coat, I'll swing it round onto my shoulders like a cape, turning towards you as I do it. As the coat swirls round, you nip out and dive into the back seat of the car. The coat will cover you if you time it right. Then I'll turn to the front door and lock it as if I'm locking you in. I'll get in the car, you stay low and I'll drive us out.'

I stopped pacing and looked at him. 'Okay?'

'Sounds a bit risky to me.'

'Would you rather stay here?'

His head dropped again and he went silent. I walked back to the window, looked out and then turned to Greene. 'Ready?'

'Now?'

'Best time. I don't see either of them at the moment.'

'Okay.' He looked scared.

We went through the routine and Greene bolted into the car like a rat down a hole. 'Drive, for God's sake!' he yelped.

I accelerated away, wipers swishing, along the edge of the wood, leaving it to the birds, the badgers and the foxes.

There were no pavements on the country road and the grass verges were soaked after the rain. I swung out to avoid splashing an old gent walking his dog. The sun was well up now and steam rose from the wet tarmac, some patches were already dry. Most of the clouds had drifted to the west and as we rounded the bend approaching the lock-keeper's house the sky was blue and clear. Coasting down the hill I braked steadily till we stopped in the curve of the lay-by in front of the canal bridge.

Greene was still lying down in the back; he'd been worried in case we'd been followed. 'You can come out now.'

'Where are we?' he asked, still prone.

'Home. Back at your boat.'

'Anything behind us?'

Most of your nerve if you ever had any, I thought. 'Nothing.' I said.

'Nothing followed us?'

'Nope.'

I heard the springs creak as he sat up and I looked round at him. The bright daylight showed the effects of the heavy night on his face and the tough morning he'd put in.

'You all right?' I asked, not caring what the answer was.

'For now I am but I've just been thinking, if they

found me at your place, what's to stop them finding me here?'

'Nothing, I suppose.'

He frowned and ran his fingers through his hair. 'Do you think they could?'

'They seem smart enough.'

'Shit! I'd better start looking for somewhere else . . . I'd better tell Sk . . .' He stopped himself.

'You'd better tell who?'

'Nobody. Forget it.' He got out. I rolled the window down and looked up at him. 'Who else is involved?'

He turned away and started walking to the boat. 'What about *The Sporting Life* piece?' I asked.

'Cancel it,' he called back. 'I don't want it printed.'

'I'll save it then, it'll make a good obituary.' I didn't mean him to hear it but he faltered slightly before stepping onto the boat and disappearing through the green and yellow door.

CHAPTER TWENTY-SEVEN

Half a mile back up the hill I'd noticed the ruins of some buildings. I drove there. They lay a hundred yards off the road. The blocks scattered around were of thick sandstone and there were enough of them left to show that the building had been laid out in an L shape of about fifty yards a side. Away from the rubble, diagonally opposite the point of the L, was the shell of a burned-out barn. Parking behind it I got out and took my binoculars from the boot.

The broken uneven spars of wood, charred a velvety black, looked like some crazy graph against the blue of the sky. The fire must have started high up, maybe in the hayloft, and burned its way down. By the time the firemen arrived they'd only been able to save five or six feet of the walls.

I picked my way through the grass and weeds sprouting from the gaps in the sandstone and sat down on the blocks which had formed the cornerstones of the old building. Sloping gently away downhill towards the canal the grass was squared off into fields by lines of hedgerow. The only trees were off to my left by the road so I had an unrestricted view. Raising my binoculars I focused on Greene's boat. It looked deserted. He was still inside – I hoped.

There was now only one boat beside Greene's, its grey tarpaulin gathering a spread of bird droppings.

I scanned the canal and the bridge and the lock,

sweeping back and forth, watching for activity from Greene's boat. It began rolling slightly in the still water. Greene was moving around inside.

I kept the boat in the bright optics. Greene came out, jumped to the towpath and made for the bridge, walking quickly. He wore the same clothes he'd had on last night. As he crossed the bridge I kept him in focus from the waist up. Reaching into a pocket in the leather jerkin he pulled out a piece of paper which he unfolded and read as he walked.

He crossed the road and went through the gate of the lock-keeper's cottage. As he walked on the paved path it was strange, seeing him so close, not to hear his boot-heels click.

He knocked on the door and waited. Thirty seconds, no reply. He knocked again, longer this time, still nothing. Searching in his trouser pocket he took something out, maybe a coin, and rapped sharply on the brass nameplate.

Someone answered this time, a lady I took to be the lock-keeper's wife. She must have been pushing seventy but she stood ramrod straight, a good eight to ten inches taller than Greene. He said his piece and she moved aside to let him in.

In less than a minute he was back out. The lady watched him till he was through the gate and back onto the road before closing the door slowly. Greene jogged back to the boat, jumped on deck and went straight inside the cabin.

The boat rolled for a minute then settled. I scanned again. The road was empty. So was the garden of the cottage. The two moored boats were the only ones on the canal.

My arms felt tired from holding the binoculars steady. I laid them down beside me for a minute and stood up from the hard stone.

I could still see the boat clearly and I began to wonder if Greene could see me. If he chose to sit at the window and pull back one of his tatty curtains he would only have to look up the hill to see that someone was there. And he might recognise me from the colour of my clothes. I moved behind a big stone block to sit on a small hill of rubble and soft dirt. Only my head and shoulders showed now and the block would make a good elbow rest when using the binoculars, though I could see enough without them. I only needed them for fine detail.

I'd been there over an hour when a lime-green Renault approached the bridge, crossed it and pulled in sharply on the grass verge. I put the glasses to my eyes and rested my elbows on the sandstone. A man got out, opened the back door and a large, thick-barrelled dog joined him. A Rottweiler.

He strode down the towpath to Greene's boat and the dog leapt on deck. His owner, Skinner, the vet, followed, wrenched open the door and went in, slamming it behind him.

Skinner was inside for about twenty minutes and when the door opened again the dog came out first, then Skinner, then Greene. They were both talking and gesturing. If they weren't arguing they sure weren't trading compliments.

Skinner finally turned and took two steps towards the side of the boat. The dog took this as the off signal and jumped onto the towpath but Skinner stopped and turned to speak to Greene again.

Greene opened his arms and shrugged in a 'what could I have done' gesture and Skinner stepped forward and poked him hard in the shoulder. Greene took a step back then suddenly started doing some finger-pointing of his own. He moved towards Skinner but any thought of making physical contact swiftly left his head when the dog leapt back onto the deck and went to its master's side. I lowered the binoculars to see the big white wet teeth.

Greene backed off. Skinner said something and Greene turned away and went inside. The animal tucked itself in at Skinner's heel as they walked to the car.

Skinner swung the car in what was meant to be a U till he found himself almost hitting the nearside of the bridge. He reversed fast, straightened up and sped away.

Three men on a summer morning . . . One in a car, angry, one in a boat, scared, one on a hill, almost happy.

The choice for me now was to leave and risk missing something or stay and see what happened next. I could go home and change into more suitable clothing, bring back a flask of tea and some food, a torch and storm-lamp. I would be gone almost two hours.

Too long.

Greene could be anywhere by the time I got back. He was panicked just now and probably wouldn't sit around much longer. I moved back to my watchtower and settled behind the stone again. I'd burst the hornet's nest, I had to wait for the sting.

Within fifteen minutes the Renault was back. Skinner couldn't have gone much further than the village. Greene emerged from the boat with a suitcase, locked the door and hurried towards the car.

Skinner was away before Greene had closed the door properly. I got up and ran to my car, the binoculars swinging from my neck and banging on my ribs.

Pulling out from behind the blackened barn I drove to the top of the track where I could just see the road through the trees. I stopped but didn't even have time to put on the handbrake before I saw the lime-green car blurring along through the trunks and flying past the entrance.

Pushing the Granada into gear I accelerated along the pot-holed track which battered the suspension into a cacophony of clunks and bangs. I checked the road to my right as I approached the exit and although it wasn't the clearest of views I could see enough to take the chance of not stopping. Swinging out onto the road the tyres squealed as they tried to bite on tarmac. I straightened her quickly and soon the only noise was the engine racing and the wind rushing past outside.

There'd been no more rain and the road was grey and dry with, I was soon to find, not enough bends to stay hidden for long. I had to keep Skinner's car in sight but I couldn't afford to get too close in case Greene saw me.

The long straight stretches were the worst, it wouldn't take Skinner long to realise the car in his mirror had been following the same road for miles. The further he went the more reason he'd have for suspicion.

Balancing that was the fact that Skinner seldom did less than eighty, meaning the road in front of him would need an awful lot more attention than the one behind. Whenever the opportunity arose I'd let another car overtake for a while. Trouble was not many others were travelling at eighty plus and if I tucked behind anyone for more than a few minutes the Renault got so far away it looked like a knot at the far end of a ribbon. There was a risk, too, that he might pull off down some side road and be long gone before I got there.

Skinner kept heading east and after two hours we reached the flat fenland of Cambridgeshire. The sun, so hot through the glass, had raised the temperature in the car till sweat prickled in my scalp and ran from my armpits down my sides. Opening the window more than a few inches seemed to slow the car down as the air rushed in. I made do with the air vents.

Still, I was feeling pretty happy with the day's work so far. Greene was obviously in something up to his neck and Skinner at least as deep from the way he'd been acting.

They were now heading for the next guy upwards in line, I was sure of that. And, I'd been following them all this time and neither had twigged. I was entitled to feel pleased.

I allowed myself the smallest of smiles and fate immediately wiped it off my face. The engine missed, picked up again for a few seconds, spluttered, then died. The oil light in the dash came on, I jabbed madly at the gas pedal, then I looked at the fuel gauge – empty. I was pumping air.

Sod's law was back.

Braking to a halt I switched on the hazard lights, jumped out and got from the boot the spare gallon I always carried. As the petrol glugged and burbled into the tank I watched across the flat land through the rippling heat haze as the Renault disappeared off the edge of the world.

The empty tank sucked at the plastic spout of the can which seemed in no particular hurry to feed it. I was tempted to pour only half the can in and get after Skinner but I knew that at the speeds I'd been doing even the full can would only take me another twenty-five miles. There might not be a petrol station for fifty.

I tipped the can and the last few drops ran down the paintwork as I pulled the spout away and shoved the cap on. I threw the can back in the boot and got in the car, turned the key and pressed the gas pedal.

The engine turned strongly but didn't catch. I tried

again. Nothing . . . the fuel wasn't through yet. Pumping the pedal hard and fast I tried to draw it quicker from the tank. Another turn . . . Still not there.

Cursing myself for letting the fuel get so low I counted the seconds out one by one, trying to be patient. I counted to ten, quickening up noticeably at seven, then turned the key again.

It started.

Shoving the stick roughly into gear I let the clutch out fast and the car bucked forward. Within twenty seconds I was doing eighty again but the road stretched long, straight and empty. They could be anywhere.

Ten miles on, the road climbed almost imperceptibly over moor-like land, treeless except for a line in the distance stretching away from the road at right angles. This row of trees was about three miles ahead on my left. There was still no sign of Skinner.

The needle on the fuel gauge kept pointing at red like some insistent schoolteacher trying to hammer home a lesson. The gallon hadn't moved it a fraction and what was left in the tank was being burned at a mighty rate. If I didn't come on a garage soon, apart from never catching up with Skinner, I'd be in for a long walk to refill the can.

The closer I came to the row of trees the more obvious was their density. Out here, in the middle of nowhere, they must have been specially planted and whoever had done that had wanted to make sure nobody would ever see what went on behind them.

I was within a hundred yards when I saw there were two rows of trees and running between them a narrow road. I slowed as I passed the entrance. Something caught my eye and I braked, not desperately, just steadily, to stop the car about a hundred yards past.

There was nothing behind me and I reversed till I reached the turn-off into the trees. A car tyre had ploughed a deep furrow through a patch of dark earth still soggy from the morning rain and in the middle of the furrow was a rabbit, its back end and rear legs badly crushed.

Its ears twitched and it tried to raise its head and look in my direction as I got out of the car and walked towards it. Squatting down I saw that the wheel had virtually flattened it from just under the ribcage down. The muddy treadmark was easily recognisable on the crushed white bob of its tail.

Reaching down with my fingers I gently raised its head high enough to get both hands round, then I broke its neck.

It couldn't have lived more than a few minutes with those injuries, which meant the car that did it must have turned up the road very fast and a very short time before I arrived. I picked up the body and laid it in the grass at the base of a tree.

Decision time. Was it Skinner's car that had taken that road? There had to be a very good chance it was. And if not? Well, it looked like I'd lost him and with only about ten miles left in the tank it didn't look likely that I'd catch him anyway.

Okay, I go in.

Decision number two. Do I walk down the road keeping to the trees or do I take the car and risk bumping into Skinner somewhere. The only way I could meet him was if he was on his way back out, which was unlikely since he'd just arrived.

If he did come back out he was still going to see my car. Driving would get me to whatever was down that road a lot quicker than walking and maybe I'd find somewhere in the trees to hide the car.

Decision made.

Turning the wheel I drove into the tunnel of trees, quietly coasting out of gear when I could. Two hundred yards away I could see the road swung to the right and I started looking for a gap in the trees I could pull into.

There was none. They were so thickly planted you couldn't have ridden a horse through them.

A hundred yards from the bend I stopped. There was no side of the road to pull into, no verge, just a solid line of tree trunks. Taking my binoculars I crossed over into the trees and began to pick my way forward in a very slow slalom.

I cut across diagonally on a line that should have brought me back onto the road after the bend, but when I reached where the road should have been I was stopped by a hedge which rose like a solid green wall. It was about twelve feet high and on my side the tree branches had been cut away completely up to that height so that none could pierce it or alter its shape.

I pushed the toe of my boot into the hedge and though it gave a bit it was strong and springy, offering enough support, with the help of a tree trunk behind me, to let me climb it.

It measured roughly five feet across at the top and easily supported my weight as I crawled onto it and lay flat to admire the view.

The road through the trees had opened out into a drive as wide as a six-lane motorway. It led towards a house, then curled round to encircle a lawn the size and shape of an Olympic running track. In the centre of the lawn stood a three-tier fountain, dry and silent.

Rising away beyond the lawn was a huge Georgian-style cream coloured house. Behind the windows were sickly green curtains. Parked in front of the huge double doors was a silver Rolls-Royce. Behind it was a lime-green Renault. Both cars were empty.

The house was not.

With my binoculars trained through the ground-floor window third on the left I could see Skinner and Greene. They were both standing. Another man was pacing, firing questions, and from what I could see he wasn't getting the answers he wanted. I wished I could lip-read.

If Skinner was trying to placate the pacing man he didn't look much placated and if Greene was trying to reassure him he didn't seem reassured. This was strange because the third man was obviously getting his point across. If he was trying to frighten the other two it looked like he was succeeding. Then again, when it came to threats nobody could communicate like Howard Stoke.

When it became clear from the body language that this was no social visit, there was nothing more to learn lying atop the hedge. Harle, Greene, Roscoe, Kruger, Skinner and now Stoke – whatever they'd been doing they'd been doing it together.

I rolled over, leaving two dents in the hedge where my elbows had rested, and made my way down.

At the junction with the main road I turned left. The road to the right had no petrol stations for a long way. It was also the road Skinner would take to go home. If I did run out of petrol again and had to hike, those two would be the last people I'd want a lift from.

Before the petrol ran out I found a village and came upon what was little more than a wooden hut by the side of the road outside of which were two of the oldest petrol pumps I'd ever seen. In pale blue metal with big lit-up lampshade tops, they matched exactly. I pulled in wondering if they were quaint display items for tourists but a boy of nineteen or so came out of the hut with a sunny, 'What'll it be, sir?'

'It'll be a tank full of four star and . . .' I went and got the empty petrol can and laid it at his feet '. . . one for the road.'

I made it home for Jackie's ten o'clock call and told her everything that had happened. At Roscoe's, she said, all was quiet.

CHAPTER TWENTY-EIGHT

The next three days were spent at the races watching Howard Stoke. I wanted to see how he ran his business, who bet with him and when and, if possible, in what amounts. I wanted to see who spoke to him but didn't have a bet. I wanted to see if Greene or Charmain would show up. Bookies operating 'on the rails' as opposed to in the betting ring itself had their pitches along the railings which separate Tattersalls' enclosure (normally the busiest one) from the Members' enclosure which was the most expensive to enter and therefore, theoretically, housed the people with most money.

Many rails bookies advertised in *The Sporting Life* which meetings they'd be attending the following week so I knew where Stoke would be each day.

From high in the stands I watched Stoke through my binoculars. He and his clerk, who marked the betting book, stood on stools.

Over the three days, I got to know most of the faces who bet with Stoke. Some were already familiar to me, some were villains of one shade or another but no more so than percentages would dictate.

No one seemed to pass anything beyond the time of day with Stoke. Even his clerk, a puny looking bald man of fifty or so in a new suit a couple of sizes too big, didn't talk much to his boss. Between races Stoke would sometimes disappear for ten minutes.

As soon as he was out of view the clerk would take

a loose cigarette from his pocket and light it with a match struck on the railings. He smoked quickly and furtively, never taking his eyes from the direction Stoke had gone in.

Stoke was a flashy dresser and wore a different suit each day, mostly pin-stripes in blues and greys. His ties were bright red or yellow and his shoes light grey.

His clerk had only one suit and from the way it didn't fit him I guessed Stoke had bought it and told him to wear it. A man aware of his image was Howard Stoke.

When he chose to be charming to his customers he seemed to do a reasonable job. The smile was wide and welcoming, especially with the occasional lady client, although as soon as they turned away the smile dropped as though someone had cut the string holding it up.

Stoke wasn't a good loser. In the first two days he had, from what I could see, four particularly bad results on which he paid out a lot of money. The last of these was in the final race at Nottingham. Of all the rails bookies he was the only one still there paying out when the rest were packed up and on their way to the car park.

His face, as he handed cash to a line of customers, a number of them strangers from whom there was little chance of winning it back, grew tight-jawed and almost purple.

When the final punter was paid and heading for the bar to celebrate, Stoke was left with a single ten-pound note in his hand. He rammed it into his jacket pocket.

His clerk closed the book and stepped stiffly down off the stool. His back was to Stoke and in what looked almost like a reflex movement, sharp and vicious, Stoke punched him hard on the back of the head.

The force of the blow knocked the clerk sprawling on

the tarmac among a litter of torn tickets and empty paper cups. Like a boxer hoping to beat the count he tried to get up but fell over again. His boss didn't even look down at him, he just stepped off the stool and strode away to the main bar.

If he'd looked back he would have seen the clerk get to his feet, stagger to the railings and ease himself down to sit on the box stool. He rubbed at his head and held it in his hands for a couple of minutes then he looked up in the direction Stoke had gone. Confident his boss was nowhere in sight he pulled a cigarette and match from his pocket and lit up.

The start of the first race at Newbury on the Friday was delayed when a horse threw his jockey on the way to the start. Most riderless horses bolt but this one seemed intent on doing damage and kicked his fallen rider savagely on the left thigh before galloping away down the course. He covered a circuit of the track slowing only occasionally to throw a kick at the running rails.

The rest of the runners circled slowly at the stalls, their jockeys dismounted, leading them round. Most of the betting had been done and the runaway was at long odds so his antics caused no late flurries in the betting ring. The loose horse had everyone's attention. The stands were two-thirds full and the bookmakers watched from their stools.

The horse was brown with one white stocking on his off hind and a white star on his forehead. He was tall but narrow and not particularly attractive to look at, nor to ride judging by the way he was behaving. His number cloth said eight and I checked my racecard. He was called Castleford.

His lad and trainer were out on the course now and Castleford galloped towards them. Suddenly he veered

219

off to the right, crashing through the plastic rails onto the steeplechase course.

His lad ducked under the rail and ran into the centre of the track waving his arms as the horse bore down on him.

The boy stood his ground and when the horse was ten yards from him he dug his feet in and stopped. The reins had come loose and were dangling and dragging on the ground. The horse lowered his head and half crab-walked over to the rails where he turned his hind legs to the lad. The boy approached cautiously, his hand out-stretched. There was a low murmur from the stands.

He got to the horse's head without being kicked and reached slowly for the loose rein, caught it and turned the horse gently back towards the paddock.

He went quietly with him and as the crowd applauded the boy reached up to pat the horse's head. Castleford turned quickly, opened his mouth and took the lad's arm between his teeth. The boy's cry could be heard high in the stands and the applause gave way to oohs and aahs.

Castleford pulled the boy off his feet and shook him like a terrier with a teddy-bear as the trainer and two groundsmen ran to help. One of the groundsmen, wielding a long-handled hoe, smashed it down on the horse's head. Castleford, stunned, let go his lad and the other groundsman dragged him away.

His friend with the hoe hit the horse again for good measure, then the trainer grabbed one end of the rein and urged the man to drop his weapon and get the other.

With one man at each side of his head holding the rein tight at the mouth, Castleford, much subdued, walked back off the course and away behind the stands. Two St John's men comforted the shocked and bleeding lad till the ambulance, fresh back from delivering the injured jockey to the doctor's room, rolled up to take him on the same journey.

As soon as the race got under way Stoke left his pitch and hurried off in the direction of the unsaddling enclosure. It was the only time I'd seen him leave during a race. Even his clerk looked surprised, so much so he even forgot to smoke.

The race had been over for a while by the time Stoke returned. A handful of punters were waiting to be paid and his clerk, for once, was pleased to see him.

When he'd paid out, Stoke made a call from the telephone on the small shelf attached to the rails. The conversation was short and when he hung up his face fronted thoughts that were miles away.

Two more races were delayed that day and the meeting ran over time by almost an hour. Stoke didn't leave his pitch again and his clerk grew nervier and more fidgety as each race passed. When the winner pulled up in the last race the clerk became almost uncontrollably on edge, stepping on and off the stool, shooting glances at Stoke. I guessed it was a bad result.

The poor clerk knew it and he looked like a frequently beaten wife awaiting her husband's return from the pub.

Stoke did pay out a lot of money but he seemed calm throughout, though the clerk kept checking along the rails to see if there were going to be any witnesses. When the last man was paid the clerk wouldn't turn his back on Stoke. He kept watching him as he stepped backwards off the stool but Stoke ignored him completely and walked away, leaving the relieved man to pack up the gear.

Trailing him to the bar I watched him go in among the soft lights and the smiling faces hazed in blue cigar smoke.

I could have used a drink myself. A long slow golden

221

whisky chilled by two fat ice cubes. I decided to have it back at the cottage as there didn't seem much to be gained from hanging around watching Stoke drink his usual quota. I hadn't really learned much over the last three days except that he was a bigger bastard than I'd thought.

I got into the car, already anticipating Jackie's call that night. Maybe she'd have picked up something worthwhile today. She'd had nothing to report the previous two evenings and in a way I was glad, at least it kept her safe.

The traffic had eased and I reached the exit within a minute of leaving my parking space, which was bad news for Phil Greene. If I'd been delayed a while I might have seen him driving in. If I'd gone for that drink maybe I'd have seen him meeting Stoke in the bar. If I hadn't gone home when I did it's just possible I could have saved his life.

Next morning half my face was shaved when the phone rang. As I lifted the receiver it slipped across the shaving cream on my fingers and clattered on the small table.

I picked it up again. 'Hallo?'

'Eddie.' The voice was tense but I recognised McCarthy.

'Morning, Mac.'

'Have you seen *The Sporting Life*?'

'They don't deliver here in the backwoods.'

'Phil Greene was killed at Newbury yesterday.'

Logic told me he was mistaken. I didn't answer.

'Eddie?'

'I'm still here . . . What happened?'

'He was savaged by a horse. They found him in its stable after racing, ribs smashed, liver punctured both arms broken – official cause of death, severe head injuries.'

222

Already it was beginning to come together. 'Was the horse called Castleford?'

'Yes. How did you know?'

'I was at Newbury yesterday. I saw the horse take a mad turn and savage his jockey and his lad.'

'That's right. Do you know who owns Castleford?'

'I don't know who owned him when he arrived at the track but I've a fair idea who owned him when he killed Phil Greene.'

'Go on.'

'Howard Stoke.'

'How the hell did you know that?'

'Adding two and two and getting the right answer – for once.'

I told him about Stoke's behaviour and how he'd followed Castleford and his trainer as the horse was led away after being caught.

'Who found Greene?' I asked.

'One of the groundsmen, checking boxes before leaving.'

'What time?'

'About eight.'

'Have you interviewed Stoke?'

'One of my men spoke to him late last night.'

'What's his story?'

'He claims he was having a drink in the bar when Greene arrived about six-fifteen and they got talking. He said Greene was boisterous, happy, and drinking large whiskies. Stoke told him about the horse he'd bought, said it was absolutely crazy and there probably wasn't a man alive who could ride him and all that Wild West stuff. Stoke said he'd had a few too many himself. Anyway, according to him, Greene started boasting that there wasn't a horse alive he couldn't ride. He said he would get him out of his box and ride him bareback into the bar.

'Stoke says he stopped all the kidding at this point and told Greene there was no way he was to go near the horse. Greene wouldn't let up and Stoke, quote, had to get serious and threaten him to stay away for his own good.

'Apparently Greene then calmed down but ten minutes later he disappeared, supposedly to the toilet. He never came back. Stoke reckons he was determined to bring the horse out, just to show he could do it. My man said Stoke seemed very upset.'

Your man is easily led, I thought.

'Did he ask Stoke why he bought the horse?'

'Yes. Stoke claims he didn't want to see the horse put down, but he didn't want it to race again either, in case it savaged anyone else.'

'Did your man believe him?'

'I think so.'

'You've got some gullible people working for you, Mac.'

'That's not exactly fair comment, Eddie, we had no reason to suspect Stoke was involved.'

'Listen, as soon as Stoke bought that horse the first thing he did when he came back to his pitch was to make a phone call which was, very probably, to arrange for Greene to come to Newbury.'

'Eddie . . .' He started back on the defensive.

'Mac, I'm sorry. You're right. Your man didn't know enough of what was going on. Forget what I said.'

'Okay.'

'Have the police interviewed Stoke?'

'They spoke to him last night. I spoke to them just before I called you. They said it's unlikely they'll be looking for anyone else but they'd wait for the verdict from the inquest.'

'Mmm.'

'As far as they're concerned, Stoke's alibi, if he

needed one, was cast iron. There were at least thirty people in that bar when Greene went out and with all the noise that had come from the table most of them probably noticed that he'd left and Stoke was still there.'

'Why do you think Stoke was generating the noise?'

'Mmm, that's a thought.'

'A thought! . . . Do me a favour, Mac, if I'm still in one piece when this is over point me in the opposite direction from Racecourse Security Services and tell me not to stop till I clear the horizon.'

He didn't reply.

'Do you know when the inquest is?'

'Probably early next week. I'll contact you as soon as I have details, okay?'

'Okay.'

'Right, I'll leave you to it then.'

'Mac, before you go . . . How did Greene get access to the racecourse stables, where were Security?'

He cleared his throat. 'We've identified a breach there which is being investigated.'

'Cut the official crap, Mac. What happened?'

'Last day of the meeting. Stoke's was the only horse still there . . .'

'And?'

'The guy on the gate skived off for a drink.'

'One of your guys?'

'It'll cost him his job.'

'It cost Greene his life.'

CHAPTER TWENTY-NINE

The inquest was on Tuesday; death by misadventure.
They buried him on Thursday. It was a warm summer
morning under a cloudless sky. The heavy scent of wild
flowers from the field next to the small cemetery drifted
across the wreaths around the graveside.

Roscoe and Stoke were there, each with his wife.
Half a dozen jockeys turned up along with the newly
elected secretary of the Jockey's Association. Two lads
from Roscoe's stable stood quietly in the background,
one wearing a violet tie and yellow shirt.

When the final prayers were said the mourners
started to drift away in small groups. I made my way
over to fall in behind Skinner's gathering.

I deliberately caught Stoke's eye, he looked smug.
Roscoe ignored me and Skinner's returned glance was
in the looks-could-kill league.

I scanned the *Life* each morning for news of Roscoe's
new stable jockey. His announcement after Greene's
death had been, 'We'll have to wait and see. It's hardly
the first thing on our minds at this sad time.'

How touching.

And, the reporter had asked, would the stable's only
patron, the elusive Mr Perlman, have a say in the choice
of new stable jockey?

'Mr Perlman,' Roscoe told him, 'leaves the handling
of all his racing affairs to me. I will choose the new
jockey.'

As yet he hadn't.

* * *

Stoke was responsible for Greene's death. I wondered
if he'd had anything to do with Harle's or had Greene
been telling me the truth about Harle being killed by
his 'business associates'?

If Stoke was controlling any hit men, why hadn't he
used them to kill Greene instead of taking a chance
himself? I needed more information on Stoke. What
was his past history? Who were his connections? How
had he got his money?

There was one person who should know Stoke better
than anyone – Charmain. I wondered if she'd talk.
She hadn't looked her best at the funeral. If Phil
Greene's drunken boasts of her being his mistress
were true then that explained why she'd looked so
distraught. But the strains of living with Stoke couldn't
be helping her either. She must have had a tough
time of it one way or another since she'd married
the guy.

He probably beat the hell out of her if she looked
the wrong way at the milkman and when he was away
racing she'd be shut in that big house in the middle of
nowhere with nothing to do but watch the trees grow
higher and thicker.

The more I thought of her the more I reckoned she'd
be sick of Stoke's idea of domestic bliss. I remembered
what she'd been like as a teenager; she wouldn't have
stood Stoke's treatment for two minutes back then. God
only knows how she'd got herself involved with him. I
wondered how much she knew, how much she'd be
willing to tell.

I checked *The Sporting Life* ad and found that Stoke
planned to be at York next Tuesday, Wednesday and
Thursday. A long way from home. I decided that on
at least one of those nights his wife would have some
company.

*   *   *

Just after ten o'clock on Friday evening, the day afte
Greene's funeral, my phone rang. Thinking it wa
Jackie, I hurried to answer.

'Hallo.'

'Eddie Malloy?'

'That's right.' I didn't recognise the accented voi
immediately.

'I have information you may want.'

The same voice I'd last heard shouting on Roscoe
answerphone. 'Kruger?' I asked.

'Yes.'

My brain raced. What the hell were these people u
to? I tried to sound cool. 'Information on what, M
Kruger?'

'On the doping ring you are trying to break.'

'Why should you want to give me information o
something you are running?'

'I am not running it, not any more.'

'They threw you out.'

'Wrong. I am stepping out. I came into this to mak
a profit, not to have people killed. You know that, M
Malloy. I am not a murderer.'

'So who is the murderer?'

'You must meet me tomorrow.'

'Sure, so I can be next in the morgue.'

'Mr Malloy, you do me a disservice, I told you . . .'

'You did me a pretty big disservice yourself fiv
years ago.'

'That was business. There was nothing personal.'

'And isn't this the same business, Mr Kruger, onl
for higher stakes?'

'They told me when I joined there would be no killin;
now three people are dead and I will not take any moi
part in it.'

His voice was calm and measured and he sounde

228

God help me, sincere. 'So what do you get out of it by giving me information?'

'I will give you evidence to convict the madman in charge and you will keep me out of it. I will be leaving the country tomorrow.'

'Why not just leave anyway if you want out? Why give me evidence on anyone?'

'Because, Mr Malloy, I want to sleep easily in my bed for the rest of my life. I will be able to do that if I know this man has been locked up for a long time.'

It was beginning to sound plausible. I knew Kruger wasn't the type, as he said, for murder. A con man, fraudster and all-round crook, but he wasn't into violence on that scale.

'If you say I'll be safe at this meeting tomorrow then you won't mind me bringing someone else along, will you?'

'No police.'

'No police, but a member of the Racecourse Security Services.'

'That is the same.'

'It's not. He has no powers of arrest other than as a citizen and that's not what I want him for.'

'Why then do you want him?'

'I want him to witness a sworn statement from you that I had nothing to do with that doping ring five years ago.'

He hesitated. 'Nothing else?'

'Nothing else.'

'You will allow me to leave when I have done that?'

'Yes.'

'All right.'

'Where will we meet?'

'Do you know the field which is used as a car park at Stratford racecourse?'

'Yes. What time?'

'Ten o'clock.'

'Okay.'

'I will see you then, and . . . Mr Malloy, no police.'

'No police.'

He hung up and I rang McCarthy and asked him to be there for nine-thirty, though I didn't tell him who we were meeting. Then I sat down with a very large drink and contemplated seriously, for the first time in five years, the prospect of riding again.

I was on a real high by the time Jackie rang at ten-thirty. She sounded anxious. 'Eddie! I've been trying to get through for ages, is everything all right?'

'Couldn't be better. The reason you couldn't get through was that I had a call that's given me the best break of the case. In fact it'll probably crack it completely . . .'

'Fantastic! Who was it?'

'Would you believe the man himself?'

'Who?'

'Kruger.'

'You're kidding!'

'Nope . . . says he wants to co-operate, have a meeting.'

'You be careful, Eddie.'

'Don't worry, he's agreed to McCarthy coming along.'

'But who'll be with this . . . Kruger? He's probably not to be trusted.'

'That's what I thought at first but I'm almost sure he's serious. I can't pass up the chance.'

'What did he say?'

'He said he was sick of the killing and wanted out, he says he'll name the ringleader.'

There was a pause. 'Jackie . . . You still there?'

'Yes, I'm here . . . Eddie, I don't like the smel of this.'

'Look, don't worry! I won't take any chances.'

'What time will you be back? Can I phone to make sure you're okay?'

'We're due to meet him at ten at Stratford racecourse but depending on how it goes I might not come straight back here. Chances are I won't. Look, don't worry, ring me tomorrow night at ten if you can.'

'Okay.'

We talked for half an hour. There was nothing to report at her end except a noticeable lack of grief at Roscoe's about Phil Greene's death. Plans for our future took up the rest of the conversation and I went to bed confident that it would all soon be over and we'd be together then.

McCarthy was there waiting at nine-thirty. So was Kruger, or at least I assumed it was his car parked in the middle of the empty field about two hundred yards away.

McCarthy pushed open his passenger door for me but I declined. 'Let's walk. It'll give me time to brief you.'

He got out and we set off through the gate towards the big black Carlton which faced us head-on. I told McCarthy why we were there. He expressed what are best described as mixed feelings.

From about fifty yards away I recognised Kruger. He was sitting quietly in the driver's seat. The engine was running. McCarthy got edgy. 'I don't like this, Eddie. Why is he parked head-on with engine running?'

'I don't know, Mac. Maybe he's cold and likes to keep his heater on.'

'Or maybe, as soon as we're close enough, he'll accelerate forward and run us down.'

'If he does, you go left and I'll go right. One of us'll survive.'

'Don't be flippant, Eddie, for all you know . . .'

'Mac . . .' We were ten yards away now. 'What's that sticking through his back window?'

'Shit!'

We both ran towards the car. McCarthy yanked the rubber hosepipe out from the small gap in the window and I pulled the driver's door open to try to haul Kruger out. But his skin was cold. He'd been dead for hours, poisoned by the exhaust fumes.

My jockey's licence, which had seemed only an arm's length away last night, had now not so much receded over the horizon as disappeared into space. I had to turn away quickly because I had a sudden urge to punch Kruger's cold blue dead face.

McCarthy switched off the engine and looked at me. 'Suicide?' he asked.

'Suicide, bollocks!' I said. 'They doped him, knocked him out or something and stuck him in there. Probably did it somewhere else and drove him here. His phone must have been bugged.'

McCarthy looked distressed and I began to wonder if this was the first corpse he'd ever seen. He leaned on the bonnet, staring down at the shiny paintwork, and said quietly, 'We'd better get the police.'

'You get the police, Mac, I'm going.'

His head snapped up. 'What are you talking about going? You're staying here to give a statement to the police.'

I marched over to face him across the bonnet and just stopped myself from grasping the wing and leaving fingerprints all over it. 'Mac, who was there when Danny Gordon was found dead?'

'You were.'

'And Alan Harle . . .?' He didn't answer. 'And now Kruger . . .?'

McCarthy shrugged. 'No matter, Eddie, you'll have to stay. It's not fair . . .'

'Not fair! Mac, grow up! Have you forgotten Detective Sergeant Cranley and what he thinks of Eddie Malloy? Just tell them you'd arranged to meet him here to get information on something you were working on. What the hell difference does it make if I'm here? Kruger's dead, he won't care!'

'All the same . . .'

'All the same nothing, Mac! If I'm here when the police arrive Cranley will lock me up for a month just for questioning! Now, I'm sick and tired of the bastard who's doing this and I'm going to find him and kick the fucking shit out of him!'

'You're shouting, Eddie.'

'Who cares?'

'Now look . . .'

'You look, McCarthy! Look at me leaving here. Now, you tell the police what you like when they get here but don't mention my name! I'm off. I am going to get whoever is doing this and the next call you get from me will be to tell you I'm holding the bastard by the balls!'

I strode back across the field, got in my car and drove, at very high speed and still boiling with anger, back to the cottage.

I spent the rest of a long day knowing it had to be Stoke. He had to be the top man. Skinner and Greene had been in terror of him, he'd engineered Greene's death and probably ordered Harle's.

The only one I couldn't positively tie him to was Roscoe but I was certain he was involved with whatever was going on at Roscoe's yard.

Seething with rage it was all I could do not to drive straight to Stoke's house and beat him to a pulp. But I had to keep control until I'd got some evidence. Surely Charmain would know something? And surely, if she was fully aware just how evil he was, she wouldn't protect him?

I'd have to get into that house and see her. Stoke probably wouldn't leave for York till Monday. This was only Saturday morning. I wondered if my temper would hold.

The anger didn't subside and when Jackie rang that night, full of hope and excitement, I was sharp with her and we had a row. In the end she hung up.

Disgusted with myself I sat down and tried to get drunk. Half a bottle of whisky later I was still quite sober, angry and bitter.

I went to bed and lay in the darkness regretting the argument with Jackie and thinking how happy we'd been last night on the phone when I'd told her we were going to meet Kruger . . .

A coldness descended on me – I told her who and I told her where and Kruger was dead when we got there. I thought back again to my suspicions of her when Harle's body was dumped on me at Kempton and the coldness turned to nausea as I faced the only logical conclusion – she was working for Stoke and Roscoe.

I lay awake for hours trying to talk myself out of it but the logic was undeniable. I should have guessed on the very first night. Why had she appeared, literally out of the blue, at the cottage? She'd said it was to warn me about Roscoe and I'd believed her.

After less than half an hour she'd launched a now obviously deliberate seduction which I was vain enough and stupid enough to be flattered by.

My last thoughts before falling asleep were that I deserved everything I'd got.

CHAPTER THIRTY

In the morning I rang McCarthy and warned him about Jackie.

'What are you going to do about it?' he asked.

'I don't know. I'm still thinking. Maybe we can use it to our advantage.'

'How?'

'I don't know yet. I'll have to think. I'm going to Suffolk tomorrow to try and see Stoke's wife. We'll just have to wait and see how things play out after that.'

'How will you get to see her with Stoke around?'

'I'm counting on him leaving for York tomorrow. He should be away for at least three days.'

'What are you hoping to get out of her?'

'She's an old girlfriend of mine, Mac; leave it to me.'

'Okay, but be careful.'

'Mac, I know there's no chance of getting my licence back now that Kruger's dead so promise me a half-hour interview with the Senior Steward when this is over. At least I can tell him what I think of him.'

'I'll see what I can do.'

I moped around for the rest of the day knowing Jackie might phone that night. If she did I knew I'd have to apologise for last night's argument and I knew I'd have to sweet talk her, to keep her believing I suspected nothing.

To do that would stick in my throat but it was necessary if I wanted to turn her treachery to my advantage at some point. She rang at five to ten and I managed to hide the bitterness in my voice and play the part well. Before she hung up she told me she loved me. Like Judas loved Jesus, I thought, and went miserably to bed.

Across the flat fenland I saw the trees when I was still miles away, the long straight rows curving when they reached the big house then finishing behind it in a straight line across. Fixed in the sky directly above the trees was the long swelling vapour trail of a jet.

It was just after one o'clock when I turned out of the sunshine into the dark tree-lined tunnel of a road. Stopping about thirty yards before the road curved round to the driveway of the house, I got out and locked the car. Keeping to the trees I walked quickly till I came to the main gates.

They were about twelve feet high, the bars ornately twisted like plaits. They peaked in spikes and were painted black. High up in the centre of each gate was a circular, coat-of-arms type design with two rearing horses, their front feet joined as though trying to push each other out of the circle. Diagonally, through circle and horses, was a knight's jousting lance. The circle and everything in it was covered in clean, unchipped gold paint. The paint on the black bars looked older.

There were no padlocks, just large keyholes: one in the centre, one at the bottom and one about seven feet up. I was as comfortably dressed as a man can be for climbing gates: cords, a loose cotton shirt and strong flexible shoes. Up the centre column where the gates joined there were enough footholds to reach the top. Crossing the spikes was going to be the tricky part.

When I reached the top I'd have to use the bar

that was set about two feet down from the spikes for stepping onto and getting a secure enough foothold to boost myself over. This could be interesting.

I started climbing and halfway up had the sudden thought that someone might be watching me from a window of the house, which was about two furlongs away. I glanced across. The view was blocked to a fair extent by the big fountain in the middle of the lawn and I felt a bit more secure.

The thought of climbing this side as a stallion and ending up on the other as a gelding made me very careful as I reached the top and stepped across the spikes onto the bar welded to the inside.

The footroom on it was two inches and bringing all my weight onto it I swung my left leg over, uttering a short prayer that the welder had been a time-served tradesman with a pride in his work.

As my left leg cleared the spikes I pushed away with the right, twisted in mid-air and landed, if not like a cat, then at least with everything in place.

Walking along the tarmac drive, the big lawn on my left, high hedge on my right, I wondered about servants. The house was certainly big enough.

The lawn had no flowers round it, nor did any border the house, so there seemed little need for a gardener. Stoke didn't seem the type to have a butler floating around and with just two to cook for I couldn't see him employing anyone for that. Maybe a maid of some sort for housework or maybe just someone who came in weekly.

The big double doors at the front of the house were firmly closed and I'd seen no sign of life at the windows as I approached. The two door knockers were of the same dark metal and I picked up the one on the right. It clattered down and seemed to echo both through and into the hall and back out towards the fountain.

I waited a full minute before trying again. The same clatter, the echo seemed quieter. Another minute ... Nothing. I tried the one on the left for luck. It brought none.

Stepping away I walked backwards and looked up at the windows. There were three rows of four on each side of the doors. All the curtains were the same horrible shade of green, a distinctive colour which scratched at a memory way in the back of my mind. All I saw in the windows were reflections of white drifting clouds. There was no sign of life.

I decided to go round the back and look for a trades-man's entrance, or something. Along the side of the house was a three-feet border of gravel chips which crunched underfoot. After a few strides I stepped onto the grass and walked the rest of the way in silence.

At the back things were nowhere near as tidy as the front. The paved yard had broken flagstones, encour-aging weeds up through the cracks. A stable block with three boxes had both half-doors of the end box lying open. The bottom door of the centre one had a deep semi-circular gap where a crib-biting horse had gnawed the wood away. There were no other signs of horses, not even a loose strand of straw.

Beside the stables was an electric mower, big and probably fairly new, but the blades were clogged with dried cuttings and oil stained the outside of the roller. Against the handle of the mower a pitchfork rested and flat on the ground beside it, spikes up, was a rake.

The windows at the back had only white net cur-tains which needed cleaning, or maybe it was the windows that were dirty. There was only one narrow single door at the back, painted cream like the rest of the building though the paint was chipped and weather-beaten.

On the wall to the right of the door, rising from

ground level for about four feet, was a big black scorch mark in the shape of a candle flame.

I lifted the metal knocker on the door but it rose stiffly and stayed still when I released it. I pushed it back down but it gave only one dull metal sound. I banged four times with the side of my fist. No answer. Again . . . Nothing. Another four thumps, this time I thought I heard a noise. Standing close I put my ear against the wooden panel . . . Silence. I listened hard, taking half a lungful of air and holding it to stop even the sound of my breathing.

I heard something.

The hairs on the back of my neck began pricking. I could feel them almost as if they were rising one at a time, stiffening away from the nerve ends at the sound I'd heard. A sound which had not come from the house. A sound which had come from behind me, from very close behind me. From low in the back of the throat of what sounded like a very large, very unfriendly animal.

As slowly as a toy soldier on dying batteries I turned my head away from the door, bringing my weight square onto my heels again as I did so. Before I could see what it was and where it was it growled again, longer this time it seemed, deeper, more drawn out, more savage. I finished turning. My back was touching the door. My hands were by my side, my head motionless on a rigid neck.

I was very still.

Only my eyes moved to see what was making the noise. They moved down and to the right and focused ten feet away and recognised the animal that was watching me. Recognised the blackness of it, broken only by the tan-coloured right leg. An animal I'd last seen bounding into a lime-green Renault. Skinner's car . . . Skinner's dog . . . Skinner's big bloody Rottweiler.

We looked at each other and there was no doubt in either of our minds who was the more afraid. The growl became constant. The dark eyes seemed to sparkle and narrow. The fleshy black lips drew back. Its teeth looked so white I could have believed they were false. If only. If only a swift kick would knock the whole set from his mouth onto the cracked paving.

It was the first time I realised that all a dog had going for it was teeth. A dog with only gums, no matter how big or how loud its bark, wouldn't scare anybody. But this one had teeth and he was scaring me.

The growl grew louder and the dog began to crouch, slowly going back on his haunches, gradually coiling. My brain searched crazily for a way out and suggested I start talking softly to him. But I rejected it, convinced that the slightest sound or movement from me would trip the switch and set him at my throat.

I suddenly remembered a defence against a mad dog that somebody had told me about when I was a kid. 'If a dog ever attacks you, goes for your throat, like, just grab its front paws as it jumps up and pull them wide apart and kick it in the chest right where the legs separate. That splits its heart in two. I know. I did it once to an Alsatian.'

I think I believed him at the time. I didn't know now but it looked like I was going to have the chance to find out. A chance I didn't fancy.

My timing and aim and nerve would have to be perfect to bring it off. And if I didn't I could say goodbye to my windpipe.

The dog was fully coiled. The growl steady and loud. I realised my left wrist was resting against the door handle. Not as slowly as I'd have liked I raised my hand, clasped the handle and turned it.

There was a click and the door opened. The relief

trickled out silently through my nostrils with the breath I'd been holding.

I considered just turning quickly and pushing through but I couldn't be sure he wouldn't be fast enough to follow me. If I could just ease it open behind me a few inches at a time till it was wide enough to slip through ... I started. One inch ... two inches ... the growl deepened; three inches ... it barked and snarled; four inches ... A noise from behind me, close to my left ear, a noise of metal on metal, the terrible spirit-sapping noise which meant there would be no five-inch opening ... the noise of a security chain taking up the slack links ... tightening, closing off my escape route. The dog was ready.

One chance. I stepped quickly away from the door, turned and slammed my shoulder against it, high up, as close to the chain as possible. The door held. I bounced back and turned as the dog sprang.

I dodged, twisting to my left. His head came up, jaws open, and he tried to snap them shut on the junction of my chest and shoulder at my right armpit. My body was still twisting and the jaws closed on fresh air but only just. The shoulder of my shirt was wet with slavering mucus.

When the dog landed he lost his balance and rolled over. I ran. The stable block was ten long strides away. I hoped to dive into the middle box through the gap left by the open half-door at the top.

I could hear the snarl of rage and the rough pads of his feet scraping the concrete as he came after me. About three yards from my take-off point he caught me. I felt his teeth pierce the flesh on the back of my left thigh and I felt the corduroy tightening quickly at the front as he gathered the loose material in his jaws. He let go my leg to rip away the rest of the cloth.

I heard it tearing and the tightness at the front

collapsed to flap loosely and I waited to feel the teeth again in my bare flesh. I stumbled, nearly went down, tried to catch my balance by grabbing at the handle of the mower, missed it and caught the wooden handle of the thing leaning against it – the pitchfork.

I couldn't regain my balance, but as I fell I kept hold of the pitchfork and pulled it out to the side as I automatically, on seeing the ground coming up, tucked my head in and rolled as I landed. I'd never thought the exercise would prove so crucial with no horses around.

As I rolled I whirled the pitchfork round at about two feet above ground level. Somewhere in the swinging arc the dog should be.

He was. I heard the thump as the shaft hit him, and the snarl of pain and anger. I came to rest sitting on the ground. The blow had knocked the dog over but he was up again and running at me. There was no time to get to my feet or even my knees and I swung the fork again, timing it, and cracked him hard on the side of the head. He yelped this time, almost like a pup, and broke off to the side to recover. I got up. He stared at me, warier now.

Backing slowly towards the open box at the end of the stable block, I was limping badly. The blood felt cold on the back of my leg as the fresh air reached it through the torn hole.

I kept backing slowly. His growl was low now, drawn out. He crouched again then started walking towards me. I held the pitchfork straight out, the spikes about four feet from his open jaws. I reached the box, backed in and, raising the fork above the height of the half-door, kept him at bay till I'd dragged the bottom half of the door closed.

It was almost five feet high with a big thick safe bolt at the top. I pushed the bolt well home then continued, for some reason, limping backwards till the rear wall of the box stopped me. With my back against it I slid down, all my energy draining as I did so. Sitting on the floor, knees bent to keep the wound off the dirt, I felt exhausted. My hands barely had the strength to shake.

I stood the pitchfork against the wall then rested my head back against it too. The box was dark and empty. Some bundled old newspapers were heaped in a corner. Nothing else. Nothing but daylight coming in through the top half of the door.

The rays of the sun came through it and warmed me and I almost smiled. Then a big black shape blocked the light as the dog cleared the bolted door in one leap and I nearly died.

From somewhere another surge of strength came and I was on my feet as he landed. For a few seconds he didn't seem to focus on me, a few seconds' adjustment from daylight to half darkness. I was only going to get one chance. Grabbing the pitchfork and throwing all my weight on my good right leg I turned, bringing the sharp prongs round and upwards in a scooping motion.

The points went in through the black hair under his big ribcage and he yelped again and snarled as he tried to turn his head and bite at the wooden shaft of this thing piercing his guts. I bent low to keep the fork in him and drove, stumbling and crying with exertion and fear towards the corner of the box. His head met one wall and his tail the other and his body curved in the middle as I forced the tines in all the way to the U shape till I heard his ribs crack and give way. I knew instantly I would never forget the noise of his howl.

The last sensation I was aware of was the points sticking into the wood as they came out the other side of his body. I held him there impaled on the fork till I was sure his breathing had stopped. Even then I left the fork in him, pinning him to the wall. I was panting hard, as much from nervous reaction as exhaustion. I finally released my grip on the fork and turned away towards the door, sickened but safe.

I heard a crack behind me and the terror surged back. I turned . . . It was the pitchfork handle hitting the floor as the weight of the dog's body pulled the tines from the wood. I limped from the box and, to be doubly sure, bolted the door behind me.

Outside again in the sunlight I breathed deep and long and leaned heavily on the mower. I didn't feel too good. The dog's dying howl and the cracking of his ribs echoed in my head.

My mouth and throat were very dry. I badly needed to drink something. I began hobbling towards the door.

As I lay back against it more through weakness than anything else it opened as far as the chain would allow. Resting my head on the cream wood I closed my eyes against the sunlight. It was warm for a minute then suddenly cool as the sun went behind the clouds. Through the gap, from somewhere inside the house, I thought I heard a call for help.

It was very faint, up on the top floor maybe, but it seemed very real. I turned, resting on my good leg, and looked again at what I could see of the security chain. The plea came again, louder this time. The chain looked solid.

Three yards along was a window at ground-floor level. I decided to get the rake and smash the glass. My leg was stiffening badly. I couldn't straighten it without almost crying out in pain. Using the rake for support I made my way to the window.

 Holding the rake like a rifle I was about to smash one of the panes of glass low down when it occurred to me to try opening the window first. It slid stiffly up for the first eighteen inches but then smoothly till it slotted behind the upper part. The gap was big and the ledge was low enough to sit up on and swing my legs through.

I closed the window from the inside. I was in a kitchen. Crossing the threadbare carpet I opened a door out into a narrow hallway. At the end of the hall another door opened into another hall, much broader, better carpeted and more ornately furnished. The tall polished wood walls boasted paintings, mostly of race-horses in the style of seventeenth- and eighteenth-century painters: animals with small narrow heads and exaggeratedly long bodies on stick-like legs.

Halfway along the hall was a staircase with around thirty steps, fairly steep, with the carpet bordered on either side by polished wood. I started climbing, listening . . . no more cries. Squeaks. Every stair squeaked. My leg was hurting. I became conscious of bleeding on the carpet. After six steps my left leg would no longer push my body up, taking the full weight. I resorted to one step at a time.

When I reached the top the muscle in my right thigh was throbbing from doing all the work. On the first floor there were eight rooms, none of them locked. The first three I searched quite thoroughly, the rest I just looked in from the open doorway. The furnishing in most of them was sparse and there was no one crying for help. I set off up the next flight.

It took me over an hour to reach the top floor, four up. I had checked all the rooms on the way. Most were empty of even a chair, many had no carpets and, although it was high summer, they seemed damp and cold. I wondered why Stoke didn't just move to a smaller house where he could afford to furnish all of it.

As I opened the door of the next room I heard a sharp intake of breath. I went in. Charmain Stoke stood by the bed looking at me. She was dressed in a long silk nightgown. Her hair, hanging loose past her shoulder-blades, shone as the sun caught it through the window behind her.

Her face was perfectly made up and her fingernails and toenails were painted pink.

On her left ankle was a broad gold bracelet. On her right ankle was a stainless steel manacle. The chain attached to it lay in coils, its tail anchored to a square steel plate bolted to a side wall a foot off the floor. The green curtains, the pale pink of her gown, the yellow of her jewellery and the silver glint of the chain and manacles were the only things in the room that weren't white.

The bed was a white four-poster with white linen and quilt. The carpet was white and deep. There was a long dressing table, two high-backed padded chairs, a chest of drawers, a wardrobe and a footstool – all were white. There was a white chandelier and a painting, or at least a white frame with a canvas of pure untouched white inside.

She stood side on to me, motionless, staring blankly at my face. A man she obviously didn't recognise stood in her bedroom bleeding on the white carpet, yet she seemed perfectly calm.

Her brow creased, quizzical, though her mind seemed miles away and she appeared to be making no conscious effort to pull her thoughts together. After a minute she spoke quietly, 'I know you.'

I nodded. 'We've met before.'

She turned to face me full on. 'Why are you here?'

I shrugged. 'I wanted to ask you some questions.'

She stared at me, unseeing, her eyes going blank again. I wondered if she was in shock. Taking two steps back, the chain clinked lightly as she sat on the bed. Pushing her hands under her thighs she swung her legs to and fro like a child and the chain moved like a caterpillar, its humps dying out six feet from her ankle.

After another minute's silence she glanced sideways at me and the patch of carpet I stood on.

'Is that blood?' Her voice still carried the flat tones of disinterest.

'I'm afraid so.'

She got up and came towards me, the chain swishing through the carpet like a pet snake. 'Let me see,' she said.

I turned and leaned against the door resting my leg on the toe of my boot to expose the injured thigh. She squatted down and I felt her gently holding apart the torn material. 'Did the dog do that?'

'Yes.'

'Where is it?'

'The dog?'

'Mmm.'

'In one of your stable boxes at the back.'

'Did you lock it in?'

I hesitated. 'It isn't your dog, is it?'

'It's Mr Skinner's.'

'Well, it's dead.'

'Did you shoot it?' Still her voice showed no emotion.

'I stabbed it with a pitchfork,' I said.

She stood up and I turned round to face her. She was smiling. 'I'm glad,' she said. 'I'm glad it's dead.'

Me, too, I thought.

She wandered over to the window and stood perfectly still, her back to me, staring out. The sunbeams pierced her gown like X-rays and I could see the outline of her body. I spoke quietly.

'Was it Howard who chained you up like that?'

She nodded. 'And Howard brought the dog,' she said, still staring out.

247

'When?' I asked.

'Yesterday.'

I limped over and stood by her side. 'Does he always do this when he goes away?'

She looked through the window at the high gates and the dark trees; the prison grounds. The sun highlighted the very fine down on her profile, more noticeable as her top lip quivered faintly. Her eyes glistened wet. 'It's been worse for a few weeks.' It came out thickly past the obvious lump in her throat.

'I'll help you if you want to get out of here,' I offered. She didn't reply, didn't turn to look at me, but the water built up in her eyes till finally she blinked, pushing out a big tear which rolled quickly down her cheek into the ridge between her lips. The tip of her tongue came out and licked it away.

Quietly, I asked again. 'Charmain, do you want me to help you get away?'

She nodded slowly and on the third nod her head stayed down and she sobbed softly.

Six inches beyond Charmain's reach with the chain fully extended, Stoke, with his usual sense of fun, had hung the manacle key on a small hook. I gave her the key and putting her foot up on the bed she freed herself.

She was brighter now, more positive. 'Can we go now?'

'You'd better get dressed. I can wait outside.'

'I haven't any clothes.'

I looked at the thin pink gown.

'It's all I have left. Howard burned all my clothes two days ago.'

'Okay, we'll have to find you something when we get out.'

She nodded briskly, waiting like a puppy for me to lead the way, and I got a glimpse of the happy schoolgirl of not that many years ago. Maybe Stoke hadn't killed her spirit completely after all.

'Right,' I said. 'Let's go.' And I turned, all the weight on my good leg, and took a step forward on the bad one which immediately balled up into twisted thigh muscles as an agonising cramp bit deep. Stumbling, I reached out towards the wall for support. I felt Charmain grab me from behind, trying to keep me upright.

'Can I sit down?' I gasped. 'I'll have to get the leg straight.'

She pulled my left arm over her shoulder and I consciously held my hand away from her breast where it would have rested. She got me to the bed and I bumped down heavily, trying to keep the leg up.

'Can you hold my foot and press the toe down? And very carefully straighten my leg . . .'

She started pushing. The pain got worse.

'Charmain! Slowly! . . . Very slowly. If I scream, stop.'

She gave a short nervous laugh.

'I mean it!'

The pain from the wound quickly overtook that from the cramp. 'Leave it!' I shouted.

'Sorry, am I going too fast?'

'No, no . . . you're doing all right but the pain's too much.'

She looked at me. I closed my eyes and clenched my teeth.

'Will I put your foot down now?'

I nodded. Sweat broke on my forehead. I opened my eyes and looked up at Charmain, at the concern on her face. I didn't delude myself that the concern was more for her escape than my survival.

'I can probably find something to bathe it . . .' she offered.

'Okay.'

'Shall I help you off with your trousers?'

I shook my head. 'Never get them on again.'

She went into what I took to be the bathroom and came out with a white towel and a porcelain bowl of hot water laced with disinfectant.

She helped me roll over to lie on my stomach, then carefully cut away the bloody material around the wound. 'This might sting a bit,' she said.

I braced myself, but not well enough. When the sting hit, my heel came up in shock and she gasped as it caught her in the stomach.

'I'm sorry! You all right?'

She coughed. 'It's okay . . . I'll try again.' She leaned from the side this time, avoiding my feet.

I spent the next two minutes trying not to scream.

CHAPTER THIRTY-ONE

Charmain supported me as I hobbled down the stairs. I pictured her trying to climb the main gate in her nightgown. I pictured me trying to climb it in a bandage and a lot of pain.

'Is there a key for the main gate?' I asked.

'I think there's one on the back ledge of the mailbox.'

There was.

We walked round the bend under the dark trees and I felt a sudden apprehension that the car might not be there but it was, exactly as I'd left it.

'Should I drive?' Charmain asked.

'I think so.' I gave her the key. She adjusted the seat and the mirror and rearranged her gown as I slowly lowered myself into the passenger seat.

Mechanically, she checked face and hair in the mirror. Some level of confidence was coming through, replacing the quiet resignation she'd shown when chained up in her room. She turned to me. 'Ready?'

For the first time in months my sense of the ridiculous took over and I laughed, albeit quietly, and rolled my head from side to side on the headrest.

Charmain didn't speak, she just looked quizzically at me, waiting for an explanation. 'Sorry,' I said. 'I can't make up my mind whether this is a murder mystery or a farce.'

'What do you mean?'

'Me bleeding through a hole in the seat of my pants, you wearing nothing but a silk nightgown ready to drive us to God only knows where and . . . you don't even remember my name.'

'I do – you're Eddie Malloy, you used to . . . fancy me at school.'

'How did you know I fancied you? I never told you.'

'You didn't have to, I . . .'

'You what?'

'Nothing. It doesn't matter . . . But I do remember you from school.'

'But that was years ago, I could have turned into a madman for all you know, I could be taking you anywhere for any purpose.'

She glanced down. 'I don't think you'd be doing much in your condition,' she said. 'I think I can cope.'

With that she started the engine, slipped into gear and released the handbrake. Then she pulled it on again and moved back into neutral. Reaching to the floor below her seat she brought out a small pink nylon case, something between a purse and a cosmetics bag.

I hadn't noticed her carrying it from the house. Unzipping it she looked inside, closed it again, replaced it under the seat then picked slowly away into a neat three point turn.

'Where are we going?' she asked.

'I don't know, let's just get away from here right now.'

She didn't look back. I did, at the big white prison with the vomit green curtains and I suddenly remembered where I'd seen that colour before – on the jockey who rode the Champion Hurdle winner, Alan Harle. The colours belonged to the phantom owner who retained him to ride all his horses – Mr Louis Perlman.

The sun was bright and the road was clear and

straight. We decided to visit the nearest hospital so I could get some treatment and Charmain, wearing an old raincoat I carried in the back, could phone a friend whom she reckoned would take her in 'till the heat died down'. God knows when that will be, I thought; once Stoke discovered she'd gone, the temperature could only go up.

'Doesn't Howard know this friend?' I asked. 'Won't he come there looking for you?'

She shook her head confidently. 'Doesn't know her; I haven't seen her myself for ages.'

Let's hope she's as charitable as you think, I was tempted to say, but I kept it to myself. She was already showing signs of nervousness in her driving, far too many glances in her rear-view mirror, for instance, so I didn't want to add to her worries.

The Greenlands Hospital Casualty Department was empty when we arrived and the doctor saw me within five minutes. Half an hour later I got back in the car and sat tenderly on eleven stitches and an anti-tetanus injection.

Two pain-killing tablets were supposed to have made things easier, as yet they hadn't.

Charmain, looking a good deal more anxious than when I'd left her, stared straight ahead through the windscreen, biting ferociously at her lip.

'What's wrong?' I asked.

'Kate's gone to Italy.'

'Your friend?'

She nodded.

'When's she due back?'

'Next month.'

I cursed silently, selfishly, knowing what the outcome of this was going to be. 'Is there anyone else?' I asked. Still not looking at me, she shook her head in short sharp jabs.

'Don't worry,' I said, with much more confidence than I felt. 'We'll find somewhere.'

She turned to me, the hunted look already etched deep in her face. 'Where?'

I shrugged. 'With me, if needs be.'

It didn't ease things for her. 'But doesn't Howard know you?'

'He knows me all right but he'd have no reason to suppose you were with me.'

Eyes vacant, she nodded slowly, not really taking it in. 'Okay,' she said, starting the car. 'Which way?'

'Head west.'

It was the best I could come up with. Going back to the cottage for any length of time was out of the question. Stoke's men would eventually come looking.

Head west and hope.

During the next hour Charmain grew increasingly nervy, biting at her nails and occasionally rubbing her mouth hard with the back of her hand like she was wiping saliva away.

When she strayed over the central white lines on the road for the second time, I spoke to her. 'You okay?'

She looked round suddenly at me as though I'd only just appeared beside her. 'Yes . . . yes. I'm okay.'

Her skin was pale. She didn't look okay. 'Is your husband going to be at York till Friday?'

'I think so.'

'What were you supposed to do for food while he was away?'

'He leaves a supply of fruit in a cupboard.'

'Fruit! For three days?'

She was right back in the seat, neck rigid, arms dead straight on the wheel as though trying to hold a runaway horse. 'Howard said it helped me keep my figure.'

'Why didn't you leave him?'

'I had my reasons.'

I waited.

'He's not an easy man to leave,' she said.

'Has he always used Skinner's dog as well as the chain?'

'Today was the first time. He told me it was there but I only half believed him.'

'What has he got on Skinner?'

'Skinner owes him a lot of money; Howard lets him run up big debts then calls in his favours.'

'What kind of favours?'

She shrugged. 'I don't know specifics but Howard's seen a lot of Skinner these past six months or so.'

These past six months . . . Felt more like years.

The talking seemed to be relaxing Charmain a little and she leaned forward into a more natural driving position. Her next question surprised me.

'Is it Skinner you're after or Howard?'

'Who do you think?'

She kept staring at the road. Since we started the conversation she hadn't looked at me. She shrugged and frowned. 'Well, I don't know.'

'But I should be after somebody?'

'You must be; people don't go around killing dogs and breaking into houses for nothing . . . And asking questions.'

'I'm trying to find out who killed Alan Harle.'

Our speed dropped suddenly as her foot eased right off the gas pedal then surged as she realised what had happened and pressed down again. Her knuckles were white on the wheel and she bit hard at her bottom lip.

'You knew Alan.' I made it a statement. Still she wouldn't look at me.

'I'm very tired,' she said. 'I feel weak. Can we stop a while?'

'Okay, pull in at the next lay-by.' That suggestion seemed to stress her even more. 'No, not a lay-by, somewhere with a toilet, somewhere I can eat. Maybe a cup of sweet tea, something like that.'

'Okay, the next place you think is suitable.'

She nodded, but the tension eased less than an ounce.

By the time we stopped at a small transport café her concentration had deteriorated so much she couldn't have driven any further.

The place looked okay for truck-drivers but not for pretty women in pink nightgowns. Charmain didn't seem to mind. If anything, her tension diminished as she reached for my old coat in the back.

'Can I use this again?' she asked.

'Why don't you stay in the car and I'll go and get some food?'

'No!' She almost shouted. 'I can't stay in the car . . . I have to go to the toilet.'

I looked at her, but she avoided my eyes. 'Okay,' I said. 'You go to the toilet, I'll get some food and drinks and meet you back here.'

She nodded, stepped out, pulling the coat round her shoulders, picked up her little pink bag and hurried off towards the white pebble-dash buildings.

Suspicion had been growing but I knew then almost for certain that she'd return calm, smiling and self-assured, courtesy of the contents of the little pink bag.

I was right.

As I limped back to the car, tea from the brimming plastic cups splashed over the sides leaving dark patches on the shallow cardboard box I carried them in. Still, I managed to keep the sandwiches dry.

Charmain sipped the tea but wouldn't eat. The colour

was back in her cheeks and she was bright and chatty. Her eyes shone.

'Pretty uplifting toilets, those,' I said.

'Mmm.' She smiled.

'Take away hunger and tension and tiredness . . . Think a visit would do my leg any good?'

She just kept smiling, reached for the recliner handle and wound the seat back. The sun shining through the side window made her close her eyes. She looked perfectly relaxed.

'I know where I can stay,' she said.

I waited.

'A friend of mine has a canal boat . . . It's on the Oxford canal near a little village.'

I wondered for a moment if she meant Skinner but I didn't think so. 'What's your friend's name?'

'Phil Greene, he's a jockey.'

I waited for it to dawn on her but it didn't. 'You've got a short memory, Charmain, Phil Greene's hardly cold in his grave. You were at the funeral.'

Eyes still closed she frowned for a few seconds then smiled again. 'It's okay, I've got a key.'

'For what?'

She opened her eyes and looked at me. 'The boat.'

'So it doesn't matter that Phil Greene's dead as long as you have a key to his boat.'

'I'm not saying it doesn't matter . . . He was a sweet kid and I know he would have wanted me to stay at the boat if I was in a spot.'

'So why didn't you think of that first before you rang your friend back there?'

She shrugged. 'I forgot.'

'You forgot or you didn't realise how short of heroin you were?'

It didn't faze her. 'What do you mean?'

'I mean that until you went into that toilet and shot

257

some of the stuff into your arm you didn't realise how little you had left.'

She looked at me. The smile had gone, replaced by a hardness. 'So?' she said.

'So, you obviously think Phil had some on the boat somewhere. What was he, your official supplier, by appointment, after Harle disappeared?'

She lay back again, closed her eyes and smiled. 'What's it to you?'

'Nothing to me. It's your life. Why should I care if you screw it up like Harle and Greene and end up the same way?'

'Don't worry, Mr . . . I've forgotten your name?'

'That's all right, you won't be seeing me again anyway once I've dropped you at the boat.'

She opened her eyes and sat up. 'You said you'd help me.'

'Don't give me the little Miss Helpless act. I'll help you hide, help you stay away from your husband for as long as I can but I won't help you kill yourself.'

'You're over-reacting.'

'Maybe, but that's the way I feel. I'm sick of all this crap. Of being scalded and bitten and shit on by idiots like Harle and Greene and you – you're not worth it.' I opened the door, struggled out and went to the driver's side.

'Move over,' I told her. 'I'll drop you at the boat.'

'But your leg!'

'Move!'

The rest of the journey took a long time. My temper had cooled quickly and the frustration had faded but the pain in my leg wouldn't go away. We stopped half a dozen times so I could rest.

Charmain didn't offer to take the wheel and I was too pig-headed to ask her. By the time we came within

triking distance of the canal night was falling. There
was no way I could face the drive back to the cottage.
needed a drink and a long deep sleep.

And I needed more answers from Mrs Stoke. I decided
o spend the night with her.

CHAPTER THIRTY-TWO

Someone was on the boat.

A thin wedge of pale yellow light was visible throug a gap in the curtains as we drove down the hill. I cut th engine and the lights and coasted silently, steering b moonlight, till we stopped by the lock-keeper's cottage

Eyes wide, Charmain tensed and stiffened in he seat.

'Who do you suppose it is?' she asked, alread whispering.

'I don't know.' Sliding the key from the ignition clicked the door open. 'Wait here,' I said.

She grabbed my arm 'Hold on!' A harsh whisper now 'Leave me the car key!'

I tried to shrug her hand off. 'No.'

'Yes!' She gripped harder. I turned to face her. Sh was corpse-pale. 'No,' I said.

'You must!'

'Why?'

'They might get you . . . I'd be stuck . . . they'd ge me too.'

'Too bad. I'm taking the key. I don't trust you.'

'I'll wait for you. Honest, I will!'

Putting the key in my pocket I prised open her gri with my right hand. 'If you weren't a junkie, Charmair I might believe you. Stay here and stay quiet. I'll b back soon.'

I hobbled down the path to the side of the boa

The night was cool and cloudless and the boat moved gently from side to side, the water lapping at it like a cat at milk.

The window at the end had been propped open. Moving towards it I heard the rising and falling tones of conversation. Crouched below the window I could hear the voices clearly. Two men. Recognisable accents: one West Midlands, the other a West Country burr.

'I thought Stoke said there was a watercock.'

'He said he thought there was. Try the kitchen.'

'The galley, you mean.'

'Bollocks.'

The boat rolled as he walked along.

'Don't see anything.'

'Have to be the acid then, won't it?'

The steps came back to the middle of the boat.

'How we gonna work it?'

'I told you, when he's out for the count we uncork the bottle and tip it over. It'll burn a big enough hole within a couple of hours to let the water in.'

'The cops won't wear the acid once they've dragged this thing back up. What would Malloy be doing with acid?'

'Could be anything, how would they know? It's not as if Malloy's gonna be here to answer questions. Obvious accident, innit? Four hundred milligrams of alcohol in his blood, pissed out of his brain . . . what else can they call it?'

'I dunno.'

'Aw, gimme a break.'

Glass clinked on glass.

'Careful!'

'No sweat.'

'What do we do if Malloy ain't home?'

'We wait. Stoke said do it before he gets back. That gives us three days.'

'He could have been out of the way ages ago when we had him over that radiator.'

'That was just a fright job. That was all we got paid for. One of my better ideas too, I'd say.'

'Yeah, really effective, Bill . . . The guy's caused nothing but trouble since.'

'Can I help it if Malloy ain't got the brains to keep his nose out of other people's business? I'll still bet he won't forget the night I nearly roasted it off his face.'

Bill, you never spoke a truer word.

The pain in my leg didn't matter any more. Heading back to the cottage I drove at speeds of up to a hundred, headlights picking out the bends just in time. I was excited. Scared, but excited.

The relief Charmain showed when I returned to the car had disappeared. The tension was back . . . and the fear.

I told her what I wanted her to do when we reached the cottage, repeating it over and over to make sure she understood. 'I'll park the car deep in the trees but facing the road, the road they'll have to come down to reach the cottage, either by car or on foot. If they walk you should be able to see them by the light of the moon but they'll probably drive. Especially when they see that the cottage is in darkness.

'Driving or walking, you'll have to be alert. If you miss them and my plans don't work out they'll probably kill me. If they pass on foot, give me thirty minutes. If you don't see the lights come on in the cottage by then, drive to the village and ring DS Cranley at this number. Tell him the men who killed Alan Harle have got Eddie Malloy and tell him where we are. Okay?'

She nodded.

'If they pass you in a car cut the time to twenty minutes maximum. Got it?'

'Yes, but what if they see me in the car as they pass?'

'They won't. If they do, then slip out into the woods, they'll never find you, and try to get back to the village.'

She started shivering.

Five hundred yards from the cottage an old cart path led off into the wood. In winter you could never have driven a car along it but in summer it was just about manageable.

I drove well down, turned off into a clearing and parked facing the road. We got out and dragged broken branches and ferns across the windscreen and side body. 'You'll have to roll down the side windows in case the moon glints on the glass.'

'Okay.'

I looked out towards the road. A moving car would be easily visible through the thin pines. I just hoped the same didn't apply to this stationary one in the woods.

I opened the passenger door for Charmain. She got in and sat clenching her left fist inside her right hand. I thought she was going to cry and I squatted down beside her and took her hands in mine. The moonlight filtering through the trees showed the goose bumps on her arms spiked with tiny hairs. Cold or fear, I couldn't help with either.

'We'll make it,' I said.

She nodded, holding back the tears.

I stood up and turned to go. 'Eddie . . .'

I looked round to see her raise a weak smile. 'Good luck,' she said.

I'd need it.

In a cupboard in the kitchen were a pair of wire-cutters and a pair of heavily padded industrial gloves. I worked in the darkness. In fifteen minutes I was ready for them.

Ready and waiting. Waiting in the alcove in the living-room twelve feet from the cold fireplace, six feet from the back of the worn sofa. Across to my left the curtains were closed on the window. One step out from where I hid and three steps to the left the door led out to the hall and the front door which I'd locked.

Waiting. Tense in the darkness. Cold. Leg aching. On the mantelpiece the clock ticked, steady and reliable . . . the only sound, the only beat. Tick tock. Tick tock. Two men. How long? Two men. How long?

Twenty minutes. Half an hour. How was Charmain holding out? Maybe they'd seen her on the way past. What if they'd caught her? What would she tell them? What would they do to her?

In her nightdress.

An owl hooted. I heard its wings in the trees. Twenty seconds later there was a noise. It seemed loud. On the roof . . . There was someone on the roof.

My heartbeat doubled.

Another noise above – scrabbling, scratching, like fingernails clawing their way up the tiles. I stopped breathing . . . I heard the wingbeat again passing the window, then silence. Thirty seconds . . . a minute. No more noise from the roof.

Then I realised what had happened. The owl, flying over, had dropped his catch then swooped down, talons open to snatch it again as it slid away down the tiles. Breathe again . . . Beat easy, heart.

The lungs breathed but the heart kept pumping fast. It must have known something because it was then I heard them coming.

Footsteps. In the loose gravel by the road . . . coming closer, so close I waited to see them pass the window. They didn't. Noises to my right, through the kitchen. They were round the back. Prowling.

I had hoped they wouldn't try the back door. If they came in that way my chances were down by fifty per cent. Coming from my right they had twice as much floor-space to cross. Twice the chance of seeing me in the narrow alcove.

I waited.

How long had it been since they passed Charmain? The longer they took coming in the less time I'd have before she headed for the village.

No more noise at the back. They must be circling the building making sure no one was at home. I was at home. So was the clock. Two men. They're here. Two men. They're here.

I heard no more footsteps, just the thin sound as the lockpick slid into the mechanism. The click as the lock turned. The creak as the door opened and the two spiders walked into the web of the fly.

They were three steps from where I stood. Everything depended on them taking those three steps in my direction. They didn't. They did something even better. They sat on the sofa.

'Let's make ourselves comfortable till our little friend comes home.'

Their little friend was a yard away thinking how much their heads above the back of the sofa resembled coconuts on a shelf. I didn't even have to step forward. In each hand I held a double loop of barbed wire, two feet in diameter.

The padded gloves protected my hands as I reached out and slipped one loop over each head. They both cried out. One full twist tightened the wire right up to the throats.

'If you even swallow I'll rip your throat open.'

I stepped in close behind them.

'Start working your way in very slow movements towards the end of the sofa.'

When they reached the end I moved to the side so I could control them more easily when they stood up.

'You're going to stand up very slowly and you're not going to do anything silly. It'll take me a tenth of a second to twist this little necklace one more time, so best behaviour unless you want to become a blood donor via your jugular. Stand up.'

They stood. 'Which one is Bill?'

'Me,' said the one on my left.

'If you raise your left hand to that wall, Bill, you'll find a light switch. Press it.'

He did and the light came on and I could almost hear Charmain's sigh of relief.

I turned his head round to look at me and I smiled as our eyes met. 'Hallo, Bill. Remember me?'

He nodded very carefully.

'I thought you might. What's your friend's name?'

'Trevor.'

'Hallo, Trevor.' I smiled. He wasn't reassured. 'I believe you were at the open-air barbecue too, the night my face was on the menu?'

Swivelling his eyes he looked at his partner.

'I'm not hearing you, Trev,' I said.

'Yes,' he croaked.

'Well, gentlemen, never let it be said that I don't return hospitality. As soon as I've made you both comfortable I'm going to put the kettle on.'

I bound them together, back to back with thirty feet of barbed wire, double twisted the ends and crimped them with pliers. Then I went to the kitchen and filled the kettle, lit the gas and put it on to boil.

I made them stand in the alcove while I stood leaning on the mantelpiece facing them. 'Why did you kill Alan Harle?'

They didn't answer.

'I don't know how much of your school physics lessons you remember but you've got as long as it takes to boil two pints of water on a full gas flame. If you're not talking by then, well, I've always supported the eye-for-an-eye theory . . . Though I think boiling water is even more painful than hot steam.'

They both flinched.

'I'll remind you of the question. Why did you kill Alan Harle?'

Silence.

'Fine. I can wait.'

I started whistling, lightly, watching them as they wondered if I'd do what I said. Whistling on in a deliberate monotone I kept it up till the kettle started whistling, low, then steadily higher.

'Catching, isn't it?'

They didn't seem to find it funny.

I carried the kettle through. Bill saw the towel wrapped round the handle. I smiled at him. 'Don't want to burn myself, it's very hot.'

His eyes widened.

I stood very close to him. The streams of blood stained his white collar and the wire was so tight round his chest he wasn't taking full breaths. I stared hard and cold and unblinking into his eyes. He knew I held the kettle somewhere below but he couldn't bend his head to look down.

'Why did you kill Alan Harle?'

He looked unsure but he obviously thought I wouldn't do it because he decided not to answer. It was a gamble. He lost.

I splashed about a cupful onto his thigh and he screamed. Trevor's body stiffened visibly at the sound.

'My aim was out a bit. I'll get it this time.'

I swung my arm back.

'No! No! I'll tell you!'

'Start telling.'

'It was a job. Just a job, a contract.'

'Who paid?'

He hesitated. I moved my arm again.

'Stoke! Howard Stoke!'

'Why did Stoke want him dead?'

'We don't ask for reasons.'

'*Why?*' I shouted in his face.

'He was screwing around with Stoke's wife.'

'Bullshit!'

'Honest!'

'How did you kill him?'

'Injected him with something Stoke gave us.'

'After chaining the poor bastard up in a filthy stable for weeks!'

'That was the way Stoke wanted it.'

'And the customer's always right, huh?'

He didn't answer.

'Harle was already injecting heroin, wasn't he?'

'Yes.'

'Where did he get it?'

'We don't know.'

'Was he dealing in it?'

'We didn't ask him any questions.'

'Don't get smart, Bill, you're on the wrong side of the wire to get smart.'

He avoided my stare. I spent another five minutes pumping them but I learned little. They didn't know much because they hadn't wanted to know. Their only interest had been money.

'Is it just Stoke you've been involved with or have you done jobs for anyone else?'

'We take it where we can find it.'

'Took.' I reminded him. Then I remembered the others who'd been attacked. 'Was it Stoke who gave you the contracts on Elrick and Ruudi Odin . . . and Danny Gordon?'

No answer.

I lifted the kettle to eye-level. 'Tell me!'

Bill looked at me. His voice was strained. 'They were just jobs, nothing personal.'

'Nothing personal! You crippled Elrick, as good as killed Odin and murdered Danny Gordon and you say it was nothing personal! You fucking bastards!' I swung the kettle and splashed another half pint of water on Bill's thighs, then did the same to Trevor. They both screamed.

My control was going and I turned and put the kettle down in the hearth because I was sorely tempted to pour the rest over their heads and they were already writhing enough. The barbs were cutting into the skin and blood was running from their throats and wrists.

I went to the phone. 'I'm just about to ring the police but I sincerely hope you bastards bleed to death before they get here.'

I rang the station and they told me Detective Sergeant Cranley was at home. They wouldn't give me his number so I told the duty sergeant where I was and what had happened and warned him that if he didn't send a squad car within half an hour they'd be picking up two corpses.

I left them both still groaning and taking shallow breaths and I went to get Charmain. She'd gone. So had the car.

CHAPTER THIRTY-THREE

I stood staring through the straight black silhouettes of the trees wondering how long ago she'd left. Wondering if she'd waited to see the light going on, to see me safe. Wondering if her nerve had simply failed or if she'd been so desperate for another fix.

Whatever, she had to be heading back to the boat ... where the heroin was, and the whisky and the acid. I was beginning to regret freeing her from that ankle chain.

I hurried back to the cottage where Bill told me, in a strangled voice, which pocket his car keys were in. The barbed wire spiked him twice before I got them out.

As I left I switched the lights off, making it even more risky for them to move around. I couldn't see their faces but as I closed the door I heard them curse.

The syringe was on the table. Charmain lay on the narrow bunk, sprawled back, her right hand above her head idly fingering the curtain, a half full glass of whisky held gently in her left.

One knee was drawn up pointing at the low ceiling, the other leg lay flat. Both were bare as the hem of her nightgown was up round her waist exposing white silk panties.

She smiled at me as I came in. 'Home is the sailor, home from the sea, and the hunter home from the hill,' she said. High as a kite.

I sat down opposite her, wincing as the hard edge of the bunk pushed into the leg wound. I looked at her. 'And the junkie?' I asked. 'Where's she home from?'

Still smiling she raised the glass and drank. 'Who cares? Who cares where the junkie's home from? Who cares? Home from the woods, the junkie's home from the woods.'

'Is this why you left?' I asked, picking up the empty syringe.

'Left what? Where? I've left a lot of places, Mr Malloy . . . a lot of places.'

Her face was pink from the warmth of the cabin. The three small gas fires along the length of the boat were lit.

'Left the woods,' I said. 'Where you were supposed to be watching out for me.'

'I watched out . . . you were okay.' The smile was dropping. 'You didn't need me any more after the light went on . . . You were the big hero then, weren't you? The big hero.'

Letting go the curtain, her right hand came down to rub her thigh. She drank again then closed her eyes and laid her head back against the pannelled wall.

She looked almost serene. You'd never have guessed how screwed up her life was.

Six feet to my left was a step down to the kitchen area where an old fridge and cooker and a sink unit with a dented draining board sat on a floor of cracked and curl-edged vinyl tiles.

Limping over I got myself a glass from the shelf above the sink. Charmain opened her eyes again as she heard the whisky being poured.

'Help yourself to a drink,' she said, not looking at me. 'Plenty for everyone.'

I sat down again, more carefully this time, and hauled my bad leg up straight on the cushions as I

271

rested my back against the corner so I faced Charmain diagonally.

Raising her glass slowly, she said, 'Cheers! Here's to the hero.'

I watched her take a big slug. 'And here's to the heroin,' I said.

Lowering her glass she half sneered, half smiled at me, wrinkling her nose. 'Very witty, Mr Malloy, very witty. You must be the smartest person out of everyone I know.' She held her glass up in mock salute. 'Smart and brave and virtuous . . .' The glass came down, the smile dropped away and she stared up at the ceiling and said, just loudly enough, 'Arsehole.'

I let it pass. She was feeling guilty about leaving me back at the cottage. The fact that she also felt obliged to me for 'rescuing' her from Stoke made her feel worse.

If you ever want someone to resent you for a long time just do them a big favour.

She wouldn't leave it alone. Turning on me again she said, 'What is it with you, Malloy? What do you get out of all this?'

I shrugged. 'My licence back, I hope.'

That silenced her for a minute. She must have been expecting me to spout some high moral reasons she could ridicule and taunt me with.

Pushing her hair back from her face she drank again and strained to think of something else to goad me into an argument.

I drank and flushed the whisky round my mouth, burning my gums, and waited for the next assault. But her frown told me the drug-clouded whisky-soaked brain was struggling to come up with anything logical.

'What do you know, anyway . . . ?' she said, staring at the wall.

Closing her eyes she rested her head against the panel, her hair rasping on the rough varnish.

'Charmain, I need your help.'

Her head came up and her eyes opened and blazed at me. 'Don't bloody patronise me!'

I shrugged. 'I didn't intend to.'

She made a face and mimicked me. 'I didn't intend to. I didn't intend to . . . You bastard!'

'To hell with this,' I said and swung my leg off the sofa. Her little pink heroin bag rested by her side. I reached across and grabbed it.

Her face froze, open-mouthed, as I sat back again clutching the bag. She stretched out a hand. 'Give me that,' she said, in a very thin voice.

'Shut up.'

She stared at me, knowing she'd pushed me too far, just as she'd done in the car that afternoon.

'I need it.' The voice was pleading now.

'Too bad.'

Unzipping the bag I took out a thumb-size, half-full phial of clear liquid. 'Where did you get it?' I asked.

The nightdress hem tumbled to her feet as she stood up quickly, still clutching her drink. 'Give me it.' The tone was strident. Her free hand reached towards me.

'Was it part of Greene's supply or did you bring it with you?'

'It's mine! Give it to me!'

Rolling it on my palm, I said, 'It's not yours. If it was yours you'd have used it in the car back in the woods and saved yourself a long drive. It's Phil Greene's . . . or it was Phil Greene's. Where was it hidden?'

She lunged towards me. Clutching the phial I pushed her away with my left hand. Losing her balance she lurched backwards and landed awkwardly on the bunk, splashing her drink on the green cushion. Struggling forward she tried to get up again.

'Sit still,' I said. 'Or I'll pour this down the sink.'

She sat still, glared at me then threw her glass at my

head. What was left of the whisky arced out and, as I ducked, I heard it sizzle against the bars of the fire. The glass hit the panel behind my head but didn't break.

Charmain sat clutching her drawn up knees and staring out of the small window into the darkness.

'Where's the rest of the supply, Charmain?'

She ignored me.

'Tell me.'

She began rocking slowly, to and fro. I got up and went to the sink. Unscrewing the lid, I tilted the phial. 'Where's the rest of it?'

She stopped rocking and stared at me wide-eyed, unbelieving.

'Don't! There isn't any more!'

'I don't believe you.' I tipped it till it was horizontal. 'Where is it?'

The horror-struck look on her face had me almost convinced she was being truthful. But I had to be sure. I let out a trickle and she screamed and ran towards me.

Falling to her knees as she reached me she hammered on the dirty tiles with her right fist.

'Please, please, please . . . that's all there is! I need it . . . For tomorrow.' She was sobbing, staring at the floor, she wouldn't look up at me.

She stopped hammering and pushed her forearms under her forehead and rocked back and forth on her knees like some demented jockey. 'Please, please, please . . .'

Screwing the cap back onto the phial I reached down slowly and helped her up. Standing in front of me with red-rimmed eyes, tear-stained face, runny nose and flakes of dirt in her hair she looked utterly dejected and beaten.

Reaching for her limp right hand I slowly brought the open palm up and placed the phial in it. She looked at me like a grateful animal newly relieved of pain, and two big tears spilled down her cheeks. Opening her arms slowly she slumped forward, head on my chest, and pulled me towards her. I put my right hand round her waist and, with my left, gently stroked the hair at the nape of her neck.

I felt, as much as heard, a long deep sigh come out of her body and the warm wetness of her tears soaked through my shirt as, very very softly, she wept.

CHAPTER THIRTY-FOUR

It took Charmain almost an hour to calm down. She'd dry her eyes and try to smile and say she was fine then burst into tears again. But at least the spite was all out of her. She looked apologetic and extremely sorry for herself though the feminine wiles still worked as she decided the troubles were ours rather than just hers.

'What are we going to do?' she asked, sipping a fresh drink.

I could play that way too.

'Before we can plan anything I need to know more about Howard and his business ... and his connections.'

She nodded slowly and after some gentle prompting told me how she'd met Howard at Sandown races three years ago when she backed a winner with him. Okay, he was much older but he had money and big cars and nice houses. She wasn't embarrassed about admitting she was a gold-digger.

She said Howard kept his business affairs pretty much to himself. Very few people visited him at home and when they did he'd never discuss business in front of her. Things had been good for the first two years. He'd taken her out, bought her things, treated her well. It all started going wrong when Harle came along.

'What happened?' I asked.

She shrugged and stared at her feet. 'We became lovers.'

'You and Harle!' I hadn't meant to sound so incredu-
lous but when I thought of them together ... Harle's
small greasy slyness and her, well, I suppose beauty
was too strong a word, but she was very attractive,
though when it sunk in that she'd slept with Harle
she seemed a lot less so ... Maybe I was just jealous.
And mad with myself. The girl I'd thought too gorgeous
to even approach at school falling for the likes of Harle
... At least she'd taken Stoke for money ...

Anyway, she caught the tone in my voice and looked
hurt then defiant. 'He was good in bed,' she said, almost
accusingly.

'You don't have to explain to me.'

'It sounded like I did.'

'My bad manners showing again. I'm sorry.'

She pouted and drank. 'You men think sex isn't
important to a woman ... well, to some of us it is
... I didn't love Alan, didn't even care all that much
for him, but he was brilliant in bed.' She drank again
and looked angry, then repeated, 'Brilliant.'

I stayed silent waiting for her to get it out of her
system. She said nothing more for a minute but I could
tell from her face it was still working on her. She was
stretched out on the bunk leaning against the wall in
pretty much the same position she'd been in when I'd
arrived, though she wasn't as relaxed now.

The phial of heroin had stayed clutched in her
hand since I'd given it back to her. I wondered if
the original fix was wearing off and how soon she'd
need another one.

'Howard was impotent,' she said quietly, staring at
her empty glass. 'From the day we were married. It
terrified him.'

I bet it did. It went along towards explaining his crazy
jealousy and manic over-protectiveness of her. 'Did he
know you were sleeping with Harle?'

She nodded very slowly. 'I think he did, but he'd never have challenged me. He was too scared of the truth.' She spoke quietly with no hint of satisfaction.

'But not too scared to make sure Harle never saw you again.'

She stared, unblinking, into her empty glass. I filled it up with what was left in the bottle.

'How did you meet Alan?' I asked.

'Howard introduced us at a party. He kept calling Alan his boy, his best boy.'

'When was this?'

'New Year's Day. We'd been to Cheltenham.'

'What was Alan doing for him? What was the connection?'

'I don't know. I assumed he was just a friend, or maybe a hanger-on. I didn't ask questions.'

'Didn't Alan tell you anything?'

'Sometimes he'd ramble on when he was drunk about how rich he was going to be, how everything was going to work out.'

'Drunk or high?'

'I don't know.'

'Was he injecting?'

Tilting her head back she rested it on the wall and closed her eyes. 'What does it matter? Alan's dead, Phil's dead . . . What's the point?'

I let it rest for a while then changed tack. 'You know Alan rode for a very rich owner?'

She nodded.

'Nobody seems to have met this guy Perlman. Didn't Alan talk about him?'

Wearily she shook her head.

'Did he ever even meet him?'

'I don't know.' She sounded very tired.

I changed tack again. 'Alan was injecting . . . I only asked you to see if you knew.'

She nodded.

'How often?'

'I don't know.'

'Did he offer you any?'

She hesitated. 'He didn't offer . . . I asked if I could try it . . . he didn't want me to . . .'

She looked down and fingered her glass.

'But you talked him into it?'

She sighed deeply. 'In the end. I tried my first fix the week he disappeared.' She looked to be going on a downer again. I kept up the questioning. 'Was Greene injecting, too?'

'No.'

'You seem pretty definite.'

'He wanted to stay clean. He'd seen Alan's behaviour when he needed a fix . . . Phil Greene didn't want to do anything that would stop him being champion jockey.'

'You seem to know a lot about his personal ambitions.'

She leaned forward far enough to sip her drink then lay back again. 'Phil had a crush on me . . .'

'And . . . ?'

'He agreed to help me after Alan disappeared.'

'You mean he agreed to get heroin for you?'

She nodded, eyes still closed.

'Who paid for it?'

She stared at me looking hurt but sounding too tired to raise any real anger. 'What the hell does that mean, Malloy?'

I shrugged. 'Heroin costs a lot of money. I just wondered who paid for it . . .'

'I paid . . . All right?'

'Okay . . .'

She settled again, closing her eyes. 'How did you meet Phil?' I asked.

'Howard brought him home for drinks after Alan disappeared.'

'Did Alan know Skinner, the vet?'

'They were connected in some way but Alan didn't like him.'

'Phil Greene was connected to Skinner too, wasn't he?'

'I think so.'

'They came to your house together last week.'

She didn't comment. 'So, we've got Alan and Phil and Skinner and Roscoe and Howard . . . all connected in some way, Alan and Phil more than anyone else because they're both dead, both murdered . . . by your husband.'

I wasn't sure how she'd react. Deep down she must have known Stoke was behind Harle's death and I suspected she knew he'd engineered Greene's death. I watched her. She didn't even blink.

'Charmain, did you hear what I said?'

She nodded.

'Am I right?'

'Aren't you always?' she murmured and turned her head away.

'Charmain, when did Howard find out about your heroin habit?'

She turned her head back but still wouldn't look at me. She stared into the fire. 'A couple of weeks ago, when Phil brought the stuff . . . I had no money. I gave him my watch to pay for it and to get some more. He said he'd wait for the money but I told him to take the watch. He shoved it into his pocket. Last week, when he came with Skinner to see Howard he accidentally pulled the watch out of his pocket . . . It fell on the floor, right at Howard's feet . . . Howard bought me that watch for our first anniversary.'

She drank.

'Phil gave him some stupid story about finding it outside in the driveway and Howard pretended to believe him ... Later, he punched the truth out of me.'

I looked at her. 'As much motive as Howard would have needed to kill him, I'd say. He probably also knew that Greene had been drinking with me and had talked too much.'

Charmain's chin dropped onto her chest. The realisation of the part she'd played in the deaths of Harle and Greene was beginning to sink in. She looked completely drained but I needed the answer to at least one more question.

'Charmain . . .' Her head stayed down. 'Do you know what Skinner's working on at Roscoe's yard? Is he making heroin or horse dope or what?'

She shook her head slowly, still not lifting it. I persevered. 'He's using the Head Lad's cottage, working on something secret. It could be the key to all this, to Harle's and Greene's deaths . . . Charmain . . . ?'

She was sobbing again in that same soft way as when I'd taken the heroin from her. I went across and stood above her, my hands on her shoulders. 'Charmain, please . . . tell me what Skinner is doing at Roscoe's?'

She leaned forward, throwing her arms around my waist, still weeping, 'I don't know . . . I don't know! Oh, Eddie, what are we going to do?' She forced me to take a step back as she stood up and put her arms around my neck.

I stood holding her for what seemed a very long time then her tear-stained face came up and her big sad eyes looked at me. As she arched her neck her pink swollen lips parted showing the tip of her tongue and she closed her eyes and kissed me, long and wet and warm.

She swept the cushions off the bunks and arranged them on the floor. Pushing at the shoulder straps of the nightgown she wriggled out of it and, bending gracefully, slipped her panties off.

She knelt, pulling me down with her and we kissed again as she undressed me. Unresisting, I let her lead, wanting to believe she was doing it because, deep down, she loved me, but knowing it was a reaction to what we'd been through tonight. A crazily overheated libido was one of the after-effects of coming safely through danger. Mine was just as hot as hers.

She was also doing it because she hoped to gain control, just as she'd tried to do with Stoke and Harle and probably Greene.

She lay flat now and pulled me alongside her. 'Oh, Eddie, this is what you wanted, isn't it? This is what you were dying for when you came into my bedroom . . . and when I was in the car . . . This is what you wanted back in the woods . . . isn't it, Eddie . . . isn't it . . . ?' She was moaning softly.

Maybe it's what I wanted, I thought, but it's not what I'm going to have, Charmain, not when you've been with scum like Stoke and chancers like Harle and idiots like Greene. Eddie Malloy doesn't play fourth in a field like that. I'd rather try to remember you the way you were.

Then Jackie's face came into my mind, Jackie the traitor, and my vengeful streak showed through. Why shouldn't I have sex with Charmain? I could tell Jackie about it and watch her face . . . How does it feel to be betrayed, Jackie?

I watched Charmain, writhing, moaning, longer and louder, 'Now, Eddie . . . please, now . . .' And I let her go and slowly and silently got to my feet and stood over her, looking down.

She lay still, staring at me, quizzically at first then her eyes focused on mine and she saw immediately how much, at that moment, I despised her and she seemed, physically, to crumple as she turned on her side drawing her knees up, her hands covering her face as the tears came. 'You bastard,' she murmured softly through her weeping. 'You dirty rotten bastard.'

And I stood there for a minute surprised at my own feeling of triumph. I knew then I'd paid her back for not loving me at school, for not wanting me when we met again, for all she'd ever done to me or could do to me in the future.

I knew it was illogical and unfair and I knew I was a bastard . . . But I felt damned good.

CHAPTER THIRTY-FIVE

I was plagued by nightmares and awoke after littl
more than an hour's sleep. Charmain still slept.

The sun was up but the boat was cold. I made a mug o
coffee and took it outside. As I walked forward the boa
rolled slightly, sending gentle ripples under a famil;
of ducks as they swam silently past into the low mis
under the bridge.

On the untrodden grass bordering the towpath th
dew was heavy. Both cars, mine parked half on th
road, half on the towpath by Charmain, were also we
with dew.

I realised how easily the cars would be spotted if an;
of Stoke's cronies were out searching and I decided t
take them into the village and leave them parked there
They would only be a taxi-ride away if I needed one.

I went to get my jacket. It would be best to move th
cars now while the village was quiet. Anyway, I had t
phone DS Cranley for an update.

Charmain was sleeping soundly when I left. I locke
the door and took the only key.

It was just after 7 a.m. when I parked the secon
car, probably a bit early to catch Cranley, but I spotte
a phone box so it was worth a try. He was at th
station.

'Where are you, Malloy?' he asked.

'A little place in the country.'

'Where?'

'I can't tell you just now. I may not be here after today. I'll let you know where I am as soon as I know it's going to be reasonably permanent.'

'That's not good enough. I want a full statement from you about last night.'

He was being remarkably polite. 'Fine, I'll call in at the station.'

'When?'

'As soon as I can.'

'Malloy!'

'Sergeant . . . look, tell me you'll pick up a bookmaker called Stoke for questioning and I'll go to the station right now.'

'For questioning on what?'

'For at least three of the murders that you and I have been fighting about since we met. Those were his two guys you picked up last night. They were out to add me to their list.'

'They're claiming you abducted them.'

'Oh, come on, Cranley! Even you can't believe that . . .'

'I'm not saying I do . . .'

'Look, pick up Stoke . . . I can get people to testify if they know he's safely locked up.'

'Come and see me, Malloy, then we'll talk about it.'

'I can't! Not now! I told you that.'

'Then it looks like I'm going to have to let your two friends here go.'

I heard a click. 'Cranley! Cranley! You bastard.'

Charmain was up and about when I got back, spooning coffee into a cup as the kettle whistled. The light covering of make-up didn't completely hide the dark rings round her eyes but she looked reasonably bright. It was hard to tell if she'd had her first fix of the day. I didn't ask.

'Coffee?' she offered.

'Please. Black, no sugar.' I sat on the bunk.

'Just as well, there's no milk.'

She poured and brought it to me then sat down on the bunk opposite and clasped her mug in both hands. 'Where've you been?'

'I took the cars into the village.'

She look puzzled.

'In case Howard's got a search party out.'

She sipped. Neither of us spoke for a minute. She seemed almost friendly and was acting as if last night hadn't happened.

'Do you think Howard will know I'm with you?' she asked.

'I hope so.'

'Why?' She looked nervous.

'Because I need him to come looking for us.' My stomach heaved as I said it, making me realise how scared I was and how tense the waiting was going to be.

'Jesus,' she said, quietly, and I knew she was scared too. 'Then what?' she asked.

'I don't know. I'm still thinking.'

She sipped her coffee. I blew on mine. We were silent again for a minute then she spoke, looking over the rim of her cup at the floor, unblinking. 'How long will it take him to find us?'

'I don't know.'

'It might be days,' she said.

'Maybe.'

'Or even a week.'

We looked at each other.

'I don't think I could stand that,' she said. 'Just sitting here knowing it could be any minute or it could be days and days.'

I nodded. I didn't think I could stand it either.

'What do you think he'll do when he gets here?'

'Charmain, I don't know yet. I'm trying to plan

286

something.' I sounded irritable though she didn't seem to notice. I got up and went to stand at the window. The hedge by the towpath blocked the view of the road and made me start worrying that Stoke might already be on his way and I wouldn't even see his car pull up.

I went outside. The air was warmer now and the low mist was lifting. I could see the road, grey and empty.

Charmain was right. Neither of us would stand days of waiting, especially if her heroin supply ran out. Rather than hide the fact that we were here I should have been advertising it. The sooner Stoke knew, the quicker he'd come.

I'd get my car back and leave it at the top of the towpath. It could only be a matter of time before one of Stoke's buddies passed by.

I told Charmain but the relief she showed was marginal, about the same as a condemned man shows when you tell him his sentence has been brought forward.

Along with my car, I brought back from the village some groceries, a pink tracksuit and yellow training shoes (size 3). The last two items were for Charmain but by the time I got back to the boat I'd decided not to give them to her.

'Why?' she asked as I stashed them in a small locker.

'Because when Howard does come . . .' I shut the clasp lock and straightened to face her '. . . I need him to think you're being held prisoner.'

'By you?'

'Yes. And there's a hell of a lot better chance of him believing it if you're locked in dressed just in your nightgown with no shoes.'

'Why do you want him to think that?'

'To protect you. So you'll have to do your bit to convince him from the moment he comes through that door.'

She was looking nervy again. 'What will you be doing?' she asked.

'I won't be here.'

She stared at me. I went to the sink and filled the kettle again and lit the stove. 'Did you notice the old barge moored just behind us?' I asked. She nodded.

'When he comes down the towpath I'll be in there. When he gets through this door I'll slip out and ring the police from the lock-keeper's cottage.'

'What if the lock-keeper isn't in?'

'We'll just have to hope he is, otherwise I'll have to drive into the village.'

'Then what?'

'You convince him I kidnapped you. Tell him I've gone to buy some booze and that I'll be back any time. I'll speak to Cranley, he'll make sure the police come quickly and quietly.' That was said with more hope than confidence.

I rinsed the coffee mugs. 'When the police get here I'll come back on board and make Howard incriminate himself loudly enough for the police to come in and get him.'

'That's silly.'

I shrugged. 'It's the best I can come up with.'

'Howard won't come alone, you know . . . he'll bring others,' she said.

'We'll have to wait and see. As long as they all come on board then I can still make the call.'

She stood, arms crossed, clutching her elbows tightly. 'What if he doesn't believe me?'

The kettle bubbled. I poured and stirred. 'You'll have to make him believe you.' I carried the drinks over and we sat down again on the bunks. She looked across at me. 'What if he shoots you as you walk through the door?'

I sipped the coffee and shook my head. 'He won't

Howard will want to see me squirm, make me suffer.'
I looked at her. 'Don't you think so?'

Despite the warmth from the fire and the hot coffee, she shivered and looked away. We both knew I
was right.

I locked Charmain in the boat, ducked through a gap
in the hedgerow and set off across the field up towards
the ruined farm I'd watched Greene and Skinner from.
The binoculars swung from my shoulder.

Reaching the rock I'd used before, I settled down
knowing I could wait days for one of Stoke's men to
come along.

Earlier that afternoon I'd gone to the lock-keeper's
cottage and asked to use the phone. In the general small
talk I found out that the couple had no plans to be away
over the weekend.

'In fact my son's coming up tomorrow to help with a
bit of work,' the tall old lady told me. At least there'd
be a phone for use when the 'emergency' came.

It was a fine warm windless evening. A tractor,
orange light flashing lazily on its roof, chugged up
the hill and turned away into a cornfield on the far
side. The only other vehicles I'd seen after half an hour
were six cars and a laundry van.

I'd been there forty minutes when I heard noises
from the direction of the canal. I focused on the boat.
It was rolling heavily and unevenly in the water. Faint
but distinctive sounds of breaking glass or crockery
reached me.

What the hell was she doing down there?

No one could have got on board without me seeing
them; she had to be making all that noise on her own.

My first inclination was to run down the hill but
what would I be running into? The noise got worse.
A metallic banging echoed as though she was hitting

the draining board with a cooking pot. Was she trying to get out? Had a fire started? Couldn't be, no smoke.

A curtain moved. I concentrated on the window and saw her hand grip the curtain and tear it down. Lowering the glasses, I stood up and started down the hill.

Charmain sat cross-legged on her bunk. A corner of the torn curtain lay over her shoulder held down by her chin which was sunk deep on her chest. Her hair had fallen forward hiding her face. Her hands, white-knuckled, were clamped to her sides as if she felt her ribcage had to be held together. She was rocking to and fro making a tuneless sound somewhere between a moan and a hum, as though she were trying to drown out something she didn't want to hear.

The damage around her couldn't have been worse if the boat had overturned twice in a storm. Every internal door lay open: lockers, cupboards, fridge, cooker, toilet. Some of the smaller ones hung only from one hinge. All looked empty; their contents were on the floor: books, magazines, towels, bedding, clothing, pictures, mirrors, twisted coathangers, lightbulbs, crockery, glasses, cutlery. Many things were broken, bent, torn, twisted, smashed, spilled.

In the kitchen area a mess of food lay over and among the wreckage. A slab of butter spread wide by a foot or a knee, blobs of corned beef with jelly still clinging, raspberry yogurt bleeding from a cracked carton, a burst loaf, bruised apples, torn teabags, a trail of coffee grains, puddles of milk and orange juice, hundreds of loose matches, many with spent black heads, and, scattered over everything like corn-coloured snowdrops, thousands of cereal flakes.

The only object I could see which wasn't on the floor was a plant pot which lay on its side on the small table next to me; the contents, a short but vicious looking actus, had been dragged out. Some of the spikes at the p were bloodstained. I righted the pot. What was left of he soil inside bore Charmain's scrabbling, desperate, eroin-seeking finger marks.

I went over to where she sat rocking. Rolling to and o with her, in the dip made by the nightgown between er open knees, was the empty heroin phial.

I squatted down in front of her, trying to look up into er face. 'Charmain, what happened? . . . I thought you ad enough to get you through?'

She didn't answer, just kept rocking. Delicately, I eached for the phial which had dropped into a fold etween her thighs. Not a drop was left. I looked closely t the cap. It was cracked.

By her side were the tattered remains of her little ink bag, the lining had been torn out. Gently, I parted er hair. A piece of the lining, sucked dry of the leaked rug, hung limply from her mouth.

Whether it was shock or the beginning of withdrawal don't know but I couldn't rouse her. She was locked way, eyes still open, in her own little world. I thought cleaning the place up then decided Stoke would e more easily convinced by our story if I left it in mess.

I sat by the window to keep watch as best I could hile Charmain rocked and swayed on her bunk. About arly evening she began moaning and whining.

I crouched in front of her. 'Charmain, are you all ght?'

Slowly, she shook her head, showing the first sign of mprehension for hours. 'I need a fix.' Her voice was nall, thin and hoarse from moaning.

I gripped her knees. 'Tough it out. We'll soon be away om here.'

She shook her head. 'Can't.'

'You can.'

'No! Get me some stuff.' She was whining now.

'Charmain, there's none to be had. You'll have t[o]
stick this out. I'll get you to hospital as soon a[s]
it's over.'

'Get me some stuff.' Same whine.

'Charmain . . .' I tried to make her look at me bu[t]
she wouldn't. I touched her chin, trying to bring it u[p]
'Charmain . . .' Slowly she straightened up and looke[d]
at me with red, pained, pleading eyes. 'Please . . .' sh[e]
moaned.

'There isn't any, Charmain. There's nowhere I ca[n]
get it. We're in the middle of the countryside, it'll soo[n]
be dark.'

She just kept staring like a frightened child. 'Just [a]
little . . .' The whine again. This was no good. I couldn[']
face many more hours of this, never mind days waitin[g]
for Stoke. Somehow I had to let him know we were her[e]
An idea came to me . . . I checked my watch . . .

'Charmain, try and take in what I'm saying to you[.']
I cupped her face in my hands. 'Try and take it in[,]
concentrate.'

I stood up slowly and gently gripped her shoulder[s]
'I'm going out for a while and for your own good I'[m]
going to lock you in. Try to stay calm and don't call o[ut]
because I can't come to you.'

She didn't look up, didn't make a sound. I squeeze[d]
her shoulders and turned towards the door, picking m[y]
way through the debris underfoot.

Locking the door behind me I stepped onto th[e]
towpath, made for the car and headed back to th[e]
cottage. Leaving Charmain alone for a couple of hou[rs]
was a gamble, but it was one I had to take.

The place was cold but I couldn't bring myself to bui[ld]
a fire, too cheery. I sat silently under the light of [a]
small lamp knowing I was making the final admissio[n]

to myself, knowing I was extinguishing the last dregs of hope for our relationship.

At 9.55 Jackie called and we spoke lovingly and I left her with the news of exactly where I was and who I was with. And I knew that, if she did her job as well as she had with Harle and Kruger, Stoke would soon be coming.

CHAPTER THIRTY-SIX

When I got back to the boat there had been no change in the pitch of Charmain's whining. I went in and tried to get through to her that Howard could be on his way and it was essential she stuck to the story we'd agreed about me kidnapping her. I was wasting my time. She took nothing in.

I doubted that Stoke would come that night. If he did I'd have real problems between Charmain and trying to rouse the lock-keeper so I could use his phone. But I couldn't take any chances so I prepared for a night on the old barge. The only consolation was that I wouldn't be in the same room as Charmain and her moaning.

By 1 a.m. the only life I'd seen was a fox trotting along the towpath. He'd stopped by the side of Charmain's boat, lifted a front paw and cocked his ears at the pathetic moaning from inside. She'd kept it up almost non-stop for two hours. The fox trotted on out of earshot. He was lucky.

I spent an uneventful night disturbed only by the cold and Charmain's whining.

When dawn came and Stoke hadn't showed, the tension eased a notch and I was sorely tempted to try to get some sleep. But I couldn't take the chance.

I could have used a cup of coffee to warm me and keep me awake but I was apprehensive about going back inside the boat. There had been no noise from Charmain for over an hour. I guessed she'd fallen asleep so I didn't want to wake her and find myself subject to another desperate pleading session.

And, Stoke could still come any minute. As soon as I walked through that door he could come coasting down the hill in his big silent Rolls. I thought about it. I thought about the hot coffee. To hell with it, I was going to make some.

Hoping not to wake Charmain I crept in quietly but I needn't have worried, she wasn't asleep. She sat on the floor by the bunk, her knees drawn up to her chest.

As soon as she saw me she scrambled to her feet and stumbled towards me, grabbing at my lapels as she reached me and staring up into my face. Her hair was matted with stale sweat and her skin was deathly pale, making the rings around her bloodshot eyes look even darker. Her breath smelled.

'Did you get any?' she whined, her eyes wide and wild looking.

I tried to ease her grip from my lapels. 'No, Charmain.'

'Yes! You must have!'

'I haven't been anywhere. I've been in the boat behind you all night . . . Freezing to bloody death.' I held her shoulders and turned her towards the bunk again. 'Come on, I'll make you a coffee.'

She tore herself away and pushed me so hard with both hands I overbalanced and fell against the table, the leg wound, again, getting the worst of it.

She stamped once and clenched her fists and leaned forward from the waist till her face was inches from mine. A vein swelled in the centre of her forehead and a dozen sprung out on her neck and, screaming every word at me she said, *I don't want a fucking coffee! I want a fix!'*

It may have been through some desire to calm her down but I think it was mostly anger that made me

stand up and slap her face as hard as I could swing
my hand.

Reeling, she staggered back against the wall, tears
welling in her mad pathetic eyes. Slowly, she let herself
slide downwards till she was sitting, knees up, on the
floor. She stayed there weeping quietly.

I made the coffee, brought a mugful for her and set
it down by her side. 'Black only, I'm afraid. You spilled
all the milk.'

Looking up at me she shifted into pleading mode
again. 'Let me go . . . please!'

I leaned back against the table. 'Where to? Where
would you go, Charmain, in that state?'

'Roscoe's.'

'Why?'

'There'll be some stuff there, I'm sure there will.
Alan might have left some, or Phil . . . Roscoe's probably
got some.'

'And do you think he'll give it to you?'

'I'll make him.'

'Sure you will. How're you going to get there?'

'Just gimme the keys, I'll drive.'

I squatted down in front of her. 'Charmain, you can
hardly walk, never mind drive.'

With both hands she rubbed her forehead, then her
eyes. 'I can,' she wept, 'I can.'

'Charmain, listen . . . listen to me. You've got to be
here when Howard comes. You've got to go through
with what we agreed . . .' She wouldn't look at me.
'He'll come before midnight tonight,' I promised. 'I'm
sure he will. Then we'll get you away from here, get
you sorted out.'

She just shook her head slowly and the quiet weeping
gave way to heavy sobbing. I was fighting a losing battle
and couldn't spend any more time trying to console her.
For all I knew Stoke was standing outside.

I turned and headed back to the old barge, locking Charmain safely in behind me.

Towards noon a combination of boredom, silence and a night without sleep had me dozing off on my feet. I decided to risk another confrontation with Charmain for the sake of a coffee and something to read. Anyway, she'd been quiet for a while, maybe she was sleeping.

Unlocking the door I tiptoed in, wary of waking her if she was asleep. I heard the metallic clunk at exactly the same time as I felt the blow and I remembered marvelling stupidly how synchronised it was as I slumped to the floor and sank into unconsciousness.

CHAPTER THIRTY-SEVEN

I opened my eyes and didn't know where I was. I closed them again for a minute. My head hurt. Opening my eyes again I stared at the ceiling, a long narrow ceiling. Was I in a hallway in some big house?

Rolling onto my stomach I slowly pushed myself up till I was kneeling. I looked around. I was still on the boat.

It was silent, deserted. No Charmain, no Stoke, no bad men. Beside me, upside down on the floor, was the steel cooking pot I'd been hit with. It wasn't even dented. Tenderly, I fingered my skull and found a painful bump above my right ear.

Carefully I got to my feet. The dizziness was slight. I walked a few steps towards the door . . . Balance was okay. I kept going and went outside. Dusk was falling. The car had gone.

I thought of the other car in the village and felt for the keys in my pocket. They'd disappeared. Charmain had taken both sets. The only place she could have gone was where she thought the heroin was – Roscoe's.

I ran towards the lock-keeper's cottage to phone a taxi in the hope he wouldn't ask for payment in advance for the fare.

The lock-keeper answered the door this time and his look said his patience was wearing thin.

'Sorry,' I said. 'Can I use your phone just one last

time?' He took on a rather mischievous look and stepped aside to let me in. 'Thanks,' I said.

The phone lay disconnected on the floor alongside its disassembled socket-box. Its white cable was being tugged along the hall and through a doorway by an unseen hand.

'Oh no . . .' I said and turned to the smiling lock-keeper.

'It's my son, you see,' he said. 'He's come to move it into the living-room for us. Save us a walk.'

'How long will it take?' I asked desperately.

'Still a good hour in it, mate,' said a voice behind me. 'Was it urgent?'

I turned. The son was as tall as his mother. I looked up at him. 'Yes, I'm afraid it was.'

He shrugged. 'Sorry.'

'It's okay.' I turned to go back out through the open door then noticed a flat-bed pick-up truck parked outside.

'Is that yours?' I asked the son.

'Yes.'

'Can I hire it from you for the evening?'

He looked at me, hesitating.

'I'll bring it back first thing in the morning.'

'How much?'

I reached for my wallet and emptied it. 'Thirty-five pounds.'

He looked at me. 'Forty,' he said.

I bit back a curse. 'I've only got thirty-five!'

He looked at me, silently. I felt in my trouser pocket and found two coins. 'Thirty-seven . . .'

He held his hand out and I gave him the money.

The truck was noisy, uncomfortable and would only top sixty going downhill. I thought of Charmain. She'd be there by now, easily. I wondered how she planned to find the stuff at Roscoe's. Would she wait till dark and try to break in? She couldn't wait. She'd be growing more desperate by the hour. Maybe she hadn't told me everything. Maybe she was tied in with Roscoe too, the same as she'd been with Harle and Greene.

The truck rattled on south-westward and my leg began to feel every ridge and pothole.

Even in the dark, driving on the road that led the last couple of miles to Roscoe's, I felt very uncomfortable at the memory of having my face scalded. The black shape of each large tree I passed reminded me of the one I'd woken up under, lying on the frosty road.

Half a mile from Roscoe's I stopped and got out. I felt only minor twinges in my leg as I climbed the small barbed wire fence and headed across the fields. No lights showed in Roscoe's house but I took a line towards the small cottage sitting alone on an incline about two hundred yards from the main stable block. The Head Lad's cottage – it, too, was in darkness.

The door was not locked. I looked around before going in. Down to my left was the stable yard, dark and almost silent. The only sound came from a box away in the corner where a shod hoof worked through straw bedding to scrape at the concrete floor. Softly, I turned the handle.

The flashlight lit up a narrow hall. There was a door on either side of me. I chose the one on the right.

The torch-beam aimed at the floor as I eased the door closed behind me. I moved the beam a yard forward and in the spotlight was a foot. I recognised the yellow training shoe which hung only on the toe. And the pale pink leg of the tracksuit that had been new the day before. As the beam moved up something glinted on the floor by her side: an empty glass phial. Her left sleeve was rolled up. Still hanging from her bare arm was the syringe, the plunger pushed fully home.

Her eyes were closed. No more cramps. No more

shivering. No more loneliness chained up in the big house. Life's agonies were over.

As I knelt in the darkness to ease the syringe from her arm someone switched the light on. I was dazzled for a second then I turned round and Howard Stoke was there by the door, his hand still on the light switch. Roscoe's strained face looked over his shoulder. Switching off the flashlight I slowly stood up.

The room was quite small. In the corner was what looked like a leather-covered doctor's 'couch'. There were racks of shelves along the top wall and more on the wall to my left. A double sink unit of stainless steel was set into a gleaming white workbench. On the bench and shelves were various bottles, none labelled, in assorted shapes. On the far end of the bench stood several racks of test-tubes and what looked like a small portable heat lamp.

Stoke and Roscoe stared at me. Stoke still held the light switch. I considered yanking the door open and running, but that was when Stoke took his hand from the switch, put it into his coat pocket and brought out a gun.

He pointed it straight at my head and I thought he was going to shoot me without saying even one word. I wanted to look at Roscoe to see if there was anything in his face to give me hope, but I couldn't make my eyes leave Stoke's trigger finger. Something told me that if I moved my eyes he'd fire.

His lips drew back from his teeth. It wasn't a smile.

'Tell me how it feels, Mister Malloy,' Stoke said. The level of control he needed to steady his voice frightened me much more than the silence had.

'How what feels?' My own control had almost gone.

'How it feels to be living the last two minutes of your life.'

'What do you want me to say? That I'm sorry about Charmain? About Phil Greene and Alan Harle?'

His reply started under control but each word jumped ten decibels. 'I want you to say you're sorry for fucking up my life!'

The gun quivered in his hand. I fought to keep cool. 'It wasn't my doing,' I said.

'Whose was it, the man in the fucking moon?'

I stayed silent. Whatever I said he was going to shoot me. Never in my life had I seen such rage in someone's face. The volcano had started erupting and it was only a matter of minutes, maybe seconds, before it blew completely.

'Look at her,' he said. I kept my eyes on the gun. 'Look at her!' he yelled. I turned and looked at Charmain.

'The stuff in that syringe, the stuff she squeezed into her arm cost me almost half a million pounds . . . Two liquid ounces . . . one single ampoule . . . five hundred thousand pounds . . .'

And four lives, I thought, but didn't say.

'. . . And that bitch shot it into one dirty vein . . . But don't think you've beaten me, Malloy . . . I'd hate you to die thinking that. Skinner didn't fuck-up completely, he did remember to write the formula down, so we will be back in business very soon. Very soon, Mister Malloy, and without you this time.'

He stepped forward and motioned Roscoe into the room. 'Where's Skinner?' Stoke asked him. I glanced at Roscoe. He looked very wary of Stoke.

'He's outside.'

'Get him in here!'

Stoke went out and came back with the vet, who darted a frightened glance at Stoke.

Stoke looked at me. 'I believe you've met Mr Skinner,' he said. I didn't reply. 'He's almost as bad as you, Malloy . . . You know how these guys with degrees are supposed to be brainy? I mean, they told me this guy was a genius when I took him on. He was smart enough to work on the ultimate drug, completely undetectable. A drug that will make me millions, give me control over all the arseholes in racing, like you, Malloy. Pretty smart, then, you'd say, eh?'

I watched him as he turned his attention to the scowling Skinner.

'. . . But not smart enough to remember to lock the fucking door behind him!'

I guessed that was how Charmain had got in.

Stoke glared at the vet, who looked away quickly, before turning his attention back to me.

'What did McCarthy tell you? You'd get your licence back if you cracked it? The Jockey Club would reconsider and all that fucking garbage? And you believed it? They took you for a mug, Malloy, and look where it's got you now . . .'

I kept watching his finger. Slowly he lowered the gun and held it out to Roscoe who'd moved away. 'Roscoe!' Stoke almost screamed. 'Take this!' Roscoe, pale-faced, hurried forward and took the gun. 'If he even moves, shoot him,' Stoke ordered.

Stoke put his hands on his hips and smiled at me. 'Cool, Malloy, very cool. I thought I'd have had you begging, thought you'd have been on your knees. You must have known I wouldn't shoot you.' He took off his coat and walked to the sink unit, talking as he went. 'No way . . . I couldn't just kill you without you suffering any pain.'

'Bad for your reputation,' I said and wished I hadn't.

'Very cool, Malloy, but very true.' His voice was much lighter now. He seemed to be enjoying the prospect of whatever he had planned.

Lifting a phial of dark liquid from a shelf he held it up. 'This is what's going to kill you, Malloy, and it's going to take weeks, maybe longer. I'm going to lock you away and come every day to watch you die, to see you suffer.'

I stared at the phial. My brain had stopped working.

'Sit down beside my wife, Mister Malloy, make yourself comfortable. And before you do, take off your jacket.' I took it off.

Stoke took his off.

'Now sit down like I told you.'

I eased myself down onto the floor beside Charmain's body. It was already cold.

'Now let's roll our sleeves up.' He rolled up his shirt-sleeves. 'Come on!' he yelled.

I rolled them up.

Carrying the liquid he came towards me moving like the eighteen-stone slob he was. As he walked, he said, 'Do you know what your friend Harle died of?'

'Heroin overdose.'

'Nope.' He stood over me, blocking out the light. I looked up at him. He smiled. 'Ever heard of Hepatitis B?'

I kept staring. He kept smiling. 'Harle had it. We did give him an overdose, two syringes full, in fact. Both needles were infected.'

My eyes were going to the glass phial as he asked, 'Guess what this is?' He held up the dark brown liquid.

I knew.

'A clever detective like you will have sussed that it's a blood sample from Harle's corpse taken shortly before we dumped him in your car.'

He bent and pulled the syringe from Charmain's arm. 'She was still alive when we got here, you know. Told us you'd be coming . . . To rescue her . . . She always was a poor judge.'

Taking the liquid back to the sink unit he dipped the

304

empty syringe in it and drew the plunger till it filled. He turned to Roscoe. 'If he moves an inch either way, kill him.'

Roscoe raised the gun. I looked at his face. It told me nothing. I didn't think he'd shoot but I didn't know.

Stoke came towards me holding the syringe up. He stopped at my feet and stood open-legged. 'Arm out.'

I didn't move.

'Hold your arm out or I'll inject it through your eye.'

Slowly I straightened my arm, open-palmed. Stoke leaned over. I glanced at Roscoe, grim-faced, still aiming. Stoke was astride my legs. He reached for my wrist, bending, slightly off-balance. I leaned towards Charmain, bent my right leg and smashed a kick so hard between Stoke's legs I literally felt his balls separate as the toe of my boot hammered deep into his scrotum. He screamed and dropped the syringe which turned once in mid-air like a dagger, then stuck into Charmain's thigh.

Stoke clutched at his groin. I reached up and grabbed the collar of his shirt and hauled him down to shield me from Roscoe. Pulling the syringe from Charmain's leg, I held it to Stoke's neck. He was groaning and breathing in short gasps.

Roscoe, gripping with both hands, still had the gun levelled. His knuckles were white as he held it at arm's length.

'Drop it or the needle goes in,' I said, trying to sound calm.

He didn't reply, just grew more tense.

'You'd have to shoot both of us,' I said.

He said nothing but I could see the panic rising in his eyes. From beneath the perfectly set fringe beads of sweat started appearing. There were dark patches, too, under his arms. His lips were parted, teeth clenched.

The jaw muscles swelled then relaxed, beating like steady pulses.

Skinner glowered at him. 'Don't let us down, Roscoe.'

'Come on, Roscoe . . .' I urged. Stoke was still fighting for breath, gasping and spluttering, very close to the needle.

'Shut up!' Roscoe said, his voice very thin and light.

I tried to weigh up the look in his eyes again and hoped it was panic rather than madness. I played on. 'What's the point? You'd have to kill us both.'

He sniffed hard. Sweat broke on his top lip now.

'Where would you go?' I asked. 'Do you think you could leave three bodies here? How will you explain all this stuff? And Harle and Greene? Why take the blame for everything Stoke's done? That's where they'll pin it . . .'

He stared at me.

'Put the gun down and call the police, tell them what Stoke's done . . . Get yourself a good lawyer, and you'll get off with five years – three, with good behaviour.'

He wavered.

'Roscoe! Shoot him!' Skinner cried.

'Don't listen to him, Roscoe . . . Okay, you'll lose your training licence, but so what? Stoke here, or Perlman, or whatever you like to call him, won't be sending you any more horses anyway.'

That seemed to do it. Slowly he straightened up and lowered the gun. The tension eased from his face to be replaced by a tired, defeated look.

Skinner moved forward and smashed the back of his hand into Roscoe's face, grabbing the gun from him as he fell. Skinner came towards me looking a lot more determined than Roscoe and almost as crazy as Stoke, who was still gasping for breath.

I held the needle closer to Stoke's throat. 'Another step, Skinner, and it goes in.'

'Who cares? Kill the bastard, I never liked him anyway, but you're dying with him, you smarmy little shit.'

He moved sideways now, towards the open door, aiming the gun at my head.

'You've got too much to lose, Skinner . . .'

'Shut it! That doesn't wash with me! I'm not some soft wimp like Roscoe! You are going to die, so say your prayers and say goodbye to your pretty little face that all the girls thought was so fucking cute when you were a big-time jockey!' He started leaning forward holding the gun straight out . . . 'Because I'm going to blow your head right off your shoulders.'

I watched his finger tighten on the trigger and closed my eyes. Then I heard a sweet soft Irish voice say, 'Don't even breathe, Mr Skinner . . . drop the gun.'

The pistol clattered to the floor and I opened my eyes to see Jackie resting both barrels of a shotgun just below Skinner's ear. The vet had gone very pale. 'Lie down on the floor next to Mr Malloy,' she said.

Skinner obeyed and she took the gun from his head and rammed it hard between his buttocks. 'Now, Mr Skinner, you tell me how it feels to have something unwanted and unexpected stuck in your arse.' She looked at me and we smiled.

Jackie got some rope from the tack room and we tied Stoke and Skinner together. She stayed covering them while I took Roscoe into another room and offered to mediate with the police on his behalf if he filled in all the missing links for me. By the time Cranley arrived he'd told me everything and promised to repeat it in court.

We gave our statements and Cranley, finally admitting defeat, said I could go. But there were only policemen milling around, cold and impersonal, so

Jackie and I decided to stay with Charmain's body till they took it away.

We sat in quiet companionship waiting for the ambulance and I tried to come to terms with the fact that it was all over. I'd expected to feel elated, to be buzzing with the satisfaction of revenge, but none of it was there.

All I felt was a deep contentment that Jackie was with me again, a massive happy relief that she hadn't betrayed me and a steadily burrowing guilt at having suspected her.

It was almost midnight, but the Red Lion in Lambourn found us a room and a bottle of Scotch. I rang McCarthy and told him the news. He said he'd be there first thing in the morning.

There was no lovemaking. When the trauma hit Jackie she got very weepy and I spent half the night comforting her and the other half coping with my deepening guilt over doubting her. Knowing she would never fogive me if she learned of my suspicions, I overcame the urge to confess.

Somewhere near dawn, in each other's arms, we slept.

CHAPTER THIRTY-EIGHT

In the morning I left Jackie asleep and McCarthy and I walked up onto the Downs. The new jumps season wasn't that far away and strings of horses, in various states of fitness, passed us going both ways. To our right, a trainer was supervising a schooling session for two 'chasers. We wandered over and stood by one of the fences.

The two horses, a bay and a chestnut, cantered past us and turned at the top. They came down towards the fence together at a fair pace, shoulder muscles bunching and ears twitching as they accelerated the last few strides in. The bay pricked his ears and flew it. The other, unsure, fiddled a bit and pecked on landing.

I recognised his rider as an old adversary from my riding days. We'd had a healthy rivalry on the course and some good crack in the pub. As they cantered past on the way back he recognised me and shouted over, 'Missing it?'

'It's the poor bloody horses that have to put up with idiots like you that's missing me,' I called after him. He laughed and cantered on.

McCarthy said, 'Well, are you going to keep me waiting all morning?'

'What . . .? Sorry, Mac, I was miles away.'

'I know, you have been since we left the hotel.'

'Mmm.'

'You said on the phone that Roscoe had filled in the missing pieces so I'd quite like to hear the full story.'

'It was more or less as we thought, except that Skinner was the instigator, which surprised me. He'd run up big gambling debts with Stoke who was ready to put the bite on him for payment. Since he was sacked by your people Skinner had been working on his own trying to come up with the perfect dope, which would have meant revenge on the Jockey Club and an end to his money worries. He soon realised he had neither the expertise nor the money and when Stoke started pressing him for payment he put the proposal that Stoke finance the research and he would do the work. That took care of the cash side of things.

'Skinner remembered Kruger's case well and knew how close he'd come to this perfect dope so he contacted him in Austria. Kruger agreed to come in as a "consultant" for a set fee and advice on which horses were to be doped. He also asked that Danny Gordon, whom he rated highly, be recruited to assist Skinner.

'Skinner himself put that proposal to Danny Gordon who agreed on condition that Elrick and Odin, who were blackmailing him for an attempted Tote fraud in Sweden years ago, were "discouraged" from their nasty habit.

'Stoke sent his two gorillas to see them and you know what happened. Once they were sorted out Gordon tried to renege on his agreement . . . Stoke had him killed. Kruger then threatened to pull out, but Skinner persuaded him that Elrick and Odin had put the hit out on Gordon, not Stoke.

'They soon realised they'd need a number of horses to experiment with under racing conditions and a trainer and jockey who'd co-operate. Skinner knew Harle and Harle knew Roscoe who had been training a couple of

310

horses under permit and giving him rides. Both agreed to take part.

'So now, as well as setting up a lab and keeping people on a payroll, Stoke had to come up with the cash to buy ten or twelve horses. He had the money to do it but was beginning to think about the risks if things didn't work out. Harle's suggestion to finance the running of the stable was that Skinner's lab could be used, in its spare time, so to speak, for manufacturing heroin.

'Harle had smuggled the stuff in from France a couple of times and knew how lucrative it would be to make it and cut out all the middlemen.'

'Wouldn't that be a specialised job, making heroin from scratch?' McCarthy asked.

'Apparently not, if you have the basic ingredients which, it seems, are more readily available in France. So Roscoe started sending horses on a fairly regular basis to run at the French provincial tracks.

'Either Skinner or Harle would accompany them and smuggle the necessary raw materials back in the horsebox. Harle was in charge of the "dealing" side and got a bit too dependent on the stuff himself. He was also creaming off some of Stoke's "profits". Stoke discovered this about the same time as Charmain admitted that Harle had got her hooked, too. Not only that but he'd seduced her. Stoke sent the boys, and Harle, as you know, was put through weeks of torture before they killed him.'

'Then Greene came in?' McCarthy asked.

'That's right, though not for the money. Young Greene was a career man and Roscoe promised him he'd be champion jockey one day if he co-operated. Trouble was, Charmain was hooked by now and needed a new supplier. She did the seducing this time and was giving Greene money to buy heroin, and sex for doing the running. Stoke found out and took a special delight in manipulating Greene into the box with the killer horse.'

'Who did they plan to replace Greene with?'

'Nobody, they knew they were very very close to the perfect formula, that's why Kruger became dispensable too. Skinner completed the first phial of the "perfect" dope yesterday morning and rushed down to the yard to tell Roscoe who immediately contacted Stoke at York. He was sufficiently excited about it to leave right away and head down here.

'But they had two pieces of bad luck – in his anxiety to tell Roscoe, Skinner left the lab door unlocked, probably around the same time that Charmain was hitting me on the head with a cooking pot. Harle must have told her they were using the lab for heroin but the stuff had all been cleared out after Harle's death. Charmain, in total desperation, lifted the only bottle that looked like heroin and injected it.'

McCarthy stared at me. 'Stoke's perfect dope?'

I nodded. 'Every drop . . . Though the formula still exists. Roscoe says he'll pass it to you to help with his plea-bargaining.'

'That's big of him. Did he happen to say if his horse was doped when it won the Champion Hurdle?'

'He claims it wasn't. Said they couldn't risk using the drug till they knew it was flawless, which makes sense. If Roscoe had been exposed early in a doping scandal it would have killed the whole plan.'

'Pretty ironic then that he bought himself some bloody good horses without even knowing it.'

'Yeah . . . anyway, Charmain lived just long enough to, inadvertently I think, warn Stoke I was coming.'

'So you were right, there never was a Perlman?' McCarthy said.

'No, I was wrong. Remember the little guy with the

glasses, the one who claimed he was Perlman when your bloke first interviewed him? Well, he was. Or at least that was his name; he worked for Stoke. You know I thought Jackie tipped them off I'd be at Kempton and that we'd be meeting Kruger?'

Mac nodded.

'It was little Perlman. He was trailing me half the time and I didn't even know it. He also bugged Kruger's phone.'

'So Jackie's completely innocent?'

I nodded, still feeling slightly ashamed. 'If you could do one thing for me, Mac, out of all this – don't ever tell anyone I suspected her.'

He smiled, but there was a mischievous glint. 'Don't worry, Eddie, soul of discretion.'

We watched the two 'chasers come down the line of fences again. The novice stood right off this time and just cleared the fence. I watched them gallop away.

'What are your plans now, Eddie?' McCarthy asked.

'My immediate plans, if I had my licence back, would be to show that clown how to school a horse.'

He looked at me. 'You really miss it, don't you?'

'More than you or your kind could ever know, Mac.'

I turned and started back for the hotel. McCarthy joined me. The sun was well up now in a clear sky. A lark rose, whistling high as we walked near its nest.

'Remember the interview with the Senior Steward you asked for?' McCarthy said.

I looked across at him. He smiled. 'Next Tuesday, ten-thirty.'

'How long for?'

'Half an hour, as we agreed.'

I nodded.

'Think it'll do any good?' he asked.

'I'll tell the bastard what I think of him. It'll get five

313

years of bitterness off my chest and then I can maybe get on with my life.'

'Don't be too hasty. Remember, Roscoe's testimony on Kruger might help you out and, there's always this . . .' He handed me a palm-sized black book about the thickness of a cigarette packet.

I stopped and riffled the handwritten pages. 'What is it?'

He smiled. 'Kruger's diary . . . From five years ago.'

I stared at him.

'It agrees with your side of the story, more or less. March twenty-third to twenty-eight are the pages you want.'

He walked on, smiling smugly.

'Mac!' I called after him. 'How long have you had this?'

He stopped and turned. 'I found it on Kruger's body the morning you ran out and left me to explain his death to the police . . . Remember?'

'You could have told me!'

He shrugged and smiled. 'Completely slipped my mind . . . See you on Tuesday.' He turned again and walked down towards the valley. I stood holding the diary.

'McCarthy . . .' I called after him, my voice carrying in the clear morning air. He kept walking.

'McCarthy . . .' I shouted at the receding figure, '. . . you're a bastard!'